APRIL OPERATION

Linda Hall

Published by
Bethel Publishing Company
1819 South Main Street
Elkhart, Indiana 46516

Cover Illustration by
Ed French

Editing by
Jill Studebaker

Printed in the United States of America

ISBN 0-934998-70-1

DEDICATION

For Rik

ACKNOWLEDGEMENTS

Thank you to Sergeant Clint Dykeman of Division 2, J Division of the Royal Canadian Mounted Police in Fredericton. Thanks for all of your help and support in the writing of these past three books. May God bless you in your well deserved retirement.

To Judy Barker of the of the Pregnancy Crisis Centre in Fredericton, thank you for sharing with me from your heart. Your deep love and concern for the unborn and their mothers is evident in your work.

To Allison Brewer of the Morgentaler Clinic in Fredericton, for giving me the grand tour of your facility, and for answering all of my probing questions with grace and dignity, I thank you.

The towns of St. Matthews, New Brunswick and Playa Brisa, Maine and all of their inhabitants are fictitious.

CHAPTER 1

On the last day of his life Dr. Douglas Shanahan planted flowers. He was doing what he modestly referred to as "puttering," but it was an artist's hands, a skilled surgeon's hands which transplanted the pink petunias and the white alyssum, the blue delphiniums and the hybrid single-leaf geraniums into the soft brown earth.

It was mild for April and he was alone with a glinting buttery sun which warmed him. He liked these times. They offered him space to meditate, time to reflect. He was kneeling next to a circular patch of garden midway between his home and the wide inlet that led into the Bay of Fundy. Through the budding elms and maples, he caught glimpses every so often of the shimmering blue water. Above and behind him was his house, a large, grand three-story wooden wide-porched structure, which was built in the mid-1800s by a sea captain for his family. Throughout the years it had served alternately as a bed and breakfast, an art museum, and at one time, a convent. It had been empty for several years before the Shanahans purchased it ten years ago.

Surrounding him on the green lawn were dozens of flats filled with little square plastic boxes of annuals and perennials. He had dropped an exorbitant amount of money earlier that morning at a garden center out on the highway.

And taking the day off to get his garden in had been a good idea. He was glad he had listened to Emma when she accosted him at the clinic yesterday.

"Dr. Shanahan, you need a day off! Dr. Lunford can handle

it. If you come in here tomorrow I will personally throw you out!" she said, wagging her finger at him.

He grinned even now at the image of Emma, all of five feet, picking him up and throwing him out. But he had no doubt that she could do it if she set her mind to it. She managed his clinic, a feisty young woman known for her fiery temperament and her brazen outspokenness.

"Okay, okay," he had said, laughing and holding up his hands in mock surrender.

One of life's greatest relaxations for him was gardening; nurturing living things, coaxing them to life with his careful hands. His entire estate was surrounded by gardens, all of them tended by Douglas or his wife Sheila. They also planted a large vegetable patch along the back and kept the clinic staff and volunteers, as well as their married daughters, well supplied with fresh tomatoes, zucchinis, carrots and beets.

Normally his wife Sheila, wearing her straw hat, trowel in hand, would be working here alongside him, but she was away for a few days visiting her sister on Prince Edward Island. And Moira Pilgrim, the woman who cleaned for them occasionally, wouldn't be here until afternoon. But he never minded being alone.

He and Sheila, married for 33 years, had two married daughters. Lois lived in St. Andrews with her husband and two children, Allison age seven and Meghan age four. Something like a shadow crossed his face when he thought of Lois. Briefly, only briefly, did he allow himself to think of his elder daughter. His other daughter Penny, stable confident Penny, lived in Bangor, Maine, with her photographer husband of eight years. The two of them had a chubby curly-headed 17 month-old daughter named Aris, who was fast becoming Douglas' favorite.

He shaded his eyes and looked up into the cloudless sky, a sky so liquid blue that it looked as if droplets of blue would fall upon the ground.

If anyone dared to comment on his lack of sons or grandsons, Douglas would wave them away, as if shooing a persistent bug.

The fates had ordained women for him, and the fates were not to be argued with. Women it was. He smiled a little. Not only did he live in a family of women, he also worked exclusively with women; all of his clinic staff, most of his volunteers and all of his patients were women.

The dirt around the pink phlox was warm on his hands and he sighed. Summer would be good, he hoped. It had been a difficult winter. New Brunswick was the last Canadian province to allow free-standing abortion clinics, a victory won only that fall. The United States had had abortion-care clinics for the last umpteen years and Douglas had always thought it was an absolute travesty that Canada lagged so far behind. Canadian women in delicate emotional states were forced to travel south across the border to get the procedure done or wait for a Canadian hospital abortion where a "committee," with confidentiality not on the menu, decided whether an abortion was called for. Canadian women deserved better.

New Brunswick, where Douglas grew up, was the last standoff. Even though his "women" called him a "pussy cat," the image he portrayed to the media was very different—Fighter! Strong willed!

During the past long winter he had had many words with New Brunswick's premier, Johnson Maddison, who had billed himself as "Canada's last pro-family leader." But Douglas abhorred his self-proclaimed title. It was as if stating that by contrast individuals such as himself were "anti-family."

"Mr. Premier," he had said on one occasion, "if being anti-family means caring for those people around you, or caring for the women and the young girls in your family who find themselves pregnant with nowhere to go and no one to care for them, or being concerned that every child has a safe and wanted place in which to be born, that women are provided with the best care possible, then, Mr. Premier, you can call me anti-family."

In January the issue had gone to New Brunswick's Supreme Court where the decision to allow free-standing abortion clinics was finally upheld. New Brunswick's first abortion clinic, therefore, was set up in the small town of St. Matthews, Douglas Shanahan's childhood home.

He chose a flat of dwarf hybrid yellow petunias to form the border for the front of the bed. In the center of the patch was a spread of phlox which was coming to life after a long winter sleep. He trimmed a few dead offshoots away, nicking his finger on a sharp branch in the process. He never wore gardening gloves. He preferred to feel the earth, warm and alive on his naked hands. A drop of blood fell from his forefinger onto a yellow petunia petal. He watched it pool, a bead of deep red dew on a bed of yellow. He watched as the edges of the droplet broke and his blood spread outward from the center, tendrils of red engulfing the entire bloom.

It's not that he particularly *liked* performing abortions—those caricatures they drew of him in the newspapers were viciously wrong—for him it was about caring, about giving women a second chance. The lesser of two evils. As he patted fresh earth up against some creeping phlox, he thought back to the time and place when he decided to become an abortion doctor.

When he was 16, he lived next door to a girl named Patty. She was a year older than he was, but they were in the same grade. They had an odd kind of friendship. It was almost as if Patty, who ran with a completely different group of classmates than the smart, serious friends that Douglas chose, could confide in him because he was somehow "safe."

It was a miserably cold and sloppy March day when Patty, shivering, confided to Douglas that she was "in trouble." He remembered her desperate words as they stood together stomping their feet under the street light. "My parents will kill me!" she had said. "They really will kill me!"

He knew her parents to be ultra-religious and extremely strict. A few weeks after that initial encounter she whispered to him not to tell anybody, especially not her parents, but her boyfriend had arranged an abortion for her. Some friend of a friend who was an intern did abortions in a clinic after hours for a fee. Her boyfriend was going to pay for it. Douglas watched down from his bedroom window when her boyfriend came to pick her up late one afternoon. He also watched when Patty came home four hours later, head down, walking slowly like an old woman, leaning on her boyfriend's arm for support. By the light of the street lamp he could see the grimace of pain on her face as she clutched her abdomen with her free hand.

The next time Douglas saw her was two days later when the ambulance came and she was rushed to the hospital, her distraught, confused parents looking on. She died later in the hospital from a massive hemorrhage and an infection which raged through her entire body.

After her funeral, Douglas decided that there would be no more Pattys. He graduated with honors in medicine at Dalhousie University in Halifax, Nova Scotia, specializing in obstetrics and gynecology. Eventually, he went into private practice as a gynecologist/obstetrician.

When the Roe vs. Wade decision was brought down in the United States, he saw it as a victory, even for Canada. He amassed an army of volunteers across the country who fought hard to make abortion accessible to Canadian women. He set up abortion clinics across the country, often defying local and provincial governments in the process. He was hailed as a pioneer, a hero in the pro-choice movement. He also knew what the anti-abortionists called him—Baby Killer! Murderer! Progenitor of the New Holocaust!

He shook his head as he rounded a pat of brown earth around the roots of small yellow and purple mottled pansies. *They know so little about me*, he thought. Then he stood up and admired his handiwork.

The bullet which felled him came from somewhere on the hills behind his estate. Later the police would fine-comb that area and find nothing. Only an instant of surprised pain registered in his mind before he bent his knees and fell forward, heavily. Later the coroner said he was probably dead even before he hit the ground. And people would tell Sheila that that was a mercy. But his own blood stained and ruined the carefully laid petunias, the newly trimmed phlox; completely obliterating the yellow flower with the finger-prick of blood, ravaging all of his living things with the blood of himself on that fine, warm April morning.

CHAPTER 2

It was almost closing time when Emma Knoll heard the news. They had had a full slate of abortions that day, women from as far away as Maine, Quebec and Nova Scotia had come, thankful for the complete confidentiality that the Shanahan Clinic provided. Then there were records to be updated, invoices to be sent, supplies to be ordered, as well as calls for information and calls for requests to speak in schools and to women's groups. The list was never-ending.

Because Dr. Shanahan had taken the day off, the abortions that day had been performed by local doctor Amos Lunford, the only other doctor in St. Matthews who worked at the clinic. Midway through the day he had been called to the hospital to perform an emergency C-section on a woman 12 weeks premature. This only served to back up the waiting room even further.

Just before lunch a very frightened looking teenage girl had walked through the door with her friend. *They usually come with friends*, thought Emma. She tearfully had said she wanted an abortion right now and Emma reached out and touched her arm. She gave her name as Nadine, adding that her parents would kill her. Emma led her back to see Sophie, the clinic nurse.

After about 20 minutes Sophie and Nadine were back in the waiting room. Nadine wiped her eyes with a Kleenex and smiled wanly. "Two weeks," Sophie told her, patting her shoulder. "Come back in two weeks." Nadine was not quite seven weeks pregnant and seven weeks was the earliest that abortions could be safely performed, when the risk to the woman was least.

Sophie told her not to worry, they would phone the school and make her excuses. Her parents need never know. Before Nadine left, heavy set motherly Sophie squeezed the shoulder of the freckled teenager. "A month from now you'll be a kid again with no worries."

Emma looked down at the schedule. It would have to be three weeks. Dr. Shanahan and Dr. Lunford would be attending a conference in Toronto. She thought how unfair it was that there were so many doctors who worked at the St. Matthews Regional Hospital, doctors who *could* help them, but didn't, so afraid were they of anti-abortion backlash. St. Matthews was such a small conservative town. Emma shook her head.

As well, the Shanahan Clinic faced constant intimidation by anti-abortion protesters who relentlessly followed the clinic patients practically through the door. They were ruthless with their stupid candlelight vigils and those disgusting glossy color leaflets of mangled baby parts they handed out. *Who paid for that stuff anyway?* She pushed a stray hair back from her forehead and frowned. There were times when Emma was so outraged that she would stomp outside and swat all the protesters away with a broom, yelling at full volume to get the blazes away from her clinic. The police had cautioned her not to do that. If protesters harassed individual patients, they had told her to just call. People had a constitutional right to protest, but they could not harass individual patients. *Yeah, you tell me the difference*, thought Emma.

Then there was the little, stooped-shoulder, gray-haired lady who sat outside of the clinic winter and summer. Either she would be walking with her cane in front of the clinic, back and forth, back and forth, or she would be just sitting there, day after day. The cops couldn't do a thing about that one, since she never ventured on clinic property, nor talked to patients. Emma had spoken to her only once. "What are you doing here?"

The woman had looked up and said, "Praying, dear, just praying. For the wee ones."

At 4:30 on that afternoon Emma walked toward the front door and made sure it was locked and secured. She closed the outside security shutters in the front and headed back to the staff room. Sophie was at the table sipping coffee from an oversized mug which read "Grandmothers are Sexy." Also in the room were two of the clinic volunteers, Kathy Baskor, who was bobbing a tea bag up and down in a mug of hot water, and Giselle Doucet, who sat at the far end of the table carefully lettering on a large sheet of pale green poster paper, a clear plastic bottle of spring water on the table beside her.

Emma sat down in one of the overstuffed chairs and slipped off her shoes. "I am so bushed. My feet are killing me and I've got a headache the size of Maine."

"Want some tea?" asked Kathy. "This bag's good for one more cup at least."

"I need something stronger than tea right now. All I can say is I'm glad it's the weekend. And I'm glad Douglas will be back on Monday. A lot of the women don't like Amos."

"I can't say I blame them," said Giselle, looking up. The poster she was working on was announcing an upcoming seminar on women's reproductive rights.

"He's not that bad," said Emma. "You just have to get to know him."

"He epitomizes all men," said Giselle. "He's rude, gruff...."

Emma looked at her. "May I remind you that aside from Douglas, he's all we've got."

Sophie looked up. "I wouldn't go to him if my feminine life depended on it." She was munching on a brownie left over from lunch.

"You guys...," said Emma, leaning forward. "Let's not tear apart Amos. We're lucky to have him. None of those other doctors in this town will come near this place...."

Emma would always remember what happened next. It would remain in her conscious mind, a still picture, a fixed image, the precise moment the camera clicked.

There was a scuttle at the back door, a knocking and frantic shouting. Kathy flew to the door and opened it. Diane, another of the volunteers, rushed in, eyes wide, hair askew, hands and arms flailing wildly. "Dead!" Her voice was frantic, hoarse. "Dead! Dead!"

"Who's dead?" demanded Emma, rising.

"Douglas! Dr. Shanahan! He was shot. On the news. Murdered!" Her voice was garbled, as if her mouth was filled with marbles.

"What are you saying?" Emma was screaming.

"He's dead! Turn the radio on!"

Kathy fumbled with the radio on the counter and finally tuned into CBC.

"...apparently died from a gunshot wound. Dr. Douglas Shanahan had successfully set up abortion clinics in all ten Canadian provinces...."

"They're wrong!" Emma was screaming. "How could he be dead? I just spoke with him this morning. He was fine then. He was going to work in his garden. How could he be dead?" The others in the room sat shocked and silent as the newscaster spoke. Only Emma went on and on. "It's not possible! It can't be true! This is insane. He was going to work in his garden."

CHAPTER 3

On the other side of town Julia Nash, director of the Pregnancy Care Centre, heard the news at about the same time. She had just put the "Closed" sign on the front door and was alone in the small, square bungalow that housed the Centre. She had decided that before she picked up her two boys at her mother's she would stay for just a few more minutes and sort through the two boxes of maternity clothes that had arrived that afternoon. Julia too, had had a busy day; calls for information, follow-up on some of their pregnant women, getting the post-abortion support group set up, calls for requests to speak at schools and church groups; the list was never-ending.

She held up a pale denim maternity smock which looked brand new. It was a youthful style and made Julia think about the teenage girl who had come in during lunch. Her name was Nadine and she had come with a friend. *They always come with friends*, thought Julia. Nadine told Julia that she was pregnant and didn't know what to do. She could have an abortion in two weeks, she had said, but now she was scared; scared of the operation, scared that her parents would find out, scared that something would go wrong and maybe she would never be able to have babies again.

"I heard that happens—that you can never have babies again." She looked at Julia mournfully.

Julia led Nadine and Nadine's friend Shelly into the counseling room, a room at the back of the Centre which was comfortably furnished with overstuffed couches, chairs, blankets and soft wall hangings. Julia was glad she had stopped at the grocery store on her way in this morning to pick up a couple of bouquets of fresh flowers.

Julia listened as Nadine told her that she had been to the Shanahan Clinic and that they had assured her the procedure was perfectly safe. They had even scheduled her for in two weeks, but now she just didn't know. She just didn't know. She kept shaking her head. Julia listened, saying little. That was the first thing. Just listen; be there while they cried. Advice and counsel would come later.

As she listened she tried not to let her anger show, but underneath, it simmered. Hundreds, thousands of needless abortions had been performed right here in St. Matthews since the Shanahan Clinic opened. But what angered her even more was that the parents didn't even have to be told. A girl needed her parents' permission to get her tonsils out, but not for an abortion. She knew some of the excuses that the clinic phoned the high school with, and it sickened her that the clinic was not only performing abortions at an alarming rate, but was driving yet another wedge between child and parent.

That became Julia's first question, "Do your parents know?"

Nadine shook her head, and Julia looked into her face, tears staining her dimpled, freckled cheeks.

"Noooo! No way. They would *never* understand!"

"Your parents may surprise you. They may be a lot more understanding than you give them credit for."

"Not my parents. No way! You don't know my parents."

Half an hour later Nadine said she had to get back to school. Julia promised to phone her that evening. They would get together over the weekend, maybe tomorrow, and Julia would even talk to her parents, if Nadine wanted. Julia knew that many parents were understanding, but some were not. The Pregnancy Care Centre had access to a number of trained counselors and pastors who helped families cope.

Her thoughts were interrupted by the ringing of the phone. Her mother.

"Julia, have you heard the news?"

Her mother's voice was strained, strange and she immediately thought of her sons, nine year-old Jeff and six year-old Joshua who had walked there together after school.

"What is it?"

"That Dr. Shanahan, the one with the abortion clinic?"

"I know who he is, Mother, I know only too well."

"He's dead, Julia."

"What are you talking about!"

"Dr. Douglas Shanahan was shot this afternoon. Murdered." Julia sat down.

"It's all over the news," her mother was saying. "Turn on your radio, dear. Douglas Shanahan was killed this morning. Shot in his garden."

Her mind reeled. Douglas Shanahan? Dead?

"Are you sure?"

"I'm sure. The news said he was shot around noon outside in his yard. They don't know who did it."

Julia placed her open palm on her forehead. She could think of nothing to say.

CHAPTER 4

By the time Emma and Julia were coming to grips with the news, Sergeant Roger Sheppard of the St. Matthews, New Brunswick detachment of the Royal Canadian Mounted Police had been on the scene for many hours and was already calling in the Ident crew from Fredericton, Saint John and Halifax to help scour the hills behind the home for anything—a cigarette butt, a gum wrapper, foot prints, spent shells, if they should be so lucky. But nothing had been left behind; only a patch of bent grass where the sniper had lain. By the position of Shanahan's body, they knew that the shot had been fired at long range by a hunting rifle. A perfect shot, right in the back of the head.

Early that afternoon Dr. Shanahan's housekeeper had made a frantic call to 911 when she found her boss sprawled across his garden patch. At first she thought he had merely collapsed, perhaps from the sun. Then she had walked closer and saw all the blood.

By 4:25 Roger knew they were dealing not with a random shooting, not a foiled burglar attempt, nor even a psychopath with a grudge. They were dealing with something far more sinister—a premeditated, carefully planned and brutal assassination. He radioed his detachment to call in to Ottawa to put out an alert to RCMP detachments, a warning to abortion clinics and physicians and health care workers who performed abortions.

He left the crime scene—headed toward the Shanahan Clinic.

CHAPTER 5

On Fridays, nine year-old Beth Knoll had dance class after school until four. Then she would walk down the hill to the clinic where her mother worked. She was looking forward to tonight because after her mother finished work they were going to McDonalds for supper. At breakfast her mother had said, "How about we go out for supper tonight? Where would you like to go?"

"McDonalds!" Beth had cheered.

At 4:04 Beth put her leotards in her Pocahontas backpack, and then said good-bye to her friend Melissa, promising to call her that night. She waved to Jane, her dance teacher, and then left.

It usually only took her 20 minutes to get to the clinic, a walk she didn't mind so much. For part of the walk she cut through the woods at the back of the school, which she liked. She imagined that fairies lived in the woods with real castles and white horses. That was how she made the trip shorter, by thinking about fairies and singing. She liked to sing. She was singing something from her new Sharon, Lois and Bram tape and trying to decide what she would get at McDonalds when the dark blue van pulled up behind her.

She never saw it, nor did she see the two black clad individuals who got out, grabbed her and covered her mouth and nose with a drug soaked cloth. She was unconscious by the time they placed her limp body in the back and sped away.

CHAPTER 6

Emma kept glancing out of the unshuttered window. Roger noticed this as he stood in the clinic staff room and questioned the five frightened and weepy women. He carefully wrote down their responses in his small notebook. They had received no threats that seemed out of the ordinary. None of their patients had reported any threats, even the pro-life contingent had remained oddly quiet during the past few weeks. "But, yes, of course the RCMP could look through their records, by all means," Emma had said, "...anything that might help to shed some light on this."

Roger recognized Emma Knoll from her pictures; small, slender, with large dark eyes and short brown hair. Whenever the media needed a pro-choice comment they called her. He knew her to be outspoken and articulate. Today, however, she was subdued and quiet, distracted almost.

It was the large nurse, Sophie, who kept talking, going on about the problem being a patriarchal society where women and women's rights are constantly being undermined and threatened. "Women are killed all the time by abusive husbands who are just a mirror reflection of society, a society which threatens and kills women!"

Roger puzzled at this since it was a man who had been shot and killed.

Roger walked toward Emma. "Ms. Knoll, are you all right?" Roger finally asked. Emma was facing the window, frowning.

She fiddled with a ring on her right hand. "My daughter should have been here half an hour ago. With all that's happened, I forgot the time."

"Your daughter?" Roger was instantly aware.

"It's not like her to be late. Douglas' death is going to upset her so. He was like a grandfather to her. I hope she doesn't hear it from somebody else."

"Maybe she's still with Jane," the long-haired woman named Kathy volunteered.

Emma shook her head. "Jane would have called me. My fear is she's heard the news somehow and is so upset that she's dawdled off somewhere."

"Maybe she's with one of her friends," said red-eyed Diane, who kept blowing her nose and wailing. Roger hadn't been able to talk to her yet.

He turned to Emma and said, "Mrs. Knoll, how old is your daughter and where is she coming from?"

"Beth is nine," said Emma, running a hand through her short hair. "And she walks down Market Street from the school. She has dance every Friday after school."

Kathy moved toward the phone. "I'll call Jane. Maybe she's still there. With all that's happened maybe she kept them." Kathy was continuing. "And with everything that's happened, the phone here hasn't stopped ringing. I bet Jane's tried to call but couldn't get through."

Emma was leaning against the wall, very still, and Roger watched as something in her began to crumple. The articulate, intelligent woman grew small before him as she hugged her chest and bent double.

Sophie ran to Emma then and hugged her, crooning, "She's all right. She's got to be all right. You'll see." And to Roger she said, "It's men. It's our patriarchal society. No one's safe. Women aren't safe."

At the phone Kathy put up her hand and mumbled a few hmm hmms. Roger could see her face grow white and then she said, "It's all right, Jane. It's not your fault. She's probably with a friend."

When she hung up, Kathy said quietly, "Jane said she left 45 minutes ago."

Kathy was back on the phone then, dialing Beth's friends in turn, while Sophie held Emma, patting her back. Diane had fallen to the floor and was sitting there cross-legged and weeping forward into her hands. A tall slim woman with wire-rimmed glasses who gave her name as Giselle, was sitting very still behind a table in front of a large poster, unmoving, face like stone.

A few minutes later, Kathy was talking quietly to Roger in the corner. "I called all of Beth's friends. She's not there. No one has seen her. I'd like it if we could look for her."

He nodded at Kathy and turned to Emma, "Mrs. Knoll, another officer should be here shortly. I'm going to head out with Miss Baskor and see if we can find your daughter. Is there a chance she's with your husband?"

"Ex," said Kathy. "But I called him. She's not there."

A few minutes later Roger and Kathy were driving very slowly up Market Street toward the school. They scanned the shop-lined street for the little girl, but did not see her. They drove from where the shops and art galleries, cafes and video stores crowded together roof-to-roof, gave way to modern lawyers' offices, dentists' offices and the large tourist center with the scale model lighthouse out front. They did not see Beth. They turned right on Thatch Road and drove slowly toward the school. They did not see Beth.

The school principal was walking toward his car when they stopped him. He had not seen Beth, he told them. Jane too, was walking toward them from the building. She hugged Kathy and said how terrible she felt about the whole thing, but that Beth had left, like she did every Friday, to walk down to the clinic. "If I had only known," she kept saying. "If I had only known I never would have let her go." And, "How awful it was about Dr. Shanahan. Wasn't that an awful thing?"

They parked the cruiser and walked the overgrown and abandoned path Beth took toward Market Street, but they did not see her.

They drove back downtown. They checked shops one by one. Kathy got out and ran the length of the wharf, walking up to people who shook their heads in answer to her question. They drove to some of Beth's friends. But everyone said sadly, "No, no one had seen her, but if they heard anything, anything at all, they'd be sure to call right away."

An hour later the two of them were back in the clinic staff room, where Emma looked up hopefully from the couch. When Kathy shook her head, Emma covered her face with trembling fingers.

Constable Francine Myers had arrived, Roger saw, and he nodded to her. Standing on the opposite side of the room, looking stunned and worried and out of place in this company of women, was a large, bearded man who extended his hand and quietly introduced himself as Glen Knoll, Beth's father. Giselle was still sitting at the table where she'd been an hour ago, running her fingers up and down a red magic marker, up and down, up and down, a vacant look in her eyes. Sophie sat next to Emma on the couch and pale-faced, tear-stained Diane was on the floor, crumpled in a ball and still wailing loudly.

CHAPTER 7

All evening Emma sat in her living room wrapped in an afghan, staring straight ahead, saying nothing, while friends moved around her, quietly making her cups of tea which she didn't drink and bringing her plates of food which she didn't eat. Kathy sat beside her, her arm around her, and Glen was across from them on the couch, elbows on his knees, his head low. Sophie wandered from room to room pronouncing judgment on the patriarchal, fundamentalists who were mainly men and mainly bent on destroying women and their rights. "What *is* their problem?" she muttered. "Abortion has been proven, *proven* to be completely safe. A woman can have four or five abortions with no ill effects. It's just men, men wanting to control women's bodies. That's what this is about. It's those anti-abortionists. They're behind this. They took her!"

Kathy gave her a look. "Sophie, we don't know that. The police haven't said anything that would link the two."

"Sophie's right," said Emma. "Think about it. Today of all days she disappears."

"Emma, she's just lost. In the woods behind the school. I specifically asked the officer if he thought there was a connection and he said he couldn't say for sure." She stroked Emma's hair. "I think this is what happened. Maybe Beth heard the news about Douglas and then just wandered into the woods. They'll find her."

"She's not lost. She *never* wanders off. She's a good kid."

"I know she is. The best," said Kathy.

Emma was shaking her head. "She wouldn't have done that. She would have come to me. She wouldn't have wandered off. If she *did* hear about Douglas, I would have been the first person she would have come to."

Glen rose heavily then and shoved his large hands into his pockets. Emma looked up at him. He was wearing a frayed gray sweater with elbow patches which she recognized from the time long ago when they were married. His gentle face looked tired, so very tired; and for a moment she wanted to be taken into his arms, buried safe within those large soft shoulders.

He said, "I can't just sit here, Emmy. I can't stay here. I've got to go look for her. I'm going out to join that search party."

*****

While Emma and her friends sat in her house, volunteer Search and Rescue teams from all over New Brunswick were being dispatched. Many of them were already on the scene, tromping methodically through the underbrush, their familiar orange jackets blazing a path.

The Coast Guard had responded, as well as fishermen who had loaned their boats and were even now shining search lights up and down the shore front. A local donut shop was providing thermoses of free coffee and boxes of donuts for the searchers. A local sandwich shop was busy making dozens of sandwiches.

And while the searchers with their high powered lights and helicopters combed the hills near St. Matthews, detectives and forensics specialists were sifting through Dr. Shanahan's estate and his clinic piece by piece, inch by inch.

All of the residents and shop keepers along Market Street and Thatch Road were questioned and re-questioned. "No," they shook their heads, "No one had seen the little girl in the blue jacket and the Pocahontas backpack skipping down the hill at four o'clock that afternoon."

Pros, thought Roger as he sat in front of his computer in the detachment office. He had already contacted Interpol in Ottawa. They were even now, gathering a list of anyone who had ever threatened an abortion worker.

Roger poured himself another cup of coffee and pulled a pink iced donut out of the box. It was going to be a long night.

*****

Julia, plus a number of local pastors, church members, Pregnancy Care Centre volunteers and members of the board of the Pregnancy Care Centre had gathered at her small house for prayer.

As Julia sat on a straight-back wooden chair, she could not stop the tears. She had never personally met Emma Knoll, even though they were constant targets of each other in the media. Emma Knoll was not the kind of person Julia would ever choose for a friend—trampling on everything that Julia held dear—yet on this night, something in her felt bruised and wounded, and so inexplicably sad. The pain she felt for this complete stranger was overwhelming.

She thought of her own two sons, terrors sometimes, but so precious to her that she would give her life for them; and she wondered about Emma Knoll. *Where was she? Was she at home, or was she out walking up and down the hills near St. Matthews? Did she have friends around her? Was there someone helping her get through this night?*

She had also never met Douglas Shanahan personally, but she knew he was married with a few grown children. *Did he have any grandchildren? Where were they on this awful night?*

Her friend Shelly, who was sitting next to her, placed her hand on Julia's shaking arm and whispered, "Julia, are you all right?"

Julia shook her head. "No, I am not all right. This is not all right. None of this is all right. None of this will ever be right again."

*****

On the internet Matt had friends, lots of them. People on the Internet liked him. On the net he was Earth Angel, that was his handle, and everyone knew him and listened to what he said. He was writing all of this to Monkey Boy, one of his internet pals. He was saying that IRL (in real life) people didn't like him a whole lot. IRL people were idiots and jerks and made fun of him at school, but on-line, "Well that's a different story. The internet is where my real friends are." Monkey Boy was writing back the same thing.

It was late at night and the house was dark, which meant his parents and bratty sister were already in bed. Not that he cared. Tonight was Friday. He could stay up all night if he wanted to. No school tomorrow. Not that he cared about school, anyway. He was in his first year of high school at St. Matthews High and he detested it.

The house was quiet, too, which meant his parents had turned off the TV in their room. He didn't see much of them anyway. They both worked all the time, and most evenings they were out. He wasn't even sure what kind of jobs they had. He knew his dad had a job with computers and his mom was some sort of secretary. That's all he knew.

He'd had his own computer for as long as he could remember. About a year ago his parents had gotten him a modem and an internet account for Christmas. And that's when he discovered a whole new part of the world and a whole new bunch of friends, people who really cared about him and listened to what he had to say. He glanced at the digital time read-out across the top of his monitor. 11:43. What in the world were helicopters doing out at this time of the night? And what's with all the lights? He got up, shut his blinds and went back to his chat line. He was trying a new chat line that WhizKid, another of his internet friends, had told him about. He logged on, and so no one could trace him, didn't give his e-mail address. He lurked for a while, but the conversation was boring, all about which soap operas were the best. Yechhh.

He left that "room," tried some "lounges," and then decided to see if he could get into a few private rooms. He and WhizKid were working on a program that, if it worked, would allow him to locate "private" rooms and then lurk without anyone even knowing he was there. He pressed the configuration of keys that WhizKid had e-mailed him and a few minutes later he was rewarded with a listing of names of private rooms currently in use. It worked! Right away he e-mailed WhizKid. "It works!" he wrote. He tried the first one on the list. Some couple trying to come up with a place to finally meet. He tried another. It was some person writing over and over again about how he was going to kill himself, and the other person kept saying, "No, no, don't do it. Life isn't that bad."

Bor-rrr-ing, thought Matt. He tried a few others, and in a room named CFLA1 he read:

Earth Mother: The mission has succeeded. He has been eradicated. We have the child. Proceed to Step 2.

Goddaughter: Can't that wait? The child is not awake yet.

Earth Mother: Our waiting or proceeding is not contingent on the child's state of consciousness.

Earth Mother! He was Earth Angel! Cool!
He read on:

Goddaughter: I don't want to wake her.

Earth Mother: Where is she now in relation to where you are?

Goddaughter: Lying on the bed beside me, I gave her her teddy bear. As soon as she awakens, I will move her to the warehouse.

Earth Mother: What teddy bear?

Goddaughter: It was in her backpack.

Earth Mother: What backpack? Take those possessions away from her immediately!

Goddaughter: I will when the effects of the drug have worn off.

Earth Mother: You have to be strong, Goddaughter.

Goddaughter: She is stirring.

Earth Mother: Then get out of there! Throw out that teddy bear and that backpack. Get rid of them.

Goddaughter: She will be afraid.

Earth Mother: What's that to you? TAKE IT AWAY FROM HER!

Mystic Queen: May I make a suggestion, Earth Mother? Let the child keep the backpack. It's far safer to have the child's effects stay with the child than throw them in some garbage bin where the police will find them. And Goddaughter, murder is never easy, all of us have to be strong. None of us are like them, able to murder day after day after day. But this plan is our destiny. We have to think of the greater good.

Goddaughter: I guess I wasn't aware of all this.

Cool! thought Matt. He would love to de-lurk for a while and ask these jokers who they were, but as soon as he did that, his presence would be known. Better to remain anonymous. At least for now. More conversation appeared across the screen:

B. Voice: Can we please get off this absurdly sentimental piece of nonsense and get on with the plans for tomorrow? Have they been finalized?

Earth Mother: The first letter will be delivered tomorrow morning early, only four hours from now. It is ready to go as we speak.

West Connect: We are ready at this end.

Goddaughter: What do I do if she wakes up?

Earth Mother: Keep quiet and take her to the warehouse. Also, we need to find the letter we sent to the pro-life contingent, the one who refused to join our organization.

Joan of Ark: I will handle it.

Goddaughter: What did you mean when you wrote, "He has been eradicated?" Who?

Mystic Queen: Didn't you fill Goddaughter in on all the specifics?

Earth Mother: I give my people just what they need for the moment. Take her to the warehouse and await our instructions.

Awesome, thought Matt. *Way cool*! He leaned forward to watch more conversation, but the screen went blank as the room was emptied. He shrugged, leaned back in his chair, stretched his arms high above his head and yawned. A box appeared on his monitor screen, "You have new mail," it read. *Cool*, thought Matt as he opened up the e-mail from WhizKid.

CHAPTER 8

It had been a long night. At about 3 a.m. Roger was leaning over the desk in his office and stifling a yawn. His eyes were gritty and bloodshot and his face felt grimed with the day's accumulated worries. He was scanning the data Interpol had faxed to him.

"Why don't you catch some shut eye, boss?" He looked up. Francine, on the night shift, stood in front of him. She always called him boss.

He smiled. She was a good head, a friendly sort, who was as new to this detachment as he was. Short, stocky with cropped blonde hair, she was as tough as any male cop he'd ever worked with. She had a black belt in judo and he knew she instructed in the local judo club a couple of evenings a week. He also knew she lived by herself in a small square house with a black lab named Peter. Other than that he didn't know too much about her. She kept pretty much to herself.

"Ah, Francine," he said, interlacing his fingers behind his head and leaning back. "I'm not counting on getting too much sleep until this is over. Are the searchers still at it?"

"Yeah," she said. "I just got back from there. They're thinking of bringing in a heat sensing device. Oh, and the donut shop brought more donuts over, in case you're interested. They're out front."

"Just what I need, more sugar." He tapped the pages of fax with his pen and said, "What do you make of all this, Francine? I'll tell you my opinion, but what do you think? Gut reaction."

"Gut reaction? That we're gonna get a call from CBC, or CTV saying they received a plain brown envelope and inside a tape or a video with a 'message for the Canadian people.'"

Roger nodded. "My thoughts, too. That little girl's been kidnapped. It's too coincidental to think she just wandered off into the woods, Yesterday afternoon of all days."

"Are you finding anything?" asked Francine.

"Pages of terrorist groups all over the world who've claimed responsibility for abortion worker killings."

"So what's the next step?"

"We start going through this list one by one. After that, I don't know. Sit tight until morning? Wait till they decide to contact us?"

"Man, I hate that," said Francine, pounding the desk with her fist. "Why can't *we* make the first move for once? Why can't *we* get on the TV and say, 'You murdering, child-abducting creeps! You walk into this town, we'll be waiting for you—you think you can get away with this, you got another thing coming!'"

"Nice try, Francine. They, however, have an innocent child."

"We're still not sure of that. Maybe she did get lost in the woods."

But Roger shook his head. "Coincidences don't happen. Not in this business."

Later when his eyes would no longer function and he'd run out of toothpicks to hold them open, he got up, stretched and walked out and across the yard to the new RCMP apartment where he was staying until his wife Kate, and their two daughters, Sara and Becky, moved out from Alberta in June. He had been promoted to Sergeant and transferred to this detachment a few months back.

Inside the small apartment, he flicked on the overhead light. *What I should do is drop right into bed*, he thought. But instead, he flicked on his little table-top computer with modem. The computer was a gift from his wife before he left, along with the modem and an internet connection, which she'd arranged with a New Brunswick internet service provider before he arrived. She had purchased the computer and the modem second hand from one of her bosses at the real estate agency where she worked as a receptionist.

"It'll really be the best way to communicate with each other when you're out there," she had told him. "And cheap, too."

Roger had just shrugged. He considered himself the computer nerd of the family. His daughters had worked with computers in school from day one and at her work, Kate communicated all over the world via computer. She could tell him what houses were for sale in St. Matthews before he even had said "yes" to the job. Even though the detachment computers were all hooked up together, that was about as far as it went for him. Theoretically, he could contact Interpol via modem, but he never did. He usually left that for someone else. But he had to admit he was getting the hang of this, even though the only people he ever sent e-mails to were Kate and the girls.

He listened to the familiar whir as the machine started up and the high tones as the modem dialed. He had two e-mails waiting for him from Kate. The first one was long and chatty and full of news about Sara and Becky plus all the happenings in Chester. They'd had two couples come look at the house, she wrote. And even though the real estate market was slow or "flat" as realtors called it, Nancy, their realtor, felt their house would sell because of its location. She wrote that she was learning a lot first-hand about selling a house; things that would put her ahead of the game if she ever did decide to go for her real estate license.

She added that Sara had received her official acceptance at the University of New Brunswick, but was now thinking of a Bible school in the States. She had talked previously about staying in Alberta, but now she had decided she would come since Mark, her boyfriend, was hoping to go to Nashville with his alternative Christian rock band, Dog Ear. She was thinking of a Bible school close to Nashville. Surprise. Surprise. She asked what Roger thought about that?

Becky was doing okay, "As well as could be expected," she wrote. Becky still wasn't keen on moving east, but Kate was coping. She "found it difficult," she wrote, "not to let Becky's bad moods get her down." Roger smiled when he read it, and a deep pang touched at the very core of his being. He shouldn't be here by himself. The three of them shouldn't be so far away. No one should have to be split up like this, even for only a few months.

He opened and read her second e-mail. By now she had heard the news about Dr. Shanahan being shot, but not about the disappearance of Beth Knoll. Kate expressed horror at the act, telling him she'd be praying for him, and that a few people had already called her asking if this St. Matthews, New Brunswick, where all this had happened was the same St. Matthews, New Brunswick, where Roger was.

Roger wrote back that he hoped Kate was fine and that Bible college, even if it was in the States, would be a wonderful idea for Sara. They should support her in her decision. He told Kate not to let Becky's moods affect her and that, "Yes, indeed, this is the same St. Matthews, New Brunswick where Dr. Shanahan was shot." He didn't mention the missing girl, nor did he say much about the shooting. Even though Kate constantly assured him otherwise, he wasn't entirely convinced that the Internet was totally secure and private. "I'll call you," he typed.

*****

Julia couldn't sleep. It was four in the morning when she stood by the open window of her darkened bedroom and gazed out into the night. Sometime during the night a wind had come up and scrabbly fingers of clouds were racing across the face of the moon. By the light of the street lamp she watched a stand of black elms, their budding branches waving like the hands of children, casting teasing shadows on the lawn.

In the distance she could hear the helicopters and occasionally a long triangle of light shone down on the dark earth.

She prayed for the little girl. She could not imagine what she would do if one of her sons were out in those woods by himself, lost in the night. She pulled her housecoat around her and shut the window, latching it tightly.

Her mother was staying with them for the night and was sleeping in the guest room downstairs. Her mother had insisted on it, phoning during the prayer meeting with, "You must be going out of your mind with worry. I'm sure those pro-abortionist people are probably blaming you by now. I know I would not feel safe under those circumstances. I've called the police to keep an eye on your house and I'll be over just as soon as I throw a few things into my train case."

When she had arrived, the prayer meeting had ended. Her mother unpacked in the guest room, then went into the kitchen and made tea and toast which she brought into the living room. Julia, intent on watching the 11 o'clock news, did not look up.

"No thanks. I'm not hungry," she said, keeping her eye on the screen. The RCMP were refusing to speculate on whether the missing girl had anything to do with the shooting death of Dr. Douglas Shanahan. Although the reporter was speculating for all her worth, drawing attention to the fact that Beth Knoll's mother Emma was an outspoken national proponent of women's reproductive rights, and that the Shanahan Clinic plus Shanahan himself had been the target of many angry protests. The station had even dug up some old footage of the original construction of the clinic four years ago. Julia leaned forward. She recognized well known pro-life activist Des Thillens who had chained himself to the fence around the clinic, not allowing construction workers to enter. Julia hadn't lived here then, but she knew that Des' membership in the local pro-life organization had been revoked shortly after that. As far as she knew, he had left the country. She had never met him, nor did she know exactly why it was that his membership was revoked.

She listened as an RCMP officer said that as far as they were concerned they were treating this just like any other homicide investigation, and presently there was no information that would link the disappearance of Beth Knoll to the murder of Dr. Douglas Shanahan, but that they were looking into all possibilities.

"Nonsense," her mother had said, placing the plate in front of Julia on the coffee table. Julia looked up, wondering what she was referring to. "You can't say you're not hungry. You must eat. Your father and I had tea and toast every single night of our lives while he was alive, God rest him. It helps with digestion and with sleep."

The newscast had shifted to the Shanahan estate, which was surrounded by yellow tape and armies of police vans. Officers with POLICE in large white letters written across the backs of their jackets walked around looking grave.

Her mother, who was breaking her toast into little pieces said, "Have some toast."

"Maybe later," said Julia.

And now, as Julia stood in front of the window in the dark of the early morning, she thought about her mother. She was her mother's only daughter. Her brother Phil and his family were missionaries in the Philippines. She only saw her brother once in a long while. He was the "star" of the family. Her mother talked about him constantly. She and her mother talked, yes, they talked, but not about anything in particular. Julia knew her mother saw her as serious and intense, while she saw her mother as flighty and unpurposed. She lived for teas and antique sales with her friends, traveling far down the New England coast with friends looking for that perfect antique china cup. Sometimes she brought things home for the boys, but they were strange things, peculiar things. Once she brought them an old and yellowed framed jigsaw puzzle of Sergeant Preston of the Yukon that she'd picked up in a flea market in Maine. Jeff looked at it and then looked up at his mother. His grandmother said that this was a part of Canada, a part of its history, to which Julia replied, "Mother, it was just a television program."

"Julia, you're so driven," her mother would sometimes say. But Julia took everything seriously, from the prayer vigils she organized, to her own personal prayer life.

Five years ago when Mason left her, it took her six weeks before she could admit to her mother over the phone that her marriage had dissolved. And even then, her mother merely chatted on about coming out to St. Matthews where she grew up, where she knew people, where she had friends. Reluctantly, Julia finally agreed. Living in Toronto on welfare as a single mom was taking its toll. She needed a new start.

Her mother had picked her up at the bus station and driven Julia and the boys to her home, chattering on and on about the weather, the architecture in St. Matthews, the fact that the Bay of Fundy was too cold for swimming, and how she hoped that didn't disappoint the boys too much since they were used to Lake Ontario. It was tea and toast that night as well.

Two years ago Julia had been offered the job as coordinator of the Pregnancy Care Centre, and she took it. She knew about pain. She knew about suffering. She'd seen her Christian, Sunday school teacher-of-a-husband leave her for another woman, another *Christian* woman. The two of them, Mason and that raven-haired woman, would sit there in church, three rows ahead of her, children spread out on either side—hers next to her and Joshua and Jeff next to him, his arms along the back of the pew. A regular Brady Bunch they were, with no one in the church even seeming to notice that anything amiss had happened at all. No one saying anything, just smiling and accepting it like this was good and proper and right. Nothing to get upset about. Happens all the time. But every night after the boys had gone to bed, Julia would hug herself into the quilt on her couch and cry there until morning.

Her new pay check enabled her to rent a small house in downtown St. Matthews and her mother gladly took the boys after school. The ripped and crumpled up piece of paper that was her life was beginning to get straightened out again, fold by fold.

The sound of the helicopters was dimming. She no longer saw the light. Maybe that meant they had found the little girl. *Oh God, please make them have found that little girl!*

CHAPTER 9

Francine had been right. At nine o'clock the following morning, Roger woke from his short sleep to the ringing of the phone at his bedside. It was Constable Steve Malone. The group claiming responsibility for the shooting had left an envelope on the desk of one of the reporters of the *St. Matthews Courier*.

"They also have the girl," said Steve.

Twenty minutes later, Roger and Steve were in a patrol car heading out to the *Courier* building a few blocks away. Steve was driving, his hands gripping the wheel tightly, his face grim. Steve was a big man in his late 20s, tall and muscular with thick red hair which he wore very short. He and his wife Cindy had a newborn baby daughter, but Roger couldn't remember her name.

Steve turned to Roger, "That reporter read me the letter over the phone...."

"You told me."

"If this letter isn't a hoax, then we're dealing with a bunch of lunatics, a crazy...." He shook his head but didn't finish the sentence.

The *St. Matthews Courier* was housed in a low, one-story building which featured a lot of brick and stone in its construction. Dwight Ingraham, the publisher of the *Courier,* met them at the front door and soberly ushered them in. "Because it was a Saturday," he explained, "the only person in was Sandy, the sports reporter, doing up the weekend sports copy for the Monday edition."

"So Sandy was the *only* one in this morning?" repeated Roger.

"That's right."

Dwight led them down a short hall and into the news room, a small room with four metal desks, a computer on each.

"Here's the letter." Dwight pointed to a single sheet of white 8 1/2 X 11 computer paper laid out on a desk. Standing to one side was Sandy, young and nervous looking.

"I never touched it," Sandy said. "After I opened it up, I never touched it at all. I just called Dwight right away." He kept running his palms up and down on his jeans as if trying to rub off something foul. "I never touched it after I opened it," he said again.

Roger and Steve bent over the piece of paper. The message was printed in all caps:

IS IT EVER RIGHT TO KILL ONE PERSON TO SAVE THE LIVES OF MILLIONS? YES!! OUR SOCIETY EXECUTES AND IMPRISONS MURDERERS AND RAPISTS WHO TAKE THE LIVES OF INNOCENT PEOPLE. BUT WE ARE LETTING PEOPLE LIVE WHO MURDER MILLIONS AND MILLIONS OF UNBORN BABIES EVERY DAY!! WE LET THEM LIVE TO MURDER AGAIN AND AGAIN AND AGAIN! WHY? BECAUSE LIBERALS AND ATHEISTS RUN OUR GOVERNMENTS AND OUR COURT SYSTEMS! LIBERALS AND ATHEISTS WHO KILL UNBORN BABIES. IT'S TIME WE PUT AN END TO THE KILLINGS. IT'S TIME WE EXECUTED THE KILLERS! SHANAHAN SHOULD HAVE DIED A THOUSAND TIMES!!!! WE HAVE BETH KNOLL. SHE IS AN INNOCENT CHILD. BUT HER MOTHER IS AN ACCESSORY TO MURDER. WE WILL KILL THIS CHILD (TO SAVE THE LIVES OF MILLIONS) IF OUR DEMANDS ARE NOT MET!!!! THESE DEMANDS WILL BE FORTHCOMING.
—THE CHRISTIAN FREEDOM LIFE ARMY

Roger hardly dared breathe, and for several minutes he stood there and read it over again, trying to absorb its horrific message.

Somehow, he had known this child had been abducted—had known it in his soul from the moment he saw Emma glance nervously down the street. Still, there was a part of him that hoped that she had just "wandered off" into the woods next to the school, and that at any moment some lumber jacketed woodsman would come carrying her into St. Matthews, all smiles. *I was out to my fish camp, and there she was, all huddled up on the porch. Lost. She's a little cold, but she's fine. Look, she's fine.*

"It was in an envelope?" asked Roger.

"Yes. In that one." Sandy pointed to the plain legal-sized white envelope which had been opened with a paper cutter. "Just like that, with no name on it. I opened it up, and then I called Dwight. I never touched it after that."

Roger knew Dwight slightly. When Roger was transferred into St. Matthews, Dwight had written a feature profile on him which was favorable and friendly. Dwight was a big, meaty man with a large-featured doughy face. Now he stood there, one arm on the young reporter's shoulder and said to Roger, "I came right down. Didn't know if this was a practical joke or not. No sense taking any chances, Saturday or no Saturday."

"Why would someone put it on my desk?" Sandy was whining. "Why'd they pick me? I don't have any connection with any of those people. It's not like I ever wrote any articles about abortion. It's not like I even have an *opinion* on the subject. I'm a sports writer." He licked his lips. His voice irritated Roger.

"It could have been random," said Roger. "It appears your desk is closest to the door."

Dwight was talking now. "You see, he's right, Sandy. No one has it in for you. Like the man says, it was probably a random thing."

"Who has keys to this building?" asked Roger straightening.

Dwight answered. "All of us; all the reporters, photographers, staff people, janitors. St. Matthews is usually a pretty safe place. Even with all of our equipment here we've never had a problem, none whatsoever."

"Does it look like anything else was tampered with? Was anything taken?"

Dwight rubbed his hand across his forehead. "To tell you the truth," he said, "I never even checked. Have you checked out back, Sandy?"

"Not me, no. I took one look at that letter and wanted to get out of here. That's when I called Dwight. At first I thought it was a joke...."

Roger interrupted him, "What time did you get here this morning?"

"Me? Oh around 8:30, maybe closer to 8:45." He glanced at Dwight.

"Did you see anything? Hear anything? Especially when you first arrived. Think back."

"No sir, I did not. Just the envelope, sitting there plain as day on my desk. That's when I opened it...."

"And at 8:30 you were the only one here?"

"Yes, sir. But it might have been 8:45."

"Was the door locked when you arrived?"

"I think so, I mean I had to use my key. I probably would have noticed if the door had been unlocked, wouldn't I? If I'd stuck my key in the lock, wouldn't I have noticed if it was already unlocked?"

"We'd like to look around," Roger said to Dwight. "We'll try to take some fingerprints from Sandy's desk, as well as near the front door area. Now, we would appreciate it if you would give us a tour of the place; doors, windows, exits, that kind of thing."

"No problem," said Dwight.

For the next half hour Dwight gave them the king's tour of the premises; doors, windows, fire escapes. But all of them were shut up tight. Neither the front nor the back door seemed tampered with. The windows looked like they hadn't been opened all winter. Roger bent down and examined the front door lock. *A cheap one*, he noted, *one a kid could pick with a credit card.* He frowned.

Before they left, Steve placed the letter and the envelope in a plastic evidence bag. After preliminary fingerprint checks in St. Matthews, the letter, along with its envelope, would be sent to the crime lab in Halifax, Nova Scotia, where it would be studied, scrutinized, examined and put through a thousand tests. Even the writing style would be analyzed by a forensic psychologist and a profile of the killer, or killers, would be drawn up. To Roger, the letter looked like it came out of a laser printer, which would make it a bit more difficult to pinpoint. Had it been typewritten it would have been easier to track down. Individual typewriters were almost as unique as fingerprints. But nobody used typewriters anymore. If the envelope had been licked when sealed, the saliva would be worth its weight in gold when it came to DNA testing.

"Can I put any of this in the paper?" asked Dwight. "I mean, you say the word and I'll keep a lid on it. We all need to work together on this. We're in this together."

"Maybe for the time being," said Roger. "Until we know what we're dealing with. Until we know it isn't a hoax."

"No use frightening people," said Steve.

"Right," said Dwight, leading them to the front door.

Before heading back to the detachment, Roger and Steve decided to do a house-to-house check on West End Boulevard near the newspaper office. This would be a fairly simple procedure as there were only three homes, one on either side of the *Courier* building and kitty corner across the street. The rest of the terrain was scrub brush and fields, an abandoned strip mall, and an empty gas station, its dried up gas pumps like dead stumps in the cracked cement. The *Courier* had moved here at a time when this part of town was the place to locate. "Good parking, low rent, the place your business can expand," the ads read. Instead, the growth of St. Matthews took off in another direction, Edge Street near the waterfront, leaving the upper west side virtually abandoned. Steve told him all of this as they walked next door.

In the small, rundown cottage to the left of the newspaper

building, an elderly lady with a thin, pinched nose and yellowing gray hair said she had seen nothing. "And I get up every morning at six to feed my birds. They're coming back, you know. The birds. I like to be up early to watch them."

"And at 6 o'clock you didn't see any strange car or person?" asked Steve.

"No, can't say as I did. Mind you, if someone'd been snooping around I'd of seen 'em. Wasn't that something, that murder yesterday? Right here in St. Matthews of all places. I never seen nothing like it. Is this anything to do with that?"

"There was a break-in at the *Courier* building last night," said Steve.

The woman clucked her tongue and muttered something about the world not being a safe place anymore. "And me up here all by myself. I live alone, you know. So much violence. I blame it on TV, you know. That's what I think is causing all this. Before TV, you think back, there was nothing like people killing each other. Nothing at all."

Roger and Steve thanked her and moved on to the duplex on the other side of the *Courier* building which was occupied by a wide-eyed young couple in their early twenties. The two of them came to the door and looked wonderingly at the uniformed men who stood there. In unison they shook their heads and said, "No," they hadn't seen anything strange. But then again, they had gotten up only a few hours ago. "We rented a couple videos last night and went to bed around two. Never saw a thing then," said the young woman.

The other side of the duplex was deserted.

The first real clue came from the house across the street. Roger and Steve could hear the loud rock music even before they headed up the walkway. After five minutes of pounding, the door was finally answered by a tall, lanky teenage boy wearing only green Adidas sweat shorts. Roger had to yell to be heard over the grating bass tones. The boy shook his head absently in answer to Roger's questions.

From somewhere behind the boy Roger heard a woman's

voice. "Turn that music down, Andy! You want to wake up the dead?" As she walked toward the door and spied the officers her eyes widened. "What's going on? My land, Andy! Get to your room, turn your music down. This instant!"

When the errant Andy had lumbered none too quickly down the hall, and the music was finally lowered to conversation levels, she turned to them and said, "I'm so sorry, it's the music, isn't it? If I tell him once, I've told him a thousand times to turn it down, but kids these days, all brain dead, but you have my word, I'll make sure he keeps it low."

Steve spoke. "We're not here about the music."

"You're not?"

Roger began, "No, we're here...."

"Is it Andy? Andy senior?" Her voice rose shrilly at the end.

"No," said Roger. "There was a break-in at the *Courier* building last night and we're here to ask you if you saw or heard anything."

She put her hand to her chest. "Oh my land. I thought it was Andy. My husband Andy. He works in the bush. I thought you were here.... I thought something had happened. Oh my land.... It's bad enough when he's gone. I've got to deal with Andy junior, all alone. You'd think I was a single mother, with Andy senior gone so much. But let me think. Last night?"

"Yes." Steve was speaking now. "Did you happen to hear or see anything out of the ordinary any time during the night?"

She stood there for several seconds, her left hand stroking her upper right arm. She was a small round-bodied woman with a pug nose and a wide mouth. She was wearing a stained tee-shirt, faded jeans and plastic flip flops. "As a matter of fact, yes I did. I don't sleep well when Andy senior's gone, what with worrying about Andy junior and all, and so I came into the living room and sat looking out."

"In the front room?" asked Roger.

"Come in, come in." She ushered them into a cramped, disheveled living room. Newspapers and magazines lay haphazardly on the floor along with coffee cups and plates which had once held food. A TV Guide lay opened and face down on the floor and the wrapping from an ice cream sandwich was crumpled on the floor next to it.

"Excuse the mess," she said, making a half-hearted attempt at straightening. "What with Andy senior being gone, I tend to let things go sometimes...." Her voice trailed off and Roger suddenly felt sorry for her. He thought of Kate, just then, a single mother of sorts, on her own coping with two teenage daughters. Was she telling people, "What with Roger gone, I tend to let things go sometimes..."?

"I was sitting right here," she said, pointing to a blanket-covered overstuffed chair which had seen better days. "It was oh, about four in the morning, so I didn't turn the lights on. I was looking across the street at the *Courier* building. A van drove up. I watched someone get out of the passenger side and then walk up to the front door. A couple minutes later he comes walking back again, gets in the van and then they take off. I never gave it another thought after that. At the time I thought to myself, 'Boy! They work late over there.'"

Roger wrote her answers in his notebook.

"You said 'he'. Was this person a man?"

She looked up at them. "You know, I'm not sure. I just assumed it was a man. It looked like a man."

"Can you describe this person?"

"Not really. It was dark. And I wasn't looking that carefully."

"Could you see what this person was wearing? Pants? A jacket? Could you see anything?"

"Nothing. But I know whoever it was wasn't wearing a dress. No, he was definitely wearing pants, maybe dark, and maybe a jacket with a hood, I think."

Roger asked, "Could you describe the way that person walked? Was he or she running?"

"No, walking."

"Walking fast, limping, anything distinctive about the walk?"

She cocked her head to one side and thought. "He walked

not exactly fast. No, I wouldn't say fast, just determined, not rushing, but walking fast."

"What about the van. Could you describe it?"

"It was a dark blue van. That's all I remember. It was dark out, so everything looked dark."

"You didn't notice the license number?" asked Steve hopefully.

"Afraid not." She frowned and hugged her arms. "Nothing. Never even looked at it. Never even considered that anyone would need to know it. I don't know if I could have seen it from here, even if I wanted to."

Steve said, "How about your son, would he have noticed anything?"

"At that time he would have been dead to the world, out like a light, but I'll call him if you want."

Andy junior had added a blue tank top to his ensemble when he returned to the living room. He shook his head. He had seen nothing, heard nothing. "I was sleeping," he said.

"You know these kids on a Friday night," she said. "Once they're asleep they're dead to the world until noon the following day."

Roger smiled. "I know. I've got two teenagers myself."

CHAPTER 10

It was Saturday. Julia's usual day for cleaning, dusting, vacuuming, laundry. And if Dr. Shanahan hadn't been killed yesterday, she would have been shaking throw rugs off the back porch and yelling at the boys to please put away their toys before they went out to play.

Instead, she was sitting with her mother at the kitchen table drinking coffee and listlessly picking apart a freshly baked blueberry muffin. Joshua and Jeff were sitting on the floor in the living room watching cartoons, aware that something very grave and different was going on.

Her mother was rambling about what constituted a perfect muffin. "The trick is not mixing the batter too much. I can always tell a muffin that the batter's been mixed too much."

Julia said, "The news said they didn't find that little girl yet."

"What a situation. What a situation. What a thing to have happen," said her mother. She was shaking her head, frowning when the phone rang.

It was a timid female voice which said, "Mrs. Nash, this is Nadine. I was in yesterday to see you?"

"Oh, Nadine. Oh yes." Julia was about to say, "I'd forgotten all about you," but stopped herself in time. She said, instead, "I'm glad you called, Nadine."

"You said you were going to call me last night? That you might call me?"

"Oh, Nadine, I'm so sorry. So much has happened since I talked with you. I'm sorry I forgot."

"That's okay, but you said you'd talk to my mom?"

"The two of us will talk to her. That includes you, too."

"Well, I was wondering about something else, too."

"Go on."

"That doctor that was killed. Do you think they'll be giving abortions in two weeks? I'm supposed to get one, but I wanted to talk to you first."

"I'm so glad you called me, Nadine."

"I was also wondering about that little girl that's lost. You haven't heard if they found her, have you?"

"No, I haven't heard. But I have been praying that she will be kept safe, wherever she is."

"Yeah, I guess. Anyway, Mrs. Nash...?"

"You can call me Julia."

"Uh, okay, but I was wondering if maybe we could meet today, like you said. If you're not too busy or anything."

"Let's meet, Nadine. How about today at the Centre at three?"

CHAPTER 11

Emma had watched the sun rise. She was in a chair by the window and was there when the dawn whitened the horizon little by little. Others around her walked carefully, quietly—making coffee, greeting visitors, accepting their pots of food, their loaves of bread, and answering the phone.

Sophie was sitting beside her now. Funny, Emma couldn't remember Kathy leaving and Sophie coming. On the coffee table in front of her a thick white candle burned. She stared at the elliptical flame, reaching upwards, perfectly still. Glen, frowning and haggard, was sitting at the kitchen table, head resting on his hands, eyes closed. Emma wondered if he was sleeping. Several seconds later she realized that he was on the phone, speaking in low tones.

Had she been asleep? Had she just wakened? But no, she had been there when the sun rose. Now it was full in the sky. Where had the last several hours gone to?

Sophie was moving toward her, a cup of coffee in her hand. "I'm glad you were finally able to get some sleep," she was saying.

Sleep? Emma was staring at the candle, at the wet pool of white wax around the wick. A perfect circle.

"That was Kathy's idea," said Sophie. "She thought we ought to light a candle and keep it lit until Beth comes home."

Emma nodded. She closed her eyes painfully and leaned her head against the back of the chair. "They haven't found Beth." It was a statement rather than a question.

Sophie shook her head slowly. "Not yet, but they will," she said.

Glen had hung up. "That was the police," he said. "They're coming over to talk to us."

The candle flame flickered a little as Glen got up and lumbered toward her. Emma held her breath. As long as the candle burned, there was hope. As long as it burned.

*****

The police officers, the same ones who had come to the clinic yesterday, were out front. Emma watched from her chair as they walked up the sidewalk. She did not move. She could not move, but stayed the way she had been all night, sitting still in her chair, knees together, hands tightly clasped in her lap.

Glen was at the door in his rumpled sweater, looking weary and gray. He was the first to speak. "You have news?"

Emma remembered the officer's name now, Sergeant Sheppard. He said, "We haven't found her, but we do have something. It could be a hoax, but we have to treat it as if it isn't. This is Constable Francine Myers, by the way."

Glen ignored the introduction. "What? What?" he said.

Sergeant Sheppard unfolded a piece of paper and spread it out on the coffee table next to the burning candle. He said, "The *St. Matthews Courier* received this anonymously last night. We're having the original examined. This is a photocopy."

Three faces, hers, Glen's and Sophie's, leaned over the coffee table and read the message. When Emma had finished, she heard a noise, a sputtering choking, a breathless wail. It was several seconds before she realized the sound was coming from herself, welling up from some place deep within her throat, some animal place, some place she could not control. A sob, a clutching at her throat. She stood up suddenly, eyes wide and rushed into the bathroom. Tears, choking, coughing, her hands trembling uncontrolably, leaning over the toilet, tears mingling with bile. She could not stop. *Stop*, she told herself. *Stop*! She could not.

Well, they had won. That much she could say for them. They had done what the thousands of protesters at the doors of her clinic had not done. They had found the one place where she hurt. They had found it and were ripping it open. With their bare hands, they were tearing out her insides, making her bleed. They had taken Beth. Beth!

"Emma." She was dimly aware of a hand touching her hair, stroking, stroking. "Emma, it's me, Kathy. I'm back. I was out getting some groceries. I read the letter, Emma. Emma, look at me. Beth will be okay. As soon as we find out what they want, we'll get it to them and then Beth will come home. We'll figure out a way to get them. We will, Emma. Look at me. You're one of the strong ones, Emma. We'll fight them. We'll do this. You have lots of friends. Lots of friends who'll help. Friends all over the country. We'll do whatever it takes."

Emma rose, flushed the toilet, rinsed out her mouth and scrubbed her face with soap. She finally asked, her voice shaky and uncertain, "Are the police still here?"

"Yes, they're still talking with Glen."

When Emma returned to the living room, Francine, the woman police officer, told Emma that someone would be staying with her, in her house 24 hours a day. In addition, the police would be monitoring her phone.

Emma nodded. She could hear Glen talking to the Sergeant. He was saying, "How have you dealt with other abductions like this?"

And the Sergeant was saying, "This doesn't happen too often here. We've had hostage situations where individuals have barricaded themselves in their houses...."

"If you've never had a situation like this before, how can you guarantee the safety of my daughter?"

The Sergeant replied softly, "We can't guarantee that, Mr. Knoll." He paused. "But what we can guarantee is that we will do our very best to find your daughter. We are, right now, bringing in experts from all over the country. And we will protect you and your family the best way that we can."

"It's a little late for that," said Glen dryly.

"I know it sounds like a cliché, but we're doing everything that we can, Mr. Knoll. This is our number one priority now."

Glen bowed his head in his hands. "I'm sorry," he said. "I'm not blaming you. It's just that I'm not used to this kind of thing."

"No one is."

Later, when Sergeant Sheppard was ready to leave, Emma looked at him. "At least she has Mrs. Jenkins."

"What?" he asked.

"Her teddy bear. She never sleeps without her teddy bear. She took him to school this morning to show Jane."

"Mrs. Jenkins?"

Emma smiled, the first time she had smiled in a day. "That was her name for the teddy bear. Mrs. Jenkins. Beth put an Anne of Green Gables dress on her bear and for some reason her name became Mrs. Jenkins."

CHAPTER 12

Back at the detachment, Constable Eric Jamison looked up from his computer screen. "Do you know how many dark blue vans there are in the province of New Brunswick? And I haven't even gotten the numbers in from Maine and Nova Scotia yet. As for Des Thillens, the guy from the news video of the protest several years ago that you told me to look up. I can't find anything on him. His New Brunswick driver's license expired four years ago and was never renewed. Not anywhere in Canada. His New Brunswick Medicare also hasn't been used in four years. The FBI is checking on him, but we haven't heard anything yet."

"So he doesn't drive anymore and hasn't gotten sick. At least not in this province."

Steve nodded. "I checked his social insurance number. His last job was four years ago in a body repair shop, Al's Garage, in St. Andrews. He was fired from that one apparently and never worked again. Never filed for unemployment, either."

Roger stood silently and said, "My guess is he's moved south. Maine, New Jersey, maybe Florida."

"What do you want me to do with all these dark colored vans?"

"Start personally checking them out."

"All of them? Do you have any idea how many there are?"

"Start with the ones in St. Matthews and work out from there."

"We don't have the manpower," protested Eric.

"We'll get it. We're getting additional help from every department in the province. This place will be like Grand Central Station for a while."

"And this list of terrorist organizations?"

"A personal check on them as well," said Roger, moving toward his office where Staff Sergeant Mal Jarvis from RCMP Division 2 in Fredericton was sitting. Roger had forgotten that earlier Kelly, their receptionist, had told him that Jarvis would be driving down today to talk to Roger about a joint plan of action. Already the media was beginning to camp out at their doors.

On the way into his office, a young female constable he didn't recognize came up to him.

"Sergeant Sheppard?" She extended her hand. "I'm Jill Mitchell from Division 2. I'm supposed to tell you that the envelope and letter are basically clean. No prints. It's already on its way down to Halifax."

Roger nodded. "We can only hope the guy licked the envelope."

"Yes sir."

After a quick fifteen minute meeting with Mal, in which they set up a cooperative plan, Roger went alone to the Shanahan estate. Although Sheila Shanahan had talked with a few officers, Roger hadn't met her yet.

Mal's last words echoed in his ears as he walked out of the detachment. "I was supposed to have next week off. Bass season opened. Even got myself a new boat."

CHAPTER 13

It was early afternoon when Roger drove up the circular drive on Edge Road toward the Shanahan estate. The sun was sending flickering shafts of light through the elms. It was warm, but then again it should be. May was only a week away.

Twenty-four hours ago Roger had driven up this same roadway in response to the frantic voice of Moira Pilgrim.

He parked the cruiser in front of the house. There were no other cars evident, although to the right of the house was an attached three car garage. The grounds around the Shanahan estate were oddly quiet, the wind had momentarily died and even the birds did not sing. It was as if the land itself were paying tribute to their slain owner, tree limbs bowing at half mast. Roger ascended the wide, newly painted, white wooden porch steps. To the left, on the wide verandah was a porch swing, cushioned in printed cotton. Sitting out there one would have a commanding view of the inlet, he noted. To the right of the door two wooden lawn chairs faced a round table. There were faint rings on the table where drinks had once sat.

The door was opened by a fair-haired woman with red eyes and pale skin who appeared to be in her late 20s. She looked tentatively at his uniform.

"I'm Sergeant Sheppard with the Royal Canadian Mounted Police here in St. Matthews. I'd like to talk to Mrs. Sheila Shanahan if I may."

"Just a minute." The woman turned, leaving him standing outside.

A few minutes later an older woman appeared. She was an attractive woman, small, with chin-length iron gray hair. Her face was smooth and strong featured. She held her head high, and even though she was clad in beige pedal pushers and a flowered blouse, she looked almost regal. She extended her hand.

"I'm Sheila Shanahan. I see you have met my daughter Lois."

Lois said nothing, just looked at him tentatively from behind her mother. In the daughter, Roger could see the mother—smooth skin, upturned nose, straight hair. But in the daughter there was nothing of the character of the mother. It was like she was a cheaply made imitation, a poor replica standing there, red-faced, blowing her nose.

Sheila ushered him into a wide polished wood foyer and then into a formal living room with bay windows which afforded a spectacular view of the Bay. Roger opened his notebook and flipped to a clean page.

"Have a seat if you wish," said Sheila.. "I would normally offer you tea, but I hope you'll forgive me if I'm not as hospitable as I usually am. The past day has taken its toll on me, I'm afraid. I've gone from incredible sadness to unbelievable outrage." She sat in a throne-like high-backed chair. Roger sat down on a love seat across from her.

"Could I ask you a few question, Mrs. Shanahan?"

"Please, call me Sheila."

"Sheila, did your husband receive any recent threats that you know about?"

She thought briefly. "Not recently. No. None that I know of." She paused. "There was all that trouble a few years ago when the clinic opened here. Des Thillens. He personally threatened Douglas. He was part of that whole group of anti-abortionists at the time. Martin Cranmore, Betsy Schellenberg; you probably have all their names. I can't remember the rest of the names of that crew. But recently, no. Things have been fairly quiet."

"Have you noticed anything different about his behavior is recent weeks? Anything you can pinpoint as strange or odd?"

She shook her head. "No, nothing."

"Any strange phone calls? Anything at all which didn't seem right? I want you to think back, Sheila."

"I can't think of a thing. I really can't." She shook her head. "If I could, believe me, I would tell you." She folded her hands in her lap and gazed down at them.

Roger turned to Lois. "How about you? Have you noticed anything different about your father lately? Have you had any conversation with him which seemed odd or strange?"

Lois shook her head, saying nothing. She was sitting in a pale green sofa and almost seemed to be disappearing into it. She looked over at her mother a few times. Then she said, "I haven't seen my father in a while."

"You live in St. Andrews?"

She shrugged. "You get busy in your life," she said. "And my father is...was always so busy with the clinic and with political things...."

Her voice trailed off.

"When was the last time you saw your father?" he asked.

Lois glanced over at her mother. "Maybe a year." She was shredding Kleenexes in her lap. Her lower lip was trembling now, too. Roger looked at her and waited. But she said no more.

"Sergeant Sheppard," said Sheila. "My daughter Lois is taking this news very badly I'm afraid. If there's nothing more you need her for, I would suggest she be allowed to leave."

Roger said fine. Once she was out of earshot, Sheila leaned toward him. "This has been most shocking for Lois. She's been through a lot lately, and is dealing with some personal problems of her own, then this on top of everything. Now, is there anything else you'd like to know about Douglas?"

"We would like to have access to any personal files that your husband may have kept here at home."

"Oh, by all means. He kept most of his patient files under lock and key down at the clinic. The only things here are some personal letters, tax stuff and the like, but you're welcome to them." She rose. "Follow me, I'll take you up to his office."

Roger followed her out into the front foyer and up a flight of stairs.

"This place used to be a convent. Did you know that? As a consequence there are a lot of very small rooms on the upper floors. Douglas and I have knocked down many walls to turn the smaller rooms into larger ones. We hope to do a bit more of that this summer."

Around the second floor landing she led him up another flight of stairs.

"Douglas is a very private person, Mr. Sheppard. I know how he is portrayed in the media, but in reality, he is reserved, almost shy. He chose the uppermost room for his study. He called it his 'Upper Room.'"

Dr. Shanahan's office was fronted by floor to ceiling cathedral shaped windows. A large wooden desk sat squarely in the center of the room, facing the view of the Bay.

"Here are his files," said Sheila, pulling open the drawer of a large wooden cabinet. "I think this is all of them."

She gathered up a handful of manila file folders and dropped them onto the desk. "Wait here a minute," she said. "I'll go get a box."

She left him standing in the room. He listened to her footfalls on the stairs. He walked over to the window and looked down. From there he had a clear view of the small garden patch where the doctor had met his demise. The ground had been combed clean. The bloodied flowers, along with the trays the plants had come in, had been sent to the crime lab. All that remained was the yellow tape, draped limply from the branches. He turned back to the room. It was a large, comfortable office that Douglas had created for himself, cavelike and cozy with dark walls and plush Oriental rugs on the hardwood floor. Roger did not see a computer and wondered if Douglas had one hidden behind a wooden cabinet somewhere.

A few minutes later Sheila returned with a box which she efficiently put the files in. "There," she said with satisfaction and handed it to him.

"Mrs. Shanahan, Sheila, does your husband have a computer at home?"

"Computer?" She shook her head and laughed. "Heavens no. You are talking about my husband. *My* husband is totally computer illiterate." She was laughing, now; a pleasant sound.

"He had one down at the clinic, but I'm sure Emma has already given you access to the files on it. But as for home, heaven's no."

Roger smiled, "A man after my own heart."

She was suddenly serious. "Can I ask about Beth? Have you located her yet?"

"I'm afraid not."

A look of genuine sadness crossed her face.

He said, "It's a strong possibility that the people who did this to your husband have kidnapped Beth. That's a strong possibility. Something we're looking into now."

"Oh my dear, no," said Sheila. "I've got to see Emma. She must be frantic."

CHAPTER 14

On the way to St. Andrews, a drive of only 20 minutes, Roger thought about Lois, who lived in St. Andrews, yet by her own admission, hardly ever saw her parents. And about Dr. Shanahan's own widow Sheila, who seemed too hale and hearty, too unmoved by the death, too in control, speaking of her husband in the present tense. But people grieve in different ways. When told about the accidental death of a child, he had seen some parents totally fall apart, while others stood stolid and still, nodding and wanting to know all the details—time, cause of death—as if knowing every single detail would somehow make it easier to accept.

To his right now, was the St. Matthews Yacht Club. A few impatient boaters were out scraping the hulls of their sail boats or scrubbing the decks. Beyond, the inlet glowed golden under the sun. His thoughts went to Kate. She would like it here, he decided. She would like the Bay, the whales, the tides, the ferry rides across to picturesque islands. Suddenly he was longing for Kate, and his longing for her became like a physical thing which caught at his chest. He felt alone and solitary in this town, incomplete without Kate and the girls. Even the support of a church and pastor and a few good friends was lacking in this new place.

He had found a church that he liked, a small one, and the people seemed friendly enough. But the ultimate decision on which church to attend would have to wait until Kate and the girls moved out. He'd already decided that, so his involvement in church and the local congregation remained almost at arm's length. A few people in the congregation had invited him over for Sunday dinner, but he could sense their wariness. He was the new RCMP Sergeant.

In a round of municipal government restructuring, the town of St. Matthews had lost its local, historical, well-established, well-loved, well-respected police force, and had been forced to turn to the federal RCMP to police it for them. Initially, that decision had not gone over well in St. Matthews. Citizens' groups had protested and editorials had come out in favor of community police officers who "walked the beat." Even though across Canada the RCMP's newest mandate was "community policing," there was an innate distrust of the "feds."

In the few months since Roger had been here, the town had come to a reluctant acceptance of the RCMP and an almost grudging pride in the new RCMP detachment building. There were five officers in the detachment; like himself all new to St. Matthews. There was Roger, Corporal Jack Boyce, and Constables Francine Myers, Steve Malone and Eric Jamison. In addition, Kelly McLean, a bouncy red-head from Nova Scotia, was the detachment receptionist. Thankfully, in the cuts, none of the former local police force had lost their jobs, but had been transferred to Fredericton, Halifax and Toronto.

There were things about Alberta that he missed. He missed, especially, the friendship he and Kate had developed with Constable Roberta St. Marie. Occasionally he heard from her. She was enjoying her new posting in the Northwest Territories. "A lot of alcohol and drug related problems," she had written, "...and domestic violence. It's a challenge."

In the horizon now, off the Bay to the south, Roger saw a bank of clouds rising in a straight line in the low sky. So, the brief good weather wasn't going to last.

He turned into the tourist town of St. Andrews and drove along the water front, passing artists' studios, craft stores, novelty shops, and outdoor cafes which featured lobster rolls and cappuccinos and catered to the backpacking crowd in the summer.

Al's Body Shop was located two streets away from the

picturesque water front drive. He pulled into the parking lot and went inside to find Al.

A young man wearing thick glasses and a grease smeared t-shirt said, "You want Al? I'll get him."

A few minutes later, Al came in; medium height, broad shoulders and a deeply rutted grizzled face.

"Yeah, what's all this about?" He was wiping his hands on a sheet of garage-issue paper toweling.

"Sergeant Roger Sheppard, St. Matthews RCMP. I'd like to ask you a few questions about a person you had in your employ at one time, a Des Thillens."

"Des?" Al looked up surprised. "You want to know about Des? That was ancient history, my friend."

"The last time he worked for you was four years ago, is that right?"

"Yeah, around then."

"How long did he work for you?" asked Roger.

"Couple, three years, maybe less."

"You fired him I understand."

"You understand right. That man wasn't right in the head, that much I knew."

"How so?"

Al dropped the paper towel in the garbage. "Always seeing visions and stuff. Aliens, that kind of thing. Said he was abducted. When all of this stuff started affecting his work, I had to let him go."

"How did it affect his work?" Roger was writing furiously in his notebook. Aliens?

"Half the time he wouldn't even come in. He was always off at some protest or another. Said God told him he had to obey God rather than me."

"Rather than men."

"What?"

"Obey God rather than men. That's the quote."

The man shrugged. "Whatever."

"Do you know what kinds of protests he was involved in?"

"Anything going. Save the whales, save the seals, save the codfish, save the sea kelp. Look, what's this all about anyway?"

"We're trying to locate Mr. Thillens in connection with an investigation."

"The abortion doctor murder. Yeah, well, don't look at me. I haven't seen the creep since the day I fired him. Maybe he got abducted by aliens. Try Mars if you're looking for him." He chuckled, enjoying his own little joke. He pulled out a little tube of breath mints and popped one in his mouth. "You want one?"

"No thanks. Do you know if he had any relatives or friends that he may have gone to?"

"He never had friends that I ever saw. No one in St. Andrews anyway."

"Do you have any employee records on him?"

"I could. I don't know." He turned and opened up a gray metal filing cabinet. After a few moments he handed Roger a legal-size sheet of white paper. "Here's his application. We always keep them."

"I'll make a copy and get this back to you."

Al put up his hand. "Don't bother. I don't need it back. I'll never be hiring him again. That's for sure."

Roger scanned the single sheet. It listed two previous employments; a building supply store in Moncton, New Brunswick, and a car dealership in Bangor, Maine. He listed one personal reference; Fred Forsythe, minister in Fredericton, NB. No address or phone given.

He folded up the paper and, after giving Al one of his cards and urging him to contact him if he remembered anything else, he left.

Well, that was a royal waste of 45 minutes, thought Roger to himself as he drove back to St. Matthews.

*****

Back at the detachment, he dropped Des' application form on his desk. Eric approached him carrying a handful of faxes. He had checked on the names Sheila mentioned to Roger. "Martin Cranmore lives in a cooperative farm in Montana. And no one can find Des Thillens or Betsy Schellenberg. We got a bunch of people working down the list of anti-abortion terrorist groups. So far nothing. And, oh yeah, Jack's back."

"Maybe he *did* get abducted by aliens," muttered Roger, going through his notes.

"Who, Jack?"

"No, never mind."

"Sergeant?" Kelly had appeared in the doorway of his office, an anxious look on her face. "There's a guy here from the radio station. Just came in. Says he has a tape he thinks you might be interested in."

CHAPTER 15

"All I want to know is your reaction to what's happened there in St. Matthews, from a *pro-life* point of view." The news reporter almost spat out the word "pro-life" and Julia felt her grip tighten on the kitchen phone receiver.

Her mother was at the stove making hot dogs and boxed macaroni and cheese for the boys' lunch. Josh and Jeff were in their room, where they'd been most of the morning. It was nice outside, mostly sunny and warm for April, but Julia was afraid to let the boys out. The few times they had approached her about going over to David's, she had countered with, "No, it's going to rain." They would look at each other, shrug and then walk back to their room.

Her mother had spent the morning baking gingersnaps, while Julia cleaned the house with the radio on. All the newscasts were the same—a review of the facts surrounding the murder of Douglas Shanahan, interviews with abortion workers throughout Canada, comments from women's organizations and speculation as to whether Beth Knoll's disappearance had anything to do with the murder. The newscasts were decidedly biased as she knew they would be, as they always were. After the head of the Federation of Canadian Women made a comment about "right wing fundamentalist groups" and "the same violent, anti-woman attitude which is so prevalent in the United States now needling its way into the peaceful country of Canada," Julia prayed for an opportunity to share her side, the pro-life side, the pro-women side.

Then the phone rang.

The caller had identified herself as Corinne Shipley, Women's Correspondent for *Canada Today*, Toronto. Julia was momentarily flustered. *Canada Today*? Why was someone from *Canada Today* calling her? *Canada Today*, Canada's newest newspaper, was fancying itself as the Canadian counterpart of *USA Today*. A fierce marketing campaign, complete with brightly colored kiosks on every street corner, catchy headlines and short, snappy tabloid type stories, was quickly making it Canada's hottest newspaper.

"My reaction?" Julia looked over at her mother who was methodically stirring macaroni with a wooden spoon. "Well," she said, "like everyone else, I'm stunned and horrified."

"Even though you believe that Dr. Shanahan was a murderer?"

"Pardon me?"

"A murderer. You are quoted as saying that Dr. Shanahan was a murderer."

Julia stared out the back window. In the distance she heard thunder.

"I never said that."

"But you have mentioned on more than one occasion that you believe that abortion is the 'murder of unborn babies.' I believe those were your exact words."

"I don't know if I said it like that...."

"I have it right in front of me, Mrs. Nash, an article in the *St. Matthews Courier*, dated 18 months ago...."

"I was probably misquoted there, because I wouldn't have said it exactly like that."

"In the article you say that you believe that abortion is the killing of unborn babies, and if you believe that, then it stands to reason that the person carrying out that procedure would be a murderer...."

"But, I never said...."

"You don't have to, Mrs. Nash."

"Wait a minute, I...."

"Mrs. Nash, I wanted your reaction. You said you were horrified and I find that amazing considering your past terrorist activities against pro-choice groups and abortion care workers."

"Terrorist activities?" What was the woman talking about? Julia's mother paused in her stirring and looked up at her.

"You are on a list of anti-abortion terrorist groups," said Corinne Shipley.

Julia willed her voice to remain calm. She had prayed for this opportunity and here it was. She took a breath and said, "The Pregnancy Care Centres are a string of care centers for women who want an alternative to abortion. We are located throughout North America and in Europe. When a woman comes to us we explain the abortion procedure to her. If she decides to go through with the abortion, we will not stand in her way. We will pray for her and tell her that she is always welcome back here afterward. We have an extensive post-abortion stress counseling program and are in the process of setting up a support group here. We, at the Pregnancy Care Centre, do not in any way physically restrain any woman from entering an abortion clinic. We do not judge nor condemn. Ours is a gentle ministry of counseling and prayer and healing." Julia hoped her words would satisfy this woman.

They did not. "And you're sure that all of these women will come running back to your center after their abortions?"

"No, I'm not sure, but we're there when they need us. And many do." Julia felt her voice rising. *Stay calm*, she told herself. She said, "And because of this, we are not a terrorist group. I don't know where you get your information from, but you can erase the name of the Pregnancy Care Centres from your list of anti-abortion terrorists."

"It's not the name of the Pregnancy Care Centres, nor the name of your *specific* Pregnancy Care Centre which is on the list. It's your name, personally."

"My name!"

"Yes. Mrs. Julia Marie Nash. That's your name, isn't it?"

"How did *my* name get on your list?"

Julia's mother was slowly pouring the macaroni in a colander in the sink. Julia watched the jumble of noodles squirming like a bowl of white worms. She looked away.

"First of all," said Corinne Shipley, "it's not our personal list. It belongs to the RCMP and the FBI."

"What?"

"Don't sound so shocked." The voice of Corinne Shipley was detached, faintly humorous. Julia could picture her sitting in her fancy *Canada Today* office, in a dress-for-success suit and coifed hair. "What I'm saying is that our sources here at *Canada Today* were able to secure a list of known anti-abortion terrorists from the RCMP and your name was there. That's how I got your phone number."

"But I've never even spoken to the RCMP! They wouldn't have my name. This is some kind of bizarre mistake."

"I'm afraid not, Mrs. Nash."

"But," Julia stammered, "how? Why?"

"I have no idea, Mrs. Nash. That's not my department. But let me ask you this—have you ever written any threatening letters to any abortion care workers?"

"No! Never!"

"Well, you must have done *something* to get on that list, Mrs. Nash. Your name didn't appear like magic...."

After Julia hung up she stood for several seconds shaking with rage. Did the RCMP really think she was a terrorist? A threat? Would they be coming to question her?

Ignoring the inquisitive look from her mother, who was now emptying a foil packet of cheese mix into the squirming elbows, Julia walked out of the kitchen door and stood on her back porch. A terrorist! What kind of a list was this? Then she thought about Mason. If he found out, he would use this to gain custody of the boys; after all, a *terrorist* was certainly an unfit mother. She slammed her fist into the wooden railing upsetting her bucket of clothes pins. *God, what is going on here? How could this be? Just after I prayed for an opportunity to share my side, the right side, I find I'm lumped in there with the IRA and the PLO!*

Sure, she'd written letters, lots of them, even a few personal ones to Emma Knoll, but she would never write a threatening one. The long and very detailed policy manual from the Pregnancy Care Management Board which headquartered in Minneapolis, expressly forbade this kind of thing. Theirs was a different kind of pro-life organization. She was told that over and over; theirs was a gentle, non-judgmental ministry of counseling and prayer. She bent down and plunked the clothes pins one by one into the plastic bucket. Could she lose her job over this? *Was* there a letter somewhere that she had written in the heat of the moment? But if she lost her job, how could she care for her boys. She'd have to move. She could never afford the rent payments on the place if she had to go back on welfare.

"Julia?" Her mother was standing in the doorway. "Julia, dear, is everything all right?"

"Nothing I can't handle," said Julia quietly, her face averted.

"Lunch is ready, dear. Shall I call the boys?"

"Fine. I've got to head over to the Centre now, Mom." Maybe she could find it—that incriminating letter, or whatever it was. Maybe in an old file someplace.

"But your haven't had lunch."

"I'll grab something later."

"But won't you get hungry?"

"I'll be fine."

"But Julia, you'll need to eat something...."

CHAPTER 16

There were five of them sitting in Roger's office on that graying afternoon; Roger, Francine, Corporal Jack Boyce, Emma and Glen. On the desk was a small square silver tape recorder. In his hand Roger held up a small cassette tape.

"What you will listen to is a copy," he was saying. "We've already sent the original down to Halifax to be analyzed. As I mentioned to you on the phone, it was delivered to the local CBC affiliate earlier this afternoon."

Emma and Glen were sitting next to each other, very close. Emma looked stricken and small.

"This is actually good news," Roger was explaining. "The fact that it was hand delivered could mean that Beth could be someplace close by. We've still got searchers in the woods checking all known camps and hideaways."

"Who delivered the tape?" asked Glen.

"We're checking that even now," said Roger, "questioning employees, checking for fingerprints. Everything is being done in that regard."

Glen nodded.

Roger was continuing. "Also, a lot of physical evidence can be found on the tape itself. If there is a strand of hair there, for example, or a dead skin cell, we will find it. And the voice—an awful lot will be determined from the voice."

Emma's face had turned very pale and she was swallowing shallowly. Roger said to her, "Mrs. Knoll, are you all right?"

She nodded, but said nothing.

"You don't have to go through with this."

"No," she said quietly. "I want to hear it."

"Okay, then, what I want you to listen for is voice inflection, any phrases or word patterns that strike a familiar chord. Anything. Keep in mind that they have disguised the voice. We will be calling you in again, when we get the voice de-scrambled. Are you ready?"

When they both nodded, Roger motioned to Francine, who pressed PLAY.

The voice was slow, metered, without inflection.

We are the Christian Freedom Life Army. We believe it is time for ordinary people to finally have a say in this world which is controlled by atheists and power mongers and murderers. We must stop bowing to the gods of hate and holocaust. Millions of unborn children are dying daily, torn from limb to bloody limb, tiny bodies ripped apart in pieces; arms, legs, hearts, livers, and brains. We would not allow such a bloody massacre even on our meanest streets. Yet we allow this to go on, fully funded and endorsed by our government.

Emma closed her eyes briefly and a pained look crossed her forehead.

We will stand for it no longer. Dr. Shanahan was the first. There will be others unless our demands are met.

There was a brief pause on the tape and Glen looked at Roger who raised one finger signifying "wait."

Our demands are thus: We have Beth Knoll. She is safe for the time being, and says "Hello" to her mother and father....

Emma's hand flew to her mouth. Francine moved toward her.

But, we will kill this innocent child unless all of the killing equipment in the Shanahan Clinic is destroyed completely within forty-eight hours, and...

Another brief pause.

...all of the aborturaries in Canada and the United States, those housed in clinics and those housed in hospitals, be closed for a period of three months beginning in one month, June 1. We will let Beth go after the equipment is destroyed and after we see that satisfactory progress is being made to make this the Summer of Life. We will then release Beth. But, if new equipment is purchased for the Shanahan Clinic after that point, and if all work stops on making this the Summer of Life, we will take her again. We know where she is. We know where she is at all times. Others, too, will be killed if our demands are not met. The forty-eight hours begin today, Saturday, at 1 p.m . This is the end of the message from the Christian Freedom Life Army.

Francine pressed STOP/EJECT. Glen was staring straight ahead and Emma was groaning softly into her fingers.

Roger asked, "Did anything on that tape sound at all familiar? Anything at all?"

Glen said, "It sounded sort of like a woman."

Roger nodded. "That's what we think, too. But with the voice disguised it's hard to tell. Would you like me to play it again?"

When they both nodded, Roger rewound it. By the third listening, Emma had regained much of her composure. She said, "I've got a key. We can go now and destroy the equipment."

"We've got 48 hours. Let's wait a bit."

"But they'll kill Beth."

"We've got every RCMP detachment in the province working on this, plus Interpol and the FBI. These people, the people in many of these terrorist groups, have very large egos. They go in for the dramatic. This tape is proof of that. This tape is probably not the last of their communications. We've got surveillance at every radio and TV station and newspaper in the Maritimes. They're going to slip up. And when they do, we'll be there. It's not our policy to ever give in to terrorist demands."

"So, what do Emma and I do now?" said Glen.

"Right now sit tight and report anything suspicious to us. We will have a constable coming to stay with you, Mrs. Knoll."

Glen nodded. Roger rose, signifying the end of the meeting. As Glen led Emma out, Roger called to him, "Mr. Knoll, may I have a private word with you?"

Glen looked up surprised, but then nodded and told Emma to wait for him in the lobby.

Roger closed the door. "Have a seat, Mr. Knoll. This will only take a minute."

Glen sat back down in the chair he had recently vacated. "Okay, so what do you want to tell me alone that Emma can't hear?"

"Mr. Knoll, I'd like to know about your relationship with Emma and with your daughter. You share custody, is that correct?"

"That's right. Emma and I have joint custody of Beth, although Beth lives with Emma. That's something we worked out."

"Joint custody, and yet Beth lives with Emma. Isn't that a bit odd?" Roger leaned forward.

"Not that strange," said Glen.

"Tell me about it," said Roger gently.

"Is this relevant to the case? Will telling you about my relationship with my daughter help you to find her?"

"It could."

Glen's eyes narrowed, but his story unfolded, nevertheless. He and Emma had married very young. "Emma was in her first year at the university in Fredericton when Beth was born. Not the best timing. We didn't plan it, it just happened."

The young couple was living in downtown Fredericton in an old house that had been converted to student apartments. Even with the baby, Emma was able to complete her university, relying on Glen and student day care. Glen, who was studying business, worked part-time at the Irving gas station to make ends meet.

"I look back on them now and those were the good times," he said. "Living from hand to mouth...."

After Emma and Glen finished at the university the marriage fell apart. Beth was only three then. "We were into different things with entirely different sets of friends. When we realized that, we decided to call it quits and be friends instead. There's no hard feelings, nothing like that between us."

"How did you both come to live down here?"

"That was easy. When the job of managing the clinic came up for Emma I decided I'd move close by so I could be near Beth. I live and work in St. Andrews."

"Would you say that your relationship with Emma is amicable?"

Glen eyed him quizzically. "I just told you, yes. What are you driving at?"

"So your relationship *is* amicable?"

"What does this have to do with anything? That's what I'd like to know. What does any of this history have to do with Beth?"

"Mr. Knoll, where were you yesterday when Beth disappeared?"

Glen rose. "I get it now. You're accusing me of kidnapping my own daughter! That's what this is all about! Of coming up with some fantastic scheme of letters and tapes. Why would I do that? I get to see Beth whenever I want. Emma and I are friends. I would never kidnap Beth. I would have no need to! And where would Beth be now in this fantastic twilight zone plan of yours, huh? While I'm spending every waking moment at Emmy's worried sick, and all the time you're thinking it's me? You're insane!"

"Mr. Knoll," Roger kept his voice even. "Please sit down. In a case such as this everyone is a suspect until proven otherwise, and in a case of kidnapping the first person we look at is the non-custodial parent."

"I have joint custody of Beth, I told you!"

"A kind of odd joint custody, wouldn't you say? She lives with your ex-wife in St. Matthews and you live in St. Andrews."

"That's something we worked out and I'm okay with it," he said. His large face was getting flushed and he glared at Roger.

"Mr. Knoll, please calm down." Roger made a lame attempt to smile. He would try a different tack. "I've got superiors over me. If I were to send the report on this abduction to Fredericton, the first thing the Staff Sergeant is going to say is, 'Did you interview the non-custodial parent?' And if I tell him, 'No, I figured the guy was innocent,' it's my head on the block...."

"I don't care one whit about your head. It's my daughter that's missing."

"Let me explain it in another way. Everything in this case must be done by the book. And here's why—eventually we're going to get these guys and take this case to court, and we want to win this case, and lock these people, whoever they are, away for a long, long time. We can't do that if there is even one hint of something not being done by the book."

Glen seemed grudgingly satisfied with that explanation and sat down heavily. "Okay," he said, grunting. "I am employed in the New Brunswick Department of Fisheries and Oceans in St. Andrews. I'm a statistician there. You can check that out. I was at work until a little after five yesterday afternoon when Kathy Baskor called me with the news that Beth was missing. I talked to my supervisor briefly and then drove immediately to the clinic in St. Matthews. I've got all kinds of co-workers who can vouch for the fact that I was at my desk until about 5:15."

"We will do that. Thank you, Mr. Knoll."

"You're welcome," Glen said icily. "May I go now?"

Roger nodded.

CHAPTER 17

Matt had spent pretty much the whole day at his computer. A couple of times his mother had yelled up at him to do this or that chore, but Matt had ignored her. He could hear his mother hollering again. His bratty sister was whining, too. The one voice he hadn't heard all day was his father's, which probably meant that his father was out golfing again, which would account for the fact that his mother was even madder than usual.

He leaned back in his chair and thought about his fantasy. Every time he dreamed about it, he embellished it just a bit more.

Here was his fantasy: He and his family were driving somewhere all together, his father and mother in the front seat and him and his bratty sister in the back. That in itself was strange, because he couldn't remember the last time they were all in a car together—all of them at the same time. But in his fantasy they were. They had to be for his fantasy to work. Anyway, they were driving—where didn't matter. They were rounding a curve in his fantasy and his father was driving too fast and they got hit head-on by a semi-truck. Because Matt was the only one not wearing a seat belt, he was thrown clear while the rest of his family was tragically killed. In his fantasy he always used the word "tragically." After a couple of weeks, all of the rest of his relatives and his grandparents would leave Matt alone in the house. "He behaved like a perfect adult throughout the whole ordeal," his grandmother would say of him, "...and he can take care of himself." Then he would have the house all to himself. He could do what he wanted, stay home from school if he wanted. He, of course, would inherit all of his dad's really high tech computer stuff from work. The people from his dad's office would bring it all over in boxes, asking him where he wanted it put. The entire downstairs living room would be his computer studio.

He leaned back and yawned. Right now he was working on a computer program. A couple of times he had logged on to the internet to download an application from the web, and each time he tried to find CFLA1, but nothing. But he'd find them, even if they were using a different name tonight. Maybe next time he'd even log on, with a phony ID of course, so no one could trace him.

"Yeah," he said out loud. "Earth Mother, wherever you are, you're not safe from Earth Angel! No one is!"

CHAPTER 18

The teen-aged girl sat cross-legged on the couch, her cheeks damp. Long hair partially hid her face as she bent over the glossy color pamphlet of photos which showed the various stages of pre-natal development. "I never knew it was a real baby before," she said, looking up at Julia. "It says here that it already has fingernails and a heartbeat and stuff."

Julia smiled. "And if we could hook you up to an ultrasound or a sonogram, Nadine, you could even hear that little heart beating."

The girl placed her hand on her stomach. "Two hearts beating," she said, "mine and the little baby's. Is it beating the same time as mine?"

"No, your baby's heart beats completely independently of yours. That little heart is beating a whole lot faster than yours. It would probably sound more like a flutter rather than a thump-thump."

"Wow." Then she paused. "My mom doesn't even know about this, and it's a real little person already."

"You haven't told your mother yet?"

She shook her head. Her eyes filled with tears again and she reached for another Kleenex. "I'm going to tell her tonight. I've thought it all out, sort of practiced what I'm going to say. I'm going to tell her I came here and talked to you. I decided I'm not going to have an abortion."

"Nadine," Julia leaned forward. "On the form you filled

out, I noticed the name of the church you wrote down. I don't go to that church myself, but I know your pastor's wife. She's on the board here at the Centre. Would you like to talk to her?"

Nadine looked down. "That church—I don't go there anymore. My parents do. I just wrote it down 'cause I thought you had to have a church, so I wrote that one."

"Well, I know Gloria Tilden, the pastor's wife, would be happy to talk with you anyway. She's a wonderful caring person and I know she would talk to your parents, too. She's helped me through some rough spots in my own life. Would you like me to give her a call?"

Nadine looked up uncomprehending.

Julia continued. "We like to pair every girl who comes in here with a counselor, a special friend—someone you can call, even in the middle of the night."

"I don't know. No one knows about this, especially not anyone in that church. They hate me enough as it is...." She looked up at her and Julia saw some of her own hurts reflected in those eyes.

Julia touched her arm. "I know what it's like to be looked down on. I also know that Gloria doesn't look down on anyone. In order to help people here at the Centre, you can't look down on people. That's one of our things here." Julia smiled. "Jesus never looked down on anybody. He got criticized for that. He accepted everybody just the way they were. Gloria's like that, too."

"Well, if you think...."

A quick phone call and Gloria and Nadine had made arrangements to meet an hour later at an ice cream shop. Julia smiled as she walked Nadine to the front door of the Centre. *Another baby saved—thank you, Lord*, she prayed as she waved good-bye to Nadine.

After what she had just done, how could anyone call her a terrorist?

Julia went back to the filing cabinet. Prior to Nadine's arrival, Julia had picked up the phone a few times to call the RCMP, and then had hung up again. The RCMP were new here and she didn't know any of the officers.

And if she did pick up the phone now and call the RCMP, what would she say, "I hear my name is on a list you have of anti-abortion terrorists. Would you kindly remove it?"

Yeah right. No, she couldn't call the RCMP. They were just like the media, biased against the pro-life stand. Or else why would they compile such a list? She could picture that list hanging in the police officer's coffee room somewhere with "WATCH OUT FOR THESE PEOPLE," written across the top in capital letters. Maybe they even had her picture!

Then again, maybe they didn't have a list. Maybe that Corinne Shipley lady was making it all up. So, then what—a call to the RCMP with, "Pardon me, could you tell me if you have a list of anti-abortion terrorists? And could you tell me if I'm on it? The name is Julia Marie Nash." She shook her head, *Get a grip, Julia,* she told herself. *This isn't like calling to find out if your name's on the voter's list.*

Pulling out a filing cabinet drawer, Julia felt momentarily startled. Someone had been here. She flipped through the files quickly. Things were not as she had left them yesterday; little things—papers at odd angles, the "T" file hurriedly placed before the "S". Was one of the volunteers here last night? That was probably it. She returned to the file cabinet.

There was nothing incriminating here, just the usual offers of help, requests to speak at churches, requests for workshops. She placed this year's letters back and searched in the back of the cabinet for last year's files. They weren't there. For a moment she was flustered until she remembered. A month ago, for lack of space, she had dug them out of the filing cabinet, rubberbanded them together and placed them in the back of the closet in the counseling room.

She walked to the counseling room and pulled out the black plastic garbage bags of maternity clothes. The letters were still there. She sorted through files and files of unremarkable letters and notices, nothing that would link her name, her *personal* name to any terrorist group. In the center of a clump of elastic banded letters she found an odd one that she couldn't identify. It was from some group called the Christian Freedom Life Army. She turned it over. She had forgotten about this one. She opened it up and flattened it on her knees. It was dated December of last year and along the top was a phone number and a local street address, 703 Front Street. She read:

> Dear Mrs. Nash,
> Like you, we are horrified at the ease with which Douglas Shanahan has set up his killing house here in St. Matthews. We are a group of citizens who are fed up with this and aim to do something very concrete to stop it. If you are interested in having your organization join with us, please call us at the above number. Because of the nature of our work, our meetings are clandestine, at least for now.
> Sincerely,
> E.M.

She turned the letter over. Funny, she couldn't remember this letter and had never heard of the organization, and she knew the names of just about every pro-life organization in the country. She took the letter back to the reception room and pulled out the phone book. No Christian Freedom Life Army. She looked through her directory of pro-life groups in Canada and the United States. The name was not there. Puzzled, she read through it again.

The phone rang.

"Julia, your mother's worried sick about you." It was Shelly. "She called me looking for you. She said you took off before lunch and she hasn't heard from you since."

Julia sighed, "She knows where I am."

"She said you were talking to someone on the phone about terrorists, and then you ran off...."

"I had just received a strange and maddening phone call, and I needed some time to cool off and figure out what to do."

Julia told her friend about Corinne Shipley and the joint RCMP/ FBI list of terrorists and how her name was probably on it. When she had finished Shelly began to laugh.

"This is *not* funny!"

"Julia, this *is* the funniest joke I have heard in a long time! Do you know how ridiculous you sound? Terrorists? Lists? This isn't the X-Files."

"But...."

"First of all, friend, there is no list, and second of all, even if there was a list your name wouldn't be on it. That so-called journalist was making it all up and you fell right into her trap. And third of all, Mason's not going to come out and take the boys. Now just quit worrying and listen to reason. Julia, there's no big conspiracy thing out there waiting to get you."

You had to admit, thought Julia when she hung up the phone, *Shelly really did make it seem quite logical.* It was just that she had been dealt such a poor hand of cards in her life. What little she did have, she held onto with both arms, hugging for dear life.

Julia sat down and stared across at the huge watercolor which hung on the opposite wall. A field of lilies, yellow and white, edged in silver extended until they met the sun. Along the left side of the picture a stream wound through; quiet, still, deep. And over it all was the face of Jesus, sketched lightly, almost invisible in certain lights, but there.

It had been painted by one of the mothers who had come to the Centre; broke, pregnant and physically and emotionally scarred. At the time she felt her only alternative was abortion. After talking with counselors, Tanya had decided to keep her baby and leave the abusive man she had been living with. During her pregnancy, which was fraught with physical problems, she lived with a Centre volunteer and her family. Other volunteers helped with clothes and meals. They still helped her, regularly donating baby clothes and furniture. Baby Meredith was now almost three. It was a surprise to everyone to find that Tanya had such artistic talent. But when she brought in the large watercolor she told Julia, "God takes care of the lilies. He's taken care of me."

It had been hanging in the Centre for about six months now. The lilies, the sparrow—trust was so difficult for Julia. Mason had betrayed her. She looked into the face of Jesus, depicted there by Tanya's skillful hand. Jesus, too, had been betrayed by a friend; yet He forgave. She had told Gloria once that, *Yes, she forgave Mason, or thought she did, but it was so hard to trust.* She wondered if she would ever trust anyone to that extent again.

Why couldn't she be like those lilies, so unafraid of the scorching sun, of the storms, of being trampled under foot, of being uprooted? Shelly was right, of course. The whole list thing was just another example of Julia blowing things right out of proportion.

She placed the letter in the top drawer of the desk and went home.

CHAPTER 19

An hour after Emma and Glen had left, Roger sat at his desk and wondered if he had been too hard on Glen. Maybe just a little. But there had been method to his madness. There always was an element of doubt and better to be sure, ask the hard questions and observe carefully. His observations left him with no doubt that Glen was not the murderer. He rubbed his forehead to stave off the beginnings of a headache and tried to remember the last time he had eaten. He'd call Kate tonight. Usually he called her every Saturday, and he hadn't spoken to her since all of this began.

Meanwhile, Eric was working through blue vans, Francine had Shanahan's files spread all over a table in one of the interrogation rooms, and Steve was going down through the list of anti-abortion protesters. Other officers were trying to locate anything at all about the Christian Freedom Life Army and some woman from *Canada Today* was putting together a feature story for Monday and kept calling them for information.

The 48-hour deadline plus the overcrowded conditions in the new detachment building were causing headaches, stresses and tempers to flare. People often commented on Roger's outward calm in the face of danger, but now he felt as tightly drawn as a drum. He had to be constantly on guard. Sometimes his anger did spill over. Not yet. Not in his new detachment yet. *Keep in control*, he told himself.

He shuffled through the scene of the crime report again, reading it carefully. He listened to the tape again, trying to find voice nuances, hidden meanings, and sounds behind the words that would indicate where it was taped. The room was hot and sweat beaded on his forehead.

"You look beat, if I may say so, boss," she said. "Why don't you go get something to eat?"

He looked up. Francine was standing there. "Thanks, Francine. I've been eating here."

"Yeah, donuts with pink icing and chocolate sprinkles," she grunted. "Why don't you go get something good to eat? Take half an hour. It'll do you good."

"Can't."

"Can," she said, challenging him.

Roger rubbed his hand through his short hair. His face felt gritty, his whole body cried out for a shower and a shave and supper. "Maybe you're right."

"Good. Go."

He rose. "I'll be back as quickly as I can."

"Take all the time you need, boss."

"If anyone wants, me I'm at Laverne's."

Ten minutes later, a shaved, showered and much refreshed Roger was sitting on a stool along the counter at Laverne's. Laverne's Diner was located at the end of the St. Matthews' wharf. A pale green rundown clapboard structure, it served the best home-cooked meals he had found anywhere. Out of the window at Laverne's you could watch the river flow both ways, the push of the river current against the onslaught of the Fundy tides. It was always quiet down on the wharf and you could smell the sea. Down along the shore line, just outside of St. Matthews, the radio towers rose like sentinels, picking up the radio and television signals from the U.S., bringing that culture into Canada. It was really only swimming distance from here across to the U.S. and Roger remembered stories he had been told about smuggling across this border.

There were three eating establishments on the wharf; Laverne's, an ice cream shop—still closed for the winter, and a pizza restaurant. Families usually dined in the pizza restaurant with its bright yellow awnings and all-you-can-eat lunch coupon specials. There was no ambiance to speak of in Laverne's, not even tables. Patrons sat on naugahyde stools which were patched with gray duct tape. They watched Laverne and her husband, Chick, along with an assortment of other blowzy gray-haired ladies, cook food on the six burner Moffat gas range or plop cut up potatoes on the large black gas griddle. A turkey dinner with all the trimmings was served every Monday and Friday. Tuesday and Wednesday was lobster and scallops, and Saturday supper was brown beans and scalloped potatoes. Thursday was fish and chips. They were open every day for lunch between 11 and 1 and every supper hour from 5 to 7. They were closed on Sundays.

Little squares of orange construction paper clothespinned to the aluminum hood range advertised other daily specials which included chicken fried steak, hot hamburg and lobster roll.

Roger sat down in the only available stool and Laverne handed him today's *Canada Today*.

"Didn't know if we'd see you in here today or not. Didn't see you yesterday. Had some new scallops come in. But then I said to Chick, 'I bet the new sergeant be some busy with that murder and all, for sure.'"

Laverne was a short, heavy, brillo-haired woman with an incredibly large nose which dipped in the middle before it pointed downward. Roger was quite sure he had never seen anyone with a nose like that before. He remembered reading somewhere that noses are one part of the body that never stops growing.

Her husband, Chick, was a tall, lean man with a slight stoop at the waist. His fine, gray hair stuck out at odd angles as if he were permanently grasping an electric fence.

She nodded. "I was telling Chick the day that abortion clinic opened up here, I told him, 'Chick,' I said, 'You mark my words. There's going to be trouble, you just mark my words,' and sure enough. What'll it be, the special?"

"Sounds good."

One of the things Laverne kept for her "regulars" was a full supply of current newspapers; The *St. Matthews Courier*, *The Saint John Telegraph Journal*, *The Fredericton Daily Gleaner*, *Canada Today*, and the *Globe and Mail*.

He read through the early Saturday morning edition of *Canada Today*, along with the *Globe and Mail*. The lead stories in both papers were, of course, the murder. The kidnapping of Beth hadn't been included, too new was that news. He turned to the sports section. Hockey was winding down to the Stanley Cup, the Blue Jays, who had won two consecutive World Series in a row had lost every game so far, and some basketball player was demanding $125 million to play. "Wrong job," he told Laverne. "I'm definitely in the wrong line of work."

Sitting next to him was Arnold, a retired fisherman, who'd spent most of his days out on the Bay of Fundy and had the stories to prove it. On the other side of him was a family, people he didn't recognize, a mother, father and two small girls. The girls wore matching pink dresses and asked for hot dogs, mashed potatoes and Jell-O. Laverne smilingly complied and told them not to get their dresses dirty because it would be a shame for dresses as pretty as those to get ketchup on them.

Although he missed his family, the odd thought came to him then that he was going to miss this place, this part of his life, when suppers were once again family dinners of Kate and Sara and Becky around the kitchen table. He was going to miss the banter between himself and Laverne, Chick, Arnold and the other "regulars." He would miss his daily paper, folded in thirds to the story he was reading, placed there beside his bowl of brown beans and potatoes.

Arnold speared a potato and leaned toward Roger. "Don't surprise me none that guy got his head blowed off. You bring an abortion place into this town and you're gettin' down on your knees and begging for trouble, no two ways about it. And that wife of his, struttin' herself around this place like she owned it or something."

Laverne was looking at Arnold. She said, "Arnold now, you keep your mouth shut about that. You don't know nothing."

Arnold shook his head and stirred his coffee. "I'm just saying what I know is true, that's all. That's all I'm doing here."

She turned to Roger. "Don't you listen to him, he's always talking off the top of his head."

She frowned, went back to her griddle and Roger turned to Arnold. "Dr. Shanahan grew up here, didn't he?"

"Him, yeah. I knowed him, sorta, when we were young. Rich family. But that wife of his. She's from away, she is."

Roger went back to the paper. "From away." Sheila Shanahan had lived in St. Matthews for almost 20 years and she was still considered "from away." Is that why she had developed such a cool and aristocratic exterior? How long would it take Kate and Becky and Sara to feel a part of this town? How long before *he* did?

CHAPTER 20

Beth kept asking when she could see her mother, and all the lady said was, "Maybe soon."

"Can't I at least phone her?" Beth begged.

"I already have."

"Yeah, but why can't I?"

Then the lady with the shiny black hair who said her name was Kara, just looked at her sadly and walked out of the room. Beth ran to the door, but she couldn't open it. Stuck!

She went back to the creaky metal bed with the itchy gray blanket on it and sat down. The bed had no sheets, not even a pillow case on the old smelly pillow with stripes. That's what had awakened her the previous night, the smell of that pillow. She had called loudly for her mother then, and stumbled out of bed to where she thought the door was, but it wasn't there! Where was she? She had screamed and screamed until Kara had come in. Kara was small, not much taller than Beth herself, and had the longest shiniest black hair Beth had ever seen. She turned on the light and said her name was Kara, but Beth kept looking at that hair shimmering in the light, swaying back and forth like a satin cloak. Kara sat on the edge of her bed and told her that her mother was sick and had asked her to take care of Beth for a while. "I'm just watching you temporarily."

"I need to call my mom," Beth had said importantly. "She will want to know where I am."

"That's impossible," said Kara. "Your mother will come for you in two days."

"Will I be back in time for school on Monday? I can't miss it, you know. It's my turn to read my journal in language arts."

The lady named Kara had looked away from her and her hair followed, swishing along beside her.

"You have nice hair," Beth had said.

Kara turned sharply and faced her, but said nothing.

"Could I phone my mom?"

"That's impossible."

"Where am I? Where is my mom?"

"That is not important."

"Yes, it's important!"

"That's not an issue."

"Yes, it is a shishue!"

"I will let you know when you can call her, when she is well enough for you to call her."

"Then how about my dad or Kathy?"

But Kara walked out and the door was stuck hard. Beth couldn't open it then, and she couldn't open it now. The place had a funny smell, Beth noticed, like a garage or something. She turned on the light and dug around in her backpack for her book. She lay down on her side and began to read. But she couldn't concentrate. Everything felt wrong. She thought about the characters in her book, transported to a magical place where fairies and strange looking creatures talked and helped them to know where they were.

A few minutes later Kara walked in again with two baloney sandwiches wrapped up in a napkin and laid them on the bed beside Beth. Two baloney sandwiches with nothing on them, no butter, no mayonnaise, just slices of baloney on white bread.

"This is my supper?"

"This is your supper."

"Don't I get anything else?"

Kara glared at her. Beth said, "But I'm more hungry than *this*. What about dessert? Or a glass of milk?"

"You can get water from the bathroom," said Kara quietly. Then Kara sighed and said, "Wait here."

A few minutes later Kara came back with a blueberry muffin and a glass of milk. By this time Beth had already eaten both sandwiches. She hungrily finished the muffin while Kara sat on the edge of the bed watching her.

"I'm supposed to take your teddy bear away," said Kara.

"But why?"

"You're too old to have a teddy bear."

"That's not true."

Kara sighed and in the end didn't take the bear, just picked it up, stroked its soft fur, re-arranged its dress somewhat, and placed it back down beside Beth.

When Kara left, Beth immediately ran to the door. Stuck again! *What's wrong with this stupid door*? She turned back, frustrated. She couldn't even look out of a window. There weren't any. Not even in the bathroom, just an old toilet there which was stained and smelly, and a rusty sink that dripped cold water. One thing she knew for sure, if her mother knew she was here, she would never approve. Her mother was even a little unsure about the summer camp Beth went to for a week every summer with Melissa.

"But you're in this cabin and the bathroom is outdoors and way over there," her mother had said, eyeing the place suspiciously.

"Mom, I'll be *fine!*"

Of course she had let Beth stay. At camp they swam and made handicrafts. Last year they made crosses on leather thongs out of colored beads. Each color had some sort of meaning, but Beth couldn't remember now what the colors stood for. Her cross was hanging from a thumb tack on her bulletin board at home. She was looking forward to camp again this year. Sometimes she even went to Sunday school with Melissa, but not all the time.

Last year at camp Colleen, her counselor, had told them that if they were ever afraid they should pray. Something about this whole place was making her very afraid. The last thing she remembered was walking down the street, then being grabbed, then smelling a horrible smell, and then waking up here. Beth started to cry again. Maybe she should do what Colleen said. Maybe she should pray.

CHAPTER 21

When Julia walked in through her back door Josh met her.

"Grandma's making spaghetti," he announced.

"Where were you?" asked Jeff, hopping from one foot to another.

"Working," said Julia.

"But you were gone so long," said Joshua.

Julia bent down and hugged her boys. No one would take them away from her. No one ever.

Her mother called, "I'm glad you're home, Julia. Supper's almost ready."

Her mother had gone all out; garlic bread, homemade sauce which had no doubt been simmering all afternoon, and a Caesar salad in the big wooden salad bowl which had been a wedding gift from Mason's parents. Julia wondered why she still kept it.

"You didn't have to do all this," said Julia, surveying the room.

"Do what?" Her mother looked up from the sauce.

"Make such a big supper. It looks wonderful."

"Julia, dear, I know you're under stress and pressure. I wanted to help. That's why I'm here. That's the only reason I'm here. And what would you do without me here, you being called out to work at all hours?"

Julia began hesitantly. "I'm sorry I left in such a hurry earlier. I had a disturbing phone call...something that upset me...."

Her mother waved her hand in front of her face, a gesture Julia knew to mean that further conversation would only complicate things. That was the problem, Julia reflected as she set four plates on the round table. Their discussions only went so far. Julia would begin talking, and then the hand waving would signify the end of conversation.

Her mother looked up. "Put a cloth down on that table, Julia. I got the pink one out. Oh, and that little girl, the one that was missing? She was kidnapped."

Julia stood still in the doorway, stunned. "Kidnapped!"

"It was on the news all afternoon. They sent some sort of a letter to the newspaper, the people that took her. They're the same ones who killed Shanahan."

Julia switched on the TV and flipped between cartoons, a talk show, and a sitcom involving a cartoon family who yelled a lot. But no news."

"Come and eat," called her mother.

"You sure they said she was kidnapped?" said Julia.

"Yes, I'm sure, well practically sure. Come and eat your supper. You had no lunch did you?" She shook her head. "I don't know how you manage on the little you eat."

Her mother sat near the kitchen, fussing over her not eating. Joshua and Jeff glanced at each other and Julia's own thoughts raced to her worst scenario which would be Mason taking her children and the RCMP coming to arrest her.

At six, Julia took her cup of coffee into the living room and turned on the news. The murder and kidnapping were the top stories. Some organization called the Christian Freedom Life Army was claiming responsibility for Shanahan's death, as well as the kidnapping of nine year-old Beth Knoll. Julia's coffee cup was poised somewhere between her lap and her mouth. The Christian Freedom Life Army?

"Julia?" Her mother was standing in the doorway, aproned, her hands folded in front of her. "Are you all right? Would you like some dessert?"

"I don't know." The words came from far away.

"It's strawberries and cream. I bought some fresh today."

The rest of the news was a rehash of the murder, clips of

women setting flowers down on the lawn of the Shanahan estate, interviews with the RCMP, interviews with women's leaders all over the country who were declaring next Friday a day of mourning for the nation, and news clips about terrorist organizations who had been responsible for other abortion doctors' deaths. "The Christian Freedom Life Army seems to be an unknown group not on the list of terrorist organizations," the anchor was saying.

The list! They all but admitted there was a list. She had to get back to the Centre and get the letter from the Christian Freedom Life Army. There was an address there and a phone number.

"Mom," she said rising, "I've got to go to the Centre just for a minute. I forgot something there."

"Julia, dear, you look as if you've seen a ghost."

"Maybe I have," muttered Julia, grabbing her keys from beside the door and heading out.

"I'll have coffee on when you get home...."

It was raining when Julia got in the car and swollen drops splattered against her windshield.

Julia parked and walked in through the side door. As soon as she entered she felt a presence, a lingering scent of someone else. She stood motionless for several seconds, willing herself to remain calm, willing herself to pray. She felt her body clenching, every muscle taut. Someone had been here. Someone was *still* here.

She forced herself to walk one foot in front of the other to the reception area. She opened the desk. That was when chills and nausea began to waft through her body in waves. She held onto the open desk drawer sinking, sinking to the chair.

The letter was gone!

"It's here," she said out loud. "This is ridiculous. It got shoved to the back. It's here. I put it right here. Right on top."

She pulled out the full, square desk drawer; spilling paper clips, pads of post-it notes, brochures, pens and pencils, rubber bands, and rulers. But the letter was gone. She went through each desk drawer in succession. Tearing, scrabbling with her fingers. But it was not there. She searched through her purse. She got up and searched through the counseling room files, throwing maternity clothes and baby layette contents around her in her haste, but it was not there either. It was gone!

She sank to the floor. "God, what is happening?" she moaned.

CHAPTER 22

It was midnight before Roger left the detachment and walked the few yards home to his apartment. Even though everyone was working full-tilt, they were no closer to finding the murderer or the kidnapper. Had it only been yesterday afternoon? The night was black, the downpour had stopped, but the air around him felt liquid and heavy and he waded through it as if swimming through a dream.

The air inside his apartment was no better. Muggy and closed in. There was his bed, unmade in his haste to get to the *Courier* building that morning, his t-shirt lumped on the floor, and on the dresser two half empty cans of Diet Coke, flat and warm now. He picked them up, dumped the contents into the bathroom sink and piled them against the kitchen wall with the other empty cans. He picked up his t-shirt and flung it into his pillow case of dirty clothes that leaned against the three-drawer dresser. He was tired and hot and lonely and the silence was oppressive. He dialed Kate. Busy. He turned on the TV, but the midnight offerings of witless talk shows only served to deepen his fatigue. He pressed redial. Sara answered on the first ring.

"Hi, Dad. How're you doing?"

He chatted with her for a few minutes. She was indeed thinking of attending Bible school, the same one Mark was going to in Tennessee because it would be near Nashville and Dog Ear was really going places. They were auditioning to go on tour with a well-known band, another one that Roger had never heard of, and when he told her so, she said, "I can't believe you've never heard of them. They're the hottest group around! Everyone's heard of them. They're even played on secular stations!"

Roger sighed inaudibly. He had always envisioned his smart elder daughter marrying a doctor or a lawyer or a minister. Not a pony-tailed drummer in an alternative Christian rock band named Dog Ear.

When Kate got on the phone her first words to him were, "You're tired."

"I'm dead."

"Have you gotten any sleep in the last couple days?"

"Some. Not a lot. Not enough." And then he told her about the radio tape, the letter, and the long list of blue van owners. She answered with concerned sounding "umm umms" at the appropriate times. The cordless phone to his ear, he wandered around his two rooms, picking up more dirty clothes and wishing he had done laundry *before* Shanahan was murdered. He opened up the half-sized fridge and pulled out another Diet Coke. He also grabbed a cellophane wrapped package of four Oreo cookies that he had bought on one of his rare shopping trips. To him grocery shopping was a walk through the corner convenience store.

"Are you eating all right?" Kate asked.

"I'm eating fine," he said, munching on a cookie. It was stale and somewhat hard and he tried to remember when he had purchased it. He ate it anyway. "Laverne's taking good care of me."

"Laverne? Oh, that restaurant. Well, I'm glad. When I come out I'll have to thank her."

"She wants to meet you."

"Maybe she can cook my welcoming dinner in her famous restaurant."

"It's not much of a restaurant, Kate. I've told you that. No tables, even. Tonight I sat next to Arnold."

"Nice guy? This Arnold?"

"You'll love him. He'll talk your ear off about lobstering."

"Can't wait."

Then Kate went on to talk about various people at church and in the community. She told him that the new corporal was a pleasant fellow with a couple of grown sons. He and his wife had been in to her agency to look for a house to buy.

"Why didn't you suggest ours?"

"We did. They looked at it, but want something further out of town."

Roger asked about Becky. "I'll put her on," said Kate.

Roger finished the rest of the stale cookies, crumpled up the wrapper and pitched it like a softball to the wastebasket at the end of the bed. He missed.

"Hi, Dad," said Becky.

"Hi kid, how are you?"

"Okay, I guess."

"Everything at school okay?"

"Yeah, I guess."

"I miss you, kiddo."

"Dad?"

"Yeah?"

"It's not fair that we have to move so much."

"A whole lot of things in life aren't fair. You just gotta live with them. But I think you'll like it here. The church I've been going to has a whole bunch of young people your age."

"I hate that word."

"What word?"

"Young people."

"Sorry."

"Jody's never moved in her whole life."

The conversation was not going the way he wanted. "That's unfortunately what you get for being the daughter of an RCMP officer."

"I didn't ask for this."

"I know."

Later when Roger was lying in bed, he thought about Jody's farming parents, farming the land Jody's grandparents and great-grandparents had farmed; their roots by now, as deep as the earth itself, as the crops they took off the land year after year. He thought about the sea people then, about Laverne and Chick and Arnold, in tune with the tides, taking their livelihood from the Bay as their parents had done, as their grandparents had done before them; as much at home on the boiling tides as Jody's family was on the land.

And then there were the gypsies—the strangers, the people "from away," people who either by choice or occupation moved from place to place just skimming the surfaces of the lands they inhabit. Like him. Like his family. Like Sheila?

CHAPTER 23

That night it took Matt exactly eleven minutes to locate the CFLA1 room again. Stupid people using the same name. What did they think, that someone as smart as himself wouldn't be able to figure out where they were in about five minutes? He joined in the live chat room at approximately 11:08, in time to read about some video that was going to be delivered tomorrow, and how nobody would be ready for its awful truth, and how some clinic somewhere was going to be bombed.

Matt didn't know whether these people were for real or not. Maybe they were playing a form of on-line Doom that he hadn't encountered yet, taking the names of real cities, instead of the imaginary castles and kingdoms of the game he sometimes joined. He turned his printer on and began printing off their messages as they filled the screen:

Earth Mother: The time for the bombing of the B. Clinic has been moved up. It will now be destroyed tomorrow at 6 p.m. instead of Monday. There is no need to wait.

B. Voice: The clinic is closed on Sundays.

Goddaughter: So no one will be hurt.

Earth Mother: That is not the reason I am moving it up. I don't think we are being taken seriously. I think we need to make more shows of strength.

Joan of Ark: I think you are rushing things unnecessarily for the sake of some personal agenda only you know about.

Earth Mother: Personal agenda? I'll say I have a personal

agenda and it has to do with the untold carnage of millions of unborn citizens. And who is supposed to be calling the shots here anyway?

Cool, thought Matt.

Joan of Ark: Collectively we are calling the shots. We collectively should decide and then inform the others. I don't see any reason to move that date ahead. The clinic equipment will be destroyed. The child will be delivered and then we move into phase 3.

Earth Mother: There is no need to wait.

Joan of Ark: Earth Mother, ask Goddaughter if she is ready to destroy the child, if needed. I'm afraid she is not.

Earth Mother: She is ready.

Joan of Ark: Ask her.

Earth Mother: I don't need to. I know my people.

Time to have a little fun, thought Matt, *throw them off the track*. He stretched his fingers, logged onto the chat line, giving himself the nickname Earthmother, the two words run together:

Earthmother: Go ahead. Destroy the child and the clinic and all the other stupid people walking around, including yourselves.

The screen remained blank for several seconds. No one responded. Finally:

Earth Mother: I didn't write that.

B. Voice: And who did?

Earth Mother: One of you is trying to destroy my reputation. ONE OF YOU!

Joan of Ark: Quit shouting. We let you begin this operation at your end because of Shanahan, but in light of the fact that Earth Mother is losing it, I think that was an unwise choice. I think the entire procedure should be re-thought.

    Mystic Queen: I will take care of Earth Mother.

    Earth Mother: Earth Mother doesn't need taken care of. I was the one who began this whole operation. I was the one who brought it into being. I shall be the one to complete it.

Matt was beside himself with laughter. What he should do is e-mail WhizKid about it. Maybe they could both "chat" with these morons. He printed off a few more screens of their "conversation" before he exited to visit another chat room.

CHAPTER 24

Emma rose early. Kathy had fixed her a mixture of relaxing teas the evening before and she had slept firmly, soundly, finally in her own bed. Glen had gone home, sulky and confused after being blamed for Beth's disappearance, and Emma remembered why they hadn't stuck it out. Glen didn't need a wife, he wanted a mother. Emma had told him to please go home until he cooled off, that she was too tired and too worried to have to coddle to his whining. As soon as he slammed out of the door she felt like calling him back again. But she didn't. Instead, she sat on the couch and cried for Beth, for Douglas, for Glen, for failed things and dead things and everything in her life that hadn't turned out right, until Kathy brought in a cup of tea and told her soothingly that everything was going to be all right. The candle of hope still burned.

She glanced over at the bedside clock and blinked. 6:30 a.m. She sat up. The house was quiet. Constable Jill Mitchell, the police officer who'd come last night, was in the second bedroom. Emma tiptoed beside the bedroom where Jill was staying. The door was open and Jill lay on the top of the bed, fully clothed, asleep. She passed Kathy, who was curled up and sleeping soundly under an afghan on the living room sofa.

Emma sat at her kitchen table and looked out of the window into the pale morning. A light rain was misting through the trees. A bird called. She looked at her gardens then, soggy and matted with last fall's leavings. They needed a thorough purging. Like her life, she thought ruefully. She pulled on her jeans, sneakers and an old zip-up sweatshirt of Glen's that hung on a hook by the door and went outside into the rain. In the small shed at the back of her yard she found her trowel and a rake and a cardboard box of plastic garden bags.

She needed to work, to occupy her hands. The house had to look nice. There would be people coming. People were coming even now, bringing casseroles, cakes and pots of soups. Her counters were crowded with food she couldn't eat. Reporters were coming too, and of course, the police had camped out. And Beth would be coming home soon, too. The house had to look nice for Beth.

For the next half hour she ripped out fronds and weeds, scaring up bugs and beetles who had made their homes in the warm places under the brown leaves. Eventually the front lawn was piled high with brush; she bagged some of it and some of it she readied for her composter.

She was deep in thought about what kinds of flowers she and Beth would put in the front bed when she became aware that someone was standing behind her. She looked up.

"What do you think you're doing?" It was Kathy.

"Weeding my garden. What does it look like?"

"It's pouring rain, Emma. You're soaked through. Jill was wondering where you were and you gave us both a start."

"Oh, you and that police officer are on a first name basis now, are you?"

"Come inside, your teeth are chattering. We were worried about you."

"Well, I'm so sorry," said Emma rising. "If the police were adept at doing their job, *Jill* would have noticed that I walked right past her on my way out the door. This happens to be my house and I happened to want to weed the garden like any normal person."

Kathy's voice sounded tired. "Emma, come inside. I'm making breakfast. Please. These aren't normal times. You just can't do your normal routine. Come inside."

"I just want to finish up out here."

"Emma, it's pouring rain and there's someone coming over later to see you."

"Who? Who's coming?"

"Someone who can help us find Beth."

"Who?"

"Her name is Elena Risa and she's a psychic from Maine. She often helps the police find missing children. I spoke with her a few minutes ago. She's driving. She'll be here in a couple of hours."

"Just what I need, more *people* around this place."

"But this is one person who can really help."

"Yeah, yeah," said Emma rising. "A couple of hours. That'll give me time to get this mess cleaned up, have a shower and head over to the clinic with my sledge hammer. I'll be back after that."

"What?"

"The only way I know to get Beth back is to destroy the equipment. That's what those idiots on the tape said. That's what I'm going to do, right after I finish here."

"But the police said not to...."

"And what have the wonderful police done, Kathy? They're spending their time blaming Glen when they should be out looking for my daughter. And what have the police done for us at the clinic in the past? They cannot keep the protesters away from our doors, cannot keep them from harassing my patients and this, this murder and kidnapping is just the logical result of a police force who cannot keep control of its citizens."

"Don't blame them, Emma, they're only doing their job...."

"If I have to hear that mamby pamby phrase one more time I will absolutely go crazy! *'We're only doing our job.' 'We're doing the best we can.'* Honestly, if they were doing the best they could, none of this would have happened. Terrorists only try something like this when they know the police force is weak, when they know they can get away with it."

"Listen to yourself, Emma. Do you want a police state?"

Emma was quiet for a few seconds. Then she swayed and a fresh wash of tears fell in rivulets down her cheeks. Kathy reached for her and caught her, stroking her hair as Emma wept, "What I want...what I really want...is Beth."

CHAPTER 25

Roger sat at the rear of the church on a pew which backed up against the wall. These seats were reserved for mothers with crying babies, fathers with toddlers who couldn't sit still, children with papers to color and on-duty RCMP sergeants in the middle of homicide investigations who didn't know how long they would get to sit before they would be called out.

He rubbed his eyes. Fatigue plus something else was making him more of an observer than a participant this morning. He watched the children's choir sing about the Good Samaritan, complete with actions. The congregation applauded. The youth drama team was next with a skit about figuring out just who your neighbor is and Roger thought about Emma. He had seen the desperation, the bewilderment, the confusion in that young woman. This would be the perfect opportunity for the Christian church to put aside its fears and prejudices to reach this "neighbor." But gazing ahead of him at the smiling good people sitting shoulder to shoulder in their Sunday best, he doubted that anyone would. Their "cups of cold water" would be to each other only.

Roger's reverie was interrupted by his beeper. Quietly he exited through the back, ducking past the ushers and into his patrol car where he dialed the detachment.

"Some new developments," said Jack. "Seems they've delivered a number of videos to television stations in Canada; CBC in Fredericton, CTV in Ottawa, some TV station in Bangor and to our local radio station in St. Matthews. Don't know how we rate...."

"We had Shanahan," said Roger.

Jack grunted.

Roger said, "How did they get past the security we've had set up at every radio and television station in this entire country?"

"They were delivered by courier. It was the same in every location. Small local independent courier companies in each place, hungry enough to work on Sunday—they were given cash in advance to deliver the packages which were left at a drop off spot. Here in St. Matthews it was the Johnny J's Quik Mart."

"Anybody been questioned there?"

"At Johnny J's? Yeah. But you may want to meet us down there. Guy's in a major flap. Said it was brought in by a woman dressed up in a fur coat who said she was in a hurry and needed this video, her screen test she called it, delivered by courier to the radio station this morning. Sunday of all days, and he believes her. Kept calling courier companies till he found one who would work on Sunday."

"Was anyone at the radio station this morning?"

"One guy. A technician."

In a matter of minutes Roger was standing with a number of other officers in Johnny J's, grilling a tall skinny young man with two-tone hair. The two inches closest to his scalp were a pale brown. The rest was black, making it appear that his hair was somehow not attached to his head. He touched his face in various places while he talked. He also had a nervous tic in his right eye, which may have been brought on by the two dozen police officers who had converged on the place and were firing questions at him. He swallowed and said that his name was Del Johansen, Johnny J was his father, and that he'd been alone in the store around 8 this morning when a lady had walked in....

"Can you describe this lady?" asked Roger.

"Okay, she was short with red hair, kind of looked like a hooker, if you know what I mean."

"Describe," said Jack.

"Well, okay, yeah, okay. It was sort of like her red hair was this wig, sort of like that fake shiny hair they have on dolls...."

"Okay, shiny red hair, what else?" said Jack.

"Okay, as in height, she came up to about here on me," he said, placing the edge of his palm on the front of his chest just below his neck. "She was also wearing these weirdo looking sunglasses that pointed out at the sides. And a short skirt. Man! A short, short skirt. I believed her when she said she was an actress. I mean she looked so weird."

"What exactly did she ask you to do?"

"She gave me $100 and asked me to get it couriered over to the radio station. I said 'Why don't you just take it over there yourself?' and she said that it wouldn't look right, her delivering her own video. Then she told me that it never looked right when a person delivered their own screen test to the station. But for the money, I thought, 'Why not? I can get this delivered.' She told me to keep the change. Then she sets the package down on the counter with two fifties and walks out. It never dawned on me to ask what good's a video gonna do at a radio station."

"And then she left?"

"She walked out."

"Did she get into a car?"

"Never looked at her after that."

"A girl with a 'short skirt, man, a short, short skirt' and you don't watch her leave?" said Jack.

"I didn't. I swear I didn't." He raised his hands.

"What did you do then?"

"Started phoning courier companies. I had a major problem finding a courier that would work on Sunday morning. I woulda gone myself except I hadda stay in here behind the counter. Not that we have all that much business on a Sunday morning. Finally, called a guy I know that is trying to set up his own company—courier, carpet shampooing, the works, does everything. So I call him and he says, 'Sure, why not?' I give the guy a fifty and I keep a fifty as a finder's fee."

Roger talked to him for a few more minutes, until he was satisfied that he had learned everything there was to learn from

Del Johansen at Johnny J's Quik Mart.

There would be no point in interviewing anyone at the radio station. The only one on duty was a technician named Rob Susan who just happened to be there and, "No, he didn't make a habit of coming in on a Sunday morning, just happened to be there today." Since the package was addressed to Employees of CXR, he had opened it up, plugged it into a video player and had the wisdom to immediately call the police.

That's when other detachments across the country began calling that they had received the same videos, all delivered by courier companies, all delivered by costumed individuals. In one case the deliverer of the package was dressed as the Easter Bunny, in another by someone wearing a Richard Nixon mask. The teenage girl at Molly's Diner in Toronto hadn't known who the mask was supposed to represent and described it alternately as a mask of Abraham Lincoln or maybe Ronald Reagan.

On the way back to the detachment Roger stopped at the donut shop drive-through. They had donated all of the donuts a couple nights ago. He picked up an extra large coffee.

"You want some donuts to go with that? On the house of course, like the coffee."

"Thanks. A pink one. With icing and sprinkles."

CHAPTER 26

Roger drove through the quiet Sunday morning streets back to the detachment, the video on the passenger seat beside him. The day was warm and wet and there was a dampness about it, harbinger of a long and humid summer. Roger bent back the plastic tab on the lid and took a sip. The coffee was strong, hot and good.

Ten minutes later he was sitting with a group of officers watching the video in the interrogation room. The room was overly warm and the air muggy with the smell of too close bodies. Roger was grateful that the previous week they had switched to their summer uniforms of blue trousers and short sleeved tan shirts.

He sat down, aimed the remote and pressed START. A few seconds of snowy screen were followed by a group of six costumed individuals standing in a row. There was the woman in the red hair, sunglasses and striped fur coat. There was the person in the Richard Nixon mask, and the one in the Easter Bunny suit. As well, there was someone in a Disney Snow White dress, another in a trench coat and nose and mustache glasses. The sixth one was dressed in a car suit, black tights and mask. They stood together smiling, as if posing for some circus publicity photo. Finally, the Easter Bunny stepped forward, and in a voice obviously disguised, said:

Hello world, we are the Christian Freedom Life Army. Oh, don't let our costumes fool you. Soon we will unmask. We are fighting for your rights, for the rights of your children, and we will not stop until those rights have been won. At that time, when the atheists have been dethroned from the power of the world, we will unmask and tell you who we are. But for now, we will systematically be destroying all of the baby killing aborturaries in North America, beginning with St. Matthews, where we have already gotten rid of Canada's number one threat to the unborn, Dr. Douglas Shanahan.   More will be forthcoming....

...And this is to you, Emma Knoll. You know our demands.

The Easter Bunny wagged his finger into the screen and then continued:

We haven't seen a whole lot of progress being made in the destruction of the equipment. We've been watching you. May I remind you that we have Beth. What a precious child, what a dear little soul. She is safe and sound now, but what a pity if she should have to come to some untimely end. Since you have now seen that we are serious, we will extend your deadline until 1pm Tuesday to be sure you meet our demands.

Richard Nixon clucked his tongue and the others in the group wagged their fingers into the screen. Roger felt sick.

It was Snow White's turn to speak:

On a more serious note, what we are about to show you occurs every day in killing aborturaries all over North America, right in your home town. Candid Camera, folks, here it goes.

The camera then moved from the parade of circus clowns to what looked like a hospital room. A uniformed rubber-gloved nurse whose eyes were hidden behind a rectangle of black, was holding a small, square tray with her left hand. With her right, she was placing on it what looked like tiny baby parts, first an arm, then legs, all the parts there. When the nurse seemed satisfied she dumped the works into a plastic grocery bag, tied the top and threw it against the door like the remains of a chicken dinner.

More of the same followed, trays and trays of tiny arms and legs and torsos and heads.

Roger shook his head. If they were going for shock value they certainly were succeeding.

Francine said, "This is gross. Is this staged or what?"

The video, which took around 10 minutes, ended with a shot of baby parts piled up, legs on legs, unformed skulls, hands, fingers, like those old black and white photos of places like Auschwitz. The video ended with a crudely lettered sign; ABORTION KILLS BABIES. ABORTION KILLS WOMEN. STOP THE HOLOCAUST!

After the video ended, the officers sat in silence. It was several moments before anyone spoke. Finally Roger said, "What do we do now?"

"Make copies of the tape...get still shots of the circus clowns...find out where the costumes came from, particularly the St. Matthews' fur coat...zoom in on the grocery bag and the hospital room...," were just a few of the suggestions.

Steve volunteered to go home (he lived the closest), get his home VCR, pick up a couple of blank tapes on the way and bring them back to make copies. He also said he knew a guy, Walt something, who had his own multi-media graphic arts company in St. Matthews. He would get a hold of him to see if he could do a bunch of stills from the video.

"Fine," said Roger.

CHAPTER 27

Julia stared at the light reflecting off the back of the right earring of the woman sitting in front of her in church. She watched that earring while the woman bowed her head, bent her head to look up at her husband, or sang from the choruses on the overhead. She wondered what the woman would think if she knew the person behind her was staring so intently at the back of her earring.

But when she tried to concentrate on something else, like the sermon, for instance, her mind wandered from the so-called maybe-existent list, to the letter she had found and lost, to the creepy feeling that someone had been in the Centre yesterday. The feeling that someone had been watching her, sitting in a car outside maybe, the whole time she was talking to Nadine. Watching, waiting. For what? Was it that *letter* they were searching for? The Christian Freedom Life Army. That had been the name, with a local address and phone number, but rack her brains as she might, she couldn't think of the street number.

The earring had caught on the woman's pink blouse and had flipped the wrong way forward. It hung at an odd angle now, like something gone wrong. Julia stared at it. She had to restrain herself from reaching forward and righting it.

That she hadn't gone to the police right off the bat was a mystery to her. Why hadn't she? Why on earth hadn't she? Now it was too late. If she went now, they would want to know why she had delayed. And she didn't know. Fear? Fear that she was on some list somewhere? If she called them today after church they would surely have some questions for her.

Yesterday you found a letter from the Christian Freedom Life Army and now you say it's gone? Let me check. Julia Marie Nash, divorced, right-wing, anti-abortion terrorist. That's you, right? And you're telling me someone broke into your place and took a letter? I don't think so, Ma'am.

The pastor was praying now, and Julia bowed her head and thought of the little girl, Beth. She prayed that God would keep her safe, and that God would forgive her for not calling the police, for being too *afraid* to call the police. She also prayed fervently for Emma Knoll, a person she had always regarded as the enemy.

For our struggle is not against flesh and blood, but against the rulers, the authorities, against the powers of darkness and against the spiritual forces of evil in the heavenly realms. The words of the verse in Ephesians came to her mind as she prayed. And she began to understand something. Emma was not the enemy. Douglas Shanahan was not the enemy. They were merely human beings with thoughts and fears and feelings, whose families were suffering. Deceived by the enemy, perhaps, but not the enemy.

CHAPTER 28

The trimmed lawn of the Shanahan estate was lined with flowers; some in plastic sleeves, some in tissue paper and others loose—wild flowers cut from the fields and tied together with ribbon. They lay side by side, placed there by mourners, mostly women, who bowed in attitudes of prayer before they left. Sometimes Roger would wonder about this placing of flowers at the scenes of tragedy. Where did this urge come from, to turn places of death into holy and sacred shrines?

Three cars were parked in front of the estate when Roger pulled up; a silver Crown Victoria with Prince Edward Island license plates, a dark blue Nissan with New Brunswick plates and a tan Jeep from Maine. The Jeep had a baby car seat in the back.

Roger's knock was answered by Sheila, who was dressed today in a pale yellow skirt and sweater. Head held high and eyes clear, she led him into the living room where various individuals were sitting on couches. Moira, unkempt and worried looking, was pouring tea out of a silver tea service. A tall, elderly woman who wore old fashioned combs in her soft gray hair extended her hand and introduced herself as Phyllis, Sheila's sister from Prince Edward Island.

"Nice to meet you," said Roger, taking her hand as if this were a Sunday afternoon tea party.

"Do meet my family," said Sheila. "You've met Lois. This is her husband, Rod. And this is little Meghan."

Lois sat huddled and small next to Rod, a balding man, wide

of girth with drooped shoulders. He wore a rumpled white dress shirt and tie, and looked like a traveling salesman after an unproductive day. Meghan sat between them on the couch, intently coloring in a book.

"Allison, my other granddaughter, is around somewhere. Where's Allison?"

Lois said quietly, "Upstairs, Mom. She'll be okay."

"And this is Penny and Dennis Schultz. Penny is my other daughter," said Sheila. "They drove up today from Bangor."

Penny and Dennis were sitting side by side on one of the brocade love seats. They were a matched pair, tall and slim in khaki hiking wear. Even their young child was clad in new jeans and a plaid cotton shirt. Leaning on the couch beside them was a backpack—*a poster family for L.L. Bean*, thought Roger.

Sheila asked, "Were you able to find anything in my husband's files?"

"We're still going through them."

"Are you any closer to finding out who did this?" asked Dennis.

"As a matter of fact, that's why I came. The organization, the one claiming responsibility, delivered a video to some of the TV stations. We've had some still pictures made from the video and I would like each of you to have a look. I want you to see if anything about these individuals looks familiar. Anything at all."

After the photos were handed around, Dennis was the first to speak. "Is this some kind of joke?"

"Apparently not," said Roger. "These people call themselves the Christian Freedom Life Army. They've claimed responsibility for the death of your father-in-law and the abduction of Beth Knoll."

"But why on earth are they dressed like that?" said Phyllis.

Roger shook his head. "I have no idea. So they won't be recognized? I don't know."

"Maybe the costumes *mean* something," said Penny, tapping a slender finger on the bunny. "Like the rabbit could stand for fertility. The hooker costume could stand for sex...."

"You're grasping at straws," said Rod, leaning forward, his face flushed, voice hoarse.

Sheila brought the photo up to her face. "I don't know. This one, I thought for a minute...."

"What is it, Mrs. Shanahan?"

"This masked one, I don't know. You said the pictures came from a video? Maybe seeing the video would help."

"Yes. But I must caution you that the video is very graphic."

"Graphic? In what way?"

"Pictures of, of...." Roger groped. "Unborn babies, parts, uh...."

Penny helped him, "Products of conception?"

Roger nodded. *Products of conception? Was that the politically correct term now?*

Lois' hand flew to her mouth. Rod put his arm around her, but she turned her face away from him.

Sheila stood and looked up at him, clear-eyed and intent. "I would like to see the video, officer. I would like to see it very much."

CHAPTER 29

Sunday dinner was roast beef, peas, mashed potatoes, gravy, creamed corn and green salad with an assortment of bottled dressings. Early that morning Julia had awakened to the sound of the skins being scraped from potatoes, her mother humming tunelessly in the kitchen, Sunday dinner being prepared.

Now church had finished and the four of them were sitting at the table. Jeff was spooning himself a second helping of mashed potatoes.

"You should make this, Mom. I like this," he said.

Julia tried to smile, but her mind was racing. After lunch was over and the dishes cleared, Julia waited as long as she could before she said, "Mother, I wonder if I could leave you again, just for a little while. There's an errand I've got to take care of."

Her mother put the paperback book she was reading face down on her lap and let her reading glasses, held by a chain around her neck, fall on her chest. "Work, work, work," she said. "They have you chained there, don't they? And on the Lord's Day, my goodness."

"It's not work. There's just something I have to check on. I won't be more than a couple of minutes."

"And you want to know if I'll stay with the boys?"

"They're fine, actually. They're going down to David's."

"It's this whole nasty abortion business, isn't it?"

Julia nodded.

Her mother waved her hand in front of her face, put her reading glasses back on and was already back into her novel, a historical romance from the church library, by the time Julia was out the door.

I'll make it up to her, Julia thought. *I'll make it up to all of them.* The mist had turned into a downpour. Julia started the car and put it in reverse.

She turned down Market Street and then right on Water Street, which followed the contour of the Bay, and then finally right on Front. If you turned left on Front you eventually crossed the border into Playa Brisa, Maine. Once in the U.S., Front Street became Lemon Blvd. To her left, Julia could see the square, brick customs building. Farther down she could see the American flags hanging limp in the rain. Playa Brisa was named by a Spanish sea captain who had settled his family there a couple of centuries ago. The name literally meant "beach of gentle breezes," and the town was filled with tropical sounding names like Lemon Blvd., Orange Grove Crescent and Palm Lane. Whether it was just wishful thinking on the part of the sea captain, or whether he was totally delusional, was never quite known. He had the money. He settled the town. He named the streets. A more apt name for this rugged north Maine coast would have been, "rocky beach of cold, damp rain."

Today Playa Brisa kept the name, more as a curiosity than anything else, a tourist attraction.

She turned right and drove north, leaving the customs booth behind her. Front Street was lined with older, rundown, brick buildings which leaned against each other as if for support. She drove slowly. Most of the buildings seemed to be warehouses and none seemed to be occupied. What was she looking for? A sign outside: Welcome to the offices of the Christian Freedom Life Army? She willed herself to remember the house number, but could not. She drove past the 100s. Two more blocks of brick buildings and rundown apartments. *Not the best of neighborhoods*, she thought to herself as she saw a ragged man, elbows on his knees, sitting on a stoop. In the rain, even. Up three more blocks she did a U-turn and drove back down toward Playa Brisa.

Right on Water Street, she turned up Market and drove over two blocks to where the Shanahan Clinic was located. She slowed down. The clinic was a small, modern building which stood alone on a corner. Mrs. Anglewood, the 85 year-old woman who had vowed before God that she would pray for every single individual who walked through those doors, was not there, this being Sunday.

Her friend Shelly said that whenever she even drove by the clinic she could sense evil. She and Julia had spent many an afternoon standing in front of the clinic, candles in hands, praying God would overcome the evil.

The front door of the clinic stood open. This was odd, thought Julia, who knew that the security around the building was very tight.

Curious, she pulled slowly into the lot and tentatively got out. It was then that she noticed the small white Ford parked behind a hedge. Someone was here. But should the door be open like that?

She stood for several seconds before moving toward the front door. Down the hall in the waiting room, she could see the person she knew as Emma Knoll, sitting cross-legged on the floor, head bent low, fingering a large hammer. The picture was one of such despair that Julia could only stand and stare. Emma must have heard something, because she looked up and the two women stared at each other until some recognition dawned, and the emptiness in Emma's eyes turned to fury. She rose, walked toward the door, faced Julia squarely and said, "What on *earth* do you think you are you doing here?"

Julia opened her mouth, but no sound came out. She clamped it shut. She had never stood this close to her adversary before.

"Just get out!" Emma screamed. "Get out! Leave! You have no right to be here!"

Julia backed away. *Evil*, she could hear Shelly's voice. *The presence of evil is in that place and dwells in that woman. Flee her. She is evil. Can't you sense it?* But all Julia could sense in Emma was despair and an impossible amount of pain. Julia regarded her and her trembling fingers as she held the hammer at her side. *This is not evil*, she thought. *This is a desperate woman who has lost her daughter and her friend.—For our struggle is not against flesh and blood, but against the rulers, against the authorities, against the powers of this dark world and against the spiritual forces of evil in the heavenly realms.*

Julia took a step forward. This woman, standing before her, was not evil. She was a person. "You are right," she said. "I have no right to be here. I don't know you. I can't possibly know the pain you're feeling. I just wanted you to know how sorry I was. I want you to know that a whole bunch of us are praying for you."

"You? Sorry?" Emma's voice was harsh. "You and your kind are *responsible* for this, my daughter missing and Douglas being murdered. And praying!" She spat out. "Now there's something I certainly don't need."

Julia felt tears well up in her own eyes. She blinked rapidly. Emma was continuing, "You'd put women's rights back a hundred years if you could. You, with your little house and your perfect little family, devoted husband, two point five children, what do you know about women's suffering, women being raped and then left to bear those children by themselves?"

Julia looked steadily at her and said very quietly, "I know more about all of that than you'll know. I have been on welfare. And I don't have a perfect little family. I'm a single mother, Mrs. Knoll. I'm trying to raise two little boys on my own. I've got an ex-husband who ran off with another woman. So don't talk to me about my perfect little house and my perfect little family. I may not know exactly what you are going through, but I know what pain is." Her voice broke. "I'm sorry. I'm so sorry about what's happened. I'll leave." Then she stopped. "But before I do, I have some information that may help you find Beth...."

Emma's eyes widened. She said slowly, "Come in then."

Emma led her into a room in the back. The coffee room of the abortion clinic had a stove, a small fridge and a metal table.

The walls were lined with posters and a bookshelf had pamphlets on issues such as AIDS, birth control and women's rights. On the table was an unfinished poster advertising a conference. Next to it was a package of magic markers, a ruler, a pencil and a half-empty bottle of spring water.

Emma pulled out a chair and sat down at the kitchen table. Julia looked around. *That place is evil. Don't you sense it? There is evil in that place. The fortress of the enemy.* Did she sense evil as she looked across at a trembling Emma Knoll? She wasn't sure.

Emma said, "You've got a lot of nerve coming here."

"You've got a lot of nerve inviting me in."

More silence. Then Emma looked around and said, "You've arrived at the right time. I'm about to destroy all of the equipment in this place. I even brought my trusty sledge hammer with me. Had to sneak out, though. I've got police guarding my house, listening in at my phone calls. The only privacy I have is when I lock the bathroom door, and even then they're standing outside with their ears against the door saying, 'Are you okay? Are you okay?' I threw up when they told me about Beth. I haven't eaten since. Maybe they're worried about me."

"Why?" said Julia, her voice breaking. "Why are you going to destroy the equipment?"

"You want to know why? Because that's the only way I'll get my daughter back. This *Christian* group of yours will give me my daughter back if all of the equipment is destroyed by Tuesday at one. That's their ultimatum."

Julia stared at her, mouth open.

Emma continued. "That's what they want, plus they want all the clinics all over the country to be shut down for the summer. You mean that isn't in the news yet?"

Julia shook her head. "I didn't know." Her voice broke.

Emma stood up and held the hammer over her head. "Come on, help me. That'll be great for the press—a picture of the both of us hammering abortion equipment to smithereens. Me, because I want my daughter back, and you, because of your very archaic ideas about women."

"No."

"Why not? That's what you fundamentalists want, isn't it? Take back a woman's right to her own body."

Julia groped for words. This was not the time to get into a debate. She said, "The real reason I came here is because I have information that may help you."

Emma sat back down. "Okay. What information?"

Julia told her about the letter she had found and then lost, about being sure she had been broken into and watched. She told her she had just come from driving up and down Front Street without finding anything.

Emma asked the obvious. "So, why didn't you go to the cops?"

"I told you. They think I'm a terrorist. But I'm not. I've never even *seen* a gun up close. I've got my boys to think about, and an ex-husband...." Her voice trailed off. Why was she telling all of this to Emma Knoll, of all people? *The enemy?*

More silence. Emma said quietly, "So the Christian Freedom Life Army asked you to join their little group. Why didn't you?"

"I don't know. I don't remember. Probably at the time something about it didn't sit right. But you can go to the police with it, if you want."

Emma leaned back in her chair. "The police! Those incompetent bunch of keystone cops. If they'd been doing their jobs, none of this would have happened."

Julia blinked at her.

"This is one for the books," she continued. "They wanted to pin this whole thing on my ex-husband. He's just as bumbling as all of them."

Julia's mind reeled. She hadn't heard that the husband of the abortion clinic manager was a pro-lifer. Was he? Emma answered her question.

"They think maybe he took Beth. What they don't know is that Glen is basically spineless. I would almost have to *applaud* him if he was smart enough to think up something this complicated, let alone pull it off. No, the cops are useless on this one. Besides, as everyone knows, they always lean to the side against women. That's their basic stand, they are anti-abortion, misogynist, anti-minority. I mean, just look at the ratio of female cops to male ones. That should tell you something. They don't think I should destroy this stuff, destruction of private property being against the law and all. So, I thought I'd come down here and take the law into my own hands. Get my daughter back." She paused, "You say their address is on Front Street? Front Street here?"

"Yes."

"And you can't remember it?"

Julia shook her head and looked down.

Emma leaned forward, eyes wide and bright and said, "If you find that letter, if you get that address, I want it. You've got to promise to tell me. Call me. Any time day or night." Then she paused, "No, the police are on my phone. Let's do it this way. If you find the letter, call my house, but don't say anything, just 'Hi' or something. Then I'll meet you here, in this parking lot, fifteen minutes later. Then you can give me the address."

Julia looked at her, but said nothing.

CHAPTER 30

Roger drove Sheila in his patrol car while Dennis, Penny and Rod followed in Dennis' jeep. Phyllis said that since her input probably wouldn't add anything, she would stay home with Lois and the children. Lois was still sitting in her chair, staring straight ahead, when they left.

At the detachment, Steve pulled a few extra chairs into the interrogation room where the video player was set up. He said to Roger quietly, "I brought my VCR, hooked it up to this one and made four copies already. The original's being checked for prints. Boy, that Walt really knows what he's doing. I was down to his studio. You wouldn't believe the stuff he has—computers, screens, digital cameras, all kinds of stuff. He said he could make a print of every second of camera movement. I forget what he called it, but I said I didn't think that was necessary."

"Thanks, Steve."

"We're getting more stuff in on blue vans. Getting closer. I'll fill you in later."

"Do that, thanks."

When the six of them were seated around the video, Roger said, "As I warned you, some of this stuff is pretty graphic. If at any time you want me to stop, just say so."

"Rated R then," said Rod in an attempt at levity. Dennis gave him a look. Rod was looking more and more rumpled as the day wore on and looked in stark contrast to his joggingly fit brother-in-law.

The video began; first there was the circus parade, then the pictures of body parts, the trash bags and finally the sign-ABORTION KILLS BABIES. ABORTION KILLS WOMEN. STOP THE HOLOCAUST! Roger noted Rod's increasing unease. He leaned toward Roger and said quietly, "You mind if I smoke?" He was already reaching for his shirt-pocket pack of cigarettes.

"This is a non-smoking building," said Roger.

Rod shrugged. Sheila's face was expressionless.

Roger rewound the tape and it began again.

Part way through the second go round, Sheila said, "I don't think viewing this rotten piece of propaganda over and over again will serve any useful purpose, other than to get my blood boiling more than it is. Why, a stacked up pile of bloody discarded kidneys would have the same effect. I'll be outside."

She left. Rod, reaching for his cigarettes, followed close behind.

Dennis and Penny remained, both looking very serious and sober. Dennis said, "I am a photographer by profession. You want me to have a look at the video?"

"Thanks, Mr. Schultz, I appreciate your offer. We have someone working on that now, a local photographer."

"If I can be of any help, then, just let me know."

Before they left, Roger called Sheila back in. "At the house you said you thought you recognized one of the individuals in the video. After having seen the video, have you been able to think of who it might be?"

Sheila shook her head. "It was just one of those fleeting remembrances. I can't think. Lately, I can't think. Perhaps it was nothing."

"Sometimes fleeting remembrances are all that we have to go on." He paused. "I also wanted to ask you about your daughter, Lois. She seems very distraught over the death of her father."

"Well, wouldn't you be?"

"I'm sorry. It seems more than that, somehow."

Sheila gazed at him, her head held high. "Douglas and I had a very good relationship, a marriage that outlasted most, thirty-three years. Don't think for a moment that I am unmoved by his death. We've had our share of problems, and living in this town has forced me to develop a thick skin, especially when there are merchants who refuse to serve me."

Roger listened, wondering where this was going. "My daughter Lois has always been a trial to us. As a teenager she had one difficulty after another. We thought that when she married she would settle down. She has in one respect, but it's been one trial after another for Lois and Rod. She and her father were bitterly estranged. I tried to bridge the gap, but it was there. That is why she feels his death so keenly."

"What was the nature of their estrangement?" asked Roger.

"That is personal and has no bearing on the case."

"I wish you'd let me be the judge of that, Mrs. Shanahan." He tried to speak as gently as he could.

"If you're wondering if Lois or Rod could somehow be a part of the Freedom Life Army, or whatever they are calling themselves, the answer is no. And she would never be a party to a kidnapping. I know my own daughter."

"Mrs. Shanahan...."

"No, I am firm on this. Her problems have nothing to do with her father's death, other than that she feels a keen remorse. If that is all, I will head home."

Roger let her go. He knew where to find her if he needed to.

CHAPTER 31

Roger was back at his desk, sipping cold coffee out of a paper cup, thinking about these things, when Francine and Eric came in with the news that Des Thillens had been located.

Roger looked up. "Des Thillens?"

"Found them through an uncle of his. Ran the name "Thillens" through our data banks. Came up with an uncle of his, a George Thillens, living up on the north shore now. We contacted him. Found that Des is living in his hunting camp. Constable Jay Davidson, from Saint John, and I drove out there, way up the Connor Settlement Road. Just got back. We brought them back with us. You wouldn't believe the two of them living like hermits."

"The two of who?"

"Des and that Betsy Schellenberg woman, the one who used to chain herself to abortion clinics all over the country."

Roger remembered. A dozen years ago a rag tag band of outspoken pro-lifers had actively protested against the construction of abortion clinics all over the country. Many spent short terms in prison. He could still see the news photos of Betsy, long brown hair, dark rimmed glasses, being dragged by police into waiting patrol cars. He also remembered Des Thillens in those high black army boots he always wore.

"You were out there?"

"Just got back. You were out at Shanahans."

"Any sign of the little girl?"

"None. We checked as far as we could without a search warrant, but we're certain she's not there. And the two of them seemed genuinely surprised to hear about it. They don't seem to have any contact with the outside world."

"And they're here with you now? They came willingly?"

"They seemed to. We told them they might have info we could use in this investigation."

"Bring them into my office, why don't you?"

The two that walked in looked like hippie refugees from the 1970s. Des hadn't lost any of his leanness. His handlebar mustache and ragged beard were edged in gray and gave him a dog-eared look. A tattered flannel shirt was tucked into faded blue jeans, held onto his narrow hips by a black plastic belt.

In the years since she was in the news, Betsy Schellenberg had turned plump and round-bodied. *Funny*, thought Roger, *how the genders differ. Left unmanaged, the males of the species tend to stringy, unmuscled bodies and females to round ones.* Her long hair, streaked with gray now, was tied back with a rubber band. She still wore those black glasses. He still wore the army boots. Both of them smelled like a campfire.

"Have a seat. Would you like some coffee?"

They both shook their heads simultaneously. Betsy said, "You wouldn't drink coffee either if you knew how it came to us—exploited workers in the third world...." She muttered something else that Roger didn't catch.

"Okay then," said Roger. "No coffee." He smiled. "I assume you have heard about what's been happening around here?"

"Only what that fine gentleman told us as he escorted us into town," she said.

"Why don't you tell us what the two of you have been up to the past few years. Still chaining yourselves to abortion clinics?"

Des shook his head and spoke for the first time, showing several missing teeth. "It's of no use. Those capitalists will find a way to make a buck off exploited women...."

"Miss Schellenberg?"

"Neither Des nor myself have any knowledge of what's been

happening here. I think Des will agree." She was surprisingly articulate, and then Roger remembered, Betsy Schellenberg held a Masters Degree in something like sociology. Criminology? (Surely not criminology.) She was continuing, "Neither Des nor myself would condemn what has happened, however. It's about time someone took the initiative. Dr. Shanahan had to be stopped. He was. But, officers, it wasn't us."

Roger leaned across his desk, his finger tips together. "The two of you have been out of the work force for quite some time. The two of you haven't driven cars in quite some time. The two of you have not received any medical attention in the past little while. Would you mind telling us what you *have* been doing?"

"Certainly," she said. "We have left society, as we know it. We have dropped out. Nothing changes. We can do nothing to change it...."

As she spoke, Des sat quietly running his thumb and forefinger through the cuff of his flannel shirt over and over, staring at it while she filled him in.

Five years ago when Des was fired from his job at the auto body shop in St. Andrews, Betsy was being released from prison. Des was suffering from severe depression at the time. "He was disillusioned with the cause," she explained. "It just wasn't working." About that time he also turned his back on his church, feeling as though the leaders in the established churches were not supporting his efforts. "They were getting their orders from denominational heads, not from God...."

Des had gone from odd job to odd job and from church to church. He started a newsletter called "Friends of Life," but it failed, lacking support of mainline denominations. When his membership in the pro-life organization was revoked, he suffered a nervous breakdown. He was hospitalized briefly, then he was released into Betsy's care and custody. The two took what money they had and moved into his uncle's hunting camp in the back woods of New Brunswick.

"Just in case you're wondering, our relationship is totally platonic. Des is like my brother. The woods are our church.

The trees are our altars. Our communion wine is the creek. Our bread is the flour we grind. We need no one."

Roger turned to Des, who was still running finger and thumb through his cuff hypnotically. "How are you now?" he asked.

"I'm fine, thank you very much."

"Still think about getting rid of abortion clinics?"

"That was in the past."

"Still think about getting rid of abortion doctors?"

"God will take care of them. 'Vengeance is mine, saith the Lord.'"

Betsy said, "Please leave us alone. We are simple people now. We grow our own vegetables. We plant our own crops. We grind our own flour. We raise chickens. *Please* leave us alone. We can't help you. We gave up the protests long ago. So long ago. Please let us live out our days in peace and tranquillity of nature. Des will never be the same. I have to take care of him."

Roger said, "You have not been a part of any protest of any sort during the past week?"

"Oh, how can you even ask!" Her voice was raised a decibel now. "Look at him," she said, pointing to Des. "Could he be a part of some international terrorist organization? You tell me that."

"Well, then you would have no objection to us coming to look around your place?"

"There's nothing to see!"

Roger frowned. The time clock was ticking to their ultimatum. And what did they have? Just pages and pages of computer printouts of dark blue vans, a bunch of circus terrorists and two renegade pro-life demonstrators who had been out of the picture for years.

Roger said, "Dr. Douglas Shanahan was shot on Friday."

"We don't know nothing about that, do we Betsy?"

"And Beth Knoll was taken from St. Matthews on Friday afternoon."

"Who's Beth Knoll?"

"A nine year-old child who is being held for ransom."

"We would never do that, would we Betsy?"

"I'm not blaming you," said Roger. "But, what we could use is help, names. Back when you were involved, you met and associated with a lot of individuals with similar ideals."

"What makes you think we would help you?"

"We're looking for names, Miss Schellenberg. Do you know anyone who drives a dark blue van?"

Des looked up suddenly.

The look was not lost on Roger. "What is it?"

"Nothing."

"Don't tell me nothing. As soon as I said dark blue van, your eyes snapped up."

"I don't have a van. We used to have a van, didn't we, Betsy? We had a van, but it was white. Wasn't it white, Betsy?"

Roger shook his head. Another dead end, another blind alley.

Betsy spoke, "We have to be heading back. Our chickens will need feeding."

"Fine," said Roger. "I'll drive you back, myself. Constable Jamison and I will drive you back."

"The *Sergeant* is driving us back. To what do we owe the honor?"

Roger leaned forward, "A little girl's life is in danger. If you are truly pro-life, you would help us. We need names and places. Old contacts."

"We've broken all contact with former colleagues," said Betsy.

Des said, "Betsy, it wouldn't do no harm. We got nothing to hide. Maybe we could help them. I mean, I could show them the scrapbooks and stuff."

"What scrapbooks?" asked Roger.

Betsy sighed, "Des kept scrapbooks of all the news articles of our exploits. He still goes through them occasionally. But it wouldn't be anything you hadn't seen or read or had access to elsewhere."

"But Betsy, what about the address book?" asked Des.

She looked at him, "The address book, fine, Des. Okay, you want to have the mounties over for tea, fine. Okay, Sergeant, you and yours want to come out for tea, I guess Des wants company. But you're wasting your time. We've nothing to hide. But we'll get out the scrapbooks. We'll get out the photos. We'll get out Des' address book. Fine. Just fine."

CHAPTER 32

Elena Risa was an attractive woman in her mid-forties with an exotic, European look about her; dark-skinned, slim, and wearing a silky dress in shades of brown. Her dark hair was pulled up onto the top of her head, but short wispy lengths of it framed her face. Her earrings were mismatched. In her right ear she wore what looked like a native feathered dreamcatcher and in her left she wore a series of gold hoops. She talked expressively, with delicate hand gestures, of how she had helped the police to find lost children in both Canada and the United States.

"Maybe you have heard of the case," she said, directing most of her comments toward Emma. "It was in Houston last year that a small boy was abducted by his father. In less than 24 hours I was able to locate the boy and his father, holed up in a cabin in the Arizona desert."

Emma nodded. She had not heard of the case, but felt it would be impolite to say so.

"At an early age I realized that God had blessed me with extraordinary powers. I believe that all of us have psychic inclinations to some degree, but in some the gift is more pronounced than in others. I happen to be one of those people in whom the gift has revealed itself. A long time ago I decided to use these powers for good and not for evil."

She was continuing, "It has to do with energies, when one person's energies become entwined with the surroundings."

Emma asked quietly, "How much do your charge for this?"

Elena leaned back in her chair. "Oh, no, no, no," she said, waving her jeweled fingers. "Please don't misunderstand me. That's not why I am here. I never charge for my services. Never. I've never taken a cent, not one cent, from any individual or police force. Never. This gift has been given me by God. How can I charge for such a thing?"

Emma watched her face as she talked; an animated, interesting face. Emma found it difficult to concentrate on her words. She kept watching her lips, her white teeth, her eyes. Emma thought, *This is a beautiful woman.*

Elena seemed to catch Emma's glance and reached out and touched her on the arm. "I believe I can help you find your little girl. I believe I can."

Kathy leaned forward now. "How do you go about this?" She was sitting next to Emma on the couch.

Elena leaned back. "Normally I work directly with the police force. Sometimes it becomes too traumatic for loved ones to be involved."

"Will you contact the police then?"

"I will, if you desire."

Emma said, "But surely you have an impression about Beth. Do you feel anything? Do you know anything?"

Elena shook her head. "As I said, it becomes too traumatic oftentimes for me to work directly with family members."

"Please...."

"Mrs. Knoll, if perhaps you have a photo of Beth, I could see if I receive impressions."

Emma rose and returned with Beth's school photo. She laid it down on the coffee table, next to the candle that burned. In her picture, Beth was smiling, her strawberry-blonde hair held up by two blue barrettes on either side.

Elena picked up the photo. "Oh, she is such a beautiful child."

"But do you have any impressions? Do you know where she is?" asked Emma.

Elena placed the photo on her lap and placed her fingers on either side of the picture. She closed her eyes. There was silence in the room for several seconds.

Elena looked up. "Your little girl is alive. That I know. She is alive now, but in danger. In grave danger."

Kathy said, "We'll call the police."

CHAPTER 33

Roger and Eric sat in the front seat of the detachment's four-wheel drive while Des and Betsy sat in the back.

"Just like old times, eh Betsy? You 'n me in the back of a police car," said Des.

Despite himself, Roger smiled. Through the rear view mirror he saw Betsy roll her eyes.

For the remainder of the trip, the two in the back were quiet. At one point Roger looked back to see Des with his head lolling against the back seat, eyes closed and mouth wide open. Betsy sat stiffly, frowning. Roger wished he could read her thoughts.

There was a part of him that admired those who chained themselves to abortion clinics, willing to spend time in prison for an ideal, a belief held so strongly.

There was a part of him that felt abortion really *was* the taking of human life. Deep inside he felt abortion shouldn't be a choice. It made no sense to think of it any other way. Yes, the video had been too graphic, yet he had to disagree with Sheila. He didn't think a pile of kidneys would have had quite the same effect.

He also knew it really didn't matter how he felt. He was a law enforcer, not a law maker. He had chosen his profession and if abortion was legal in Canada, then it was his job to uphold that law. As a Christian law enforcement officer, this was the kind of tension he lived with daily. He thought back to a picture that made it to the front of the *Calgary Herald*. As a young constable, he was one of a number of officers who were sent out to break up an abortion protest that was turning violent. When he arrived, the media was there in full force and one of the reporters snapped a picture of him forcing a screaming protester down into the back of a patrol car. That picture made it to the front page. Both of them, Roger Sheppard and the young screaming protester, went to the same large Calgary church.

Up ahead on the dirt road a small wooden cabin, badly in need of paint, came into view. It was fronted by a narrow ramshackle porch which was supported by cinder blocks. There were several outbuildings on the property; an outhouse with a door that hung crookedly and several wooden shacks. Next to the cabin was a creek. Roger examined the driveway carefully when he got out of the vehicle. It looked like the only other tracks had been made by the first police car. Maybe no blue vans had come to call.

Roger and Eric followed Betsy and Des up the four steps to the porch. She swung open the screen door and allowed everyone to enter before it banged behind them. Their cabin had not been locked.

"What are the outbuildings?" asked Roger.

"Sheds."

"May we have a look?"

"Be my guest, but we don't have keys."

"They're locked?" asked Roger.

"Yep. Des' uncle's stuff's in there. I don't have the foggiest what's in them. Shed stuff, I suppose. You can try to look through the windows, I suppose. The chicken coop's out there. You want to go have a look? I'll get you to feed the chickens while you're there." She pointed. "And the outhouse is over that way. Search that, be my guest. Maybe we got some important stuff buried down in there." She chuckled. When Roger and Eric did not smile, she said, "I told you officers, we live a primitive existence out here."

"Do you have a phone?" said Eric.

"No."

"Electricity?"

"No."

"Why the overhead wires, then?" he asked, looking up.

"I have no idea. Some of the people down the way have electricity, I suppose."

"I suppose," said Eric.

The cabin contained three rooms. Along the front was a living area with a wood stove, a dilapidated couch and a small wooden table. In the back were two bedrooms, one on the left and one on the right. Betsy followed his look. She said, "We are the only one's living out here. My bedroom's the one to the left and Des' is to the right. I told you we are like brother and sister."

Without saying anything, Des took a seat at the kitchen table and quietly, slowly began rolling a cigarette.

"Well, gentlemen," said Betsy. "I'd offer you something to drink but our cappuccino maker's broken."

"What I would like to see are Des' articles and photos," said Roger, ignoring her attempt at levity.

"Des, can I go and get your scrapbooks?"

Des nodded, and Betsy left. Roger could hear her rummaging around in Des' bedroom. She emerged a few minutes later with a cardboard box brimming with yellowed and dirty papers. She dropped it heavily on the table. Des stood up, stretched and said, "I'm going for a walk." He left.

For about half an hour, Roger and Eric leafed though articles yellowed and cut out from newspapers and scrapbooks. Des had written names and dates underneath the photographs, "Me and Martin in Vancouver, 1986," or "Way to go, Betsy!" or "Out of Prison, again!"

At the bottom of the box was Des' famous address book, small, black, ripped plastic. Roger leafed through it. Names of anti-abortion demonstrators leaped out at him; Martin Cranmore, Steffan Molko, Renee Blanchard. He asked if they could take the box and book with them.

"We'll return it. You don't have to worry about that," said Eric.

"It doesn't matter to me. These things are Des' and it looks like Des is overwhelmingly eager to cooperate with the authorities."

About half an hour later Roger and Eric climbed back into the four-by-four and headed for home. Des still had not returned.

"Now, those two are the strangest people I've met in a long time," said Eric.

Roger frowned, trying to keep the vehicle out of the biggest ruts. "I don't know. I plan to go through those articles and that address book with a fine tooth comb. I'd hate to think we just wasted the past two and a half hours."

Halfway into town they received the news that the Back Bay Women's Clinic in Boston had been bombed. Fortunately it was Sunday, so no one was injured. One of the videos was left at the site and a TV station in Boston was thinking of running the video in full on their late night newscast.

CHAPTER 34

A special prayer meeting was called at Julia's church following the evening service that night. By now everyone in the world had heard about the murder of Shanahan, the abduction of Beth Knoll, and the bombing of the Boston clinic.

Julia sat in a center pew, her hands folded tightly into fists as she prayed. She still wondered if she should have gone to the RCMP. Could she still go? But she had gone to Emma Knoll, and Emma Knoll was free to go to the RCMP if she wanted to. But why was there something still nagging at her? The house address. If only she could remember!

When the prayer meeting ended she didn't go straight home. Her mother was still there with the boys, and she had no desire to get into some long, drawn-out discussion about the benefits of tea and toast. Instead, she drove down Water Street and then up Front Street. *Think, Julia, think.* But the numbers were a blur to her. She pulled up behind a black pick-up truck, walked up the sidewalk to the first house, and knocked tentatively on the door. It was answered by an overweight, middle-aged man with bloodshot eyes.

"Yes?"

"I'm looking...." Julia faltered. "Do you have anyone living in this house with the initials E.M.?"

"Who are you?"

She'd never make it as a gumshoe. Her voice was small and hesitant and she gripped onto the sides of her raincoat. She went on, "I'm a friend of someone who used to live on this street, someone with the initials of E.M."

"If you're a friend of this person, how come you don't know this person's whole name?"

Boy, this guy was not going to be fooled. "Actually, it's a friend of a friend. And I only know the friend of a friend's initials."

"Little lady, I don't know what your game is...." He started to close the door.

"No, wait." Julia put up her hand. "This E.M. person is very important to me. It's vital that I locate...this person. Very important. I can't go into the details, but all I'm asking is if you ever ran into anyone on this street with the initials E.M."

He scratched his day's growth of beard with his hand and thought. Finally he said, "No, I haven't."

She reached into the pocket of her raincoat and from her wallet extracted a business card and handed it to him. "If you think of anyone by that name could you give me a call?"

He took the card and squinted at it, then held it at arms length for a second. "Pregnancy Care Centre?"

"That's where I work, yes. I'm Julia Nash. Can you call me at that number if you think about that name?"

"Yeah, sure."

He shut the door.

She went to the other houses along the street with the same story, handing out business cards like jelly beans at a parade, but no one knew anyone with the initials E.M.

CHAPTER 35

It had been another very long day, and Roger sat at his desk trying to rub the grit out of his eyes, considering the self-imposed CFLA deadline. He wondered if the entire day had been wasted, from the Shanahan family interview to the trip out to the crazies in the woods. And progress was exceedingly slow on the dark colored vans' front. Steve and Joanne, a constable from Fredericton, were working on that, personally checking into every blue van owner in the province. Others were going through Des' box and still others were working through Shanahan's personal files. So far, nothing. Earlier, he had spoken at length with the Boston detective investigating the bombing. No one was injured, but force from the bomb had blown out windows in the O'Keefe Funeral Home across the street. It was determined that video had been placed there after the bombing. A Boston television station had also received one of the notorious videos and had aired it in its entirety on their late night news program. This, of course, had set off a round of outrage from both sides of the issue. The Canadian Radio and Television Commission had banned Canadian TV stations from airing the video. This had about as much effect as thwarting a charging bear with a fly swatter, since about 90 percent of Canadians pick up U.S. television signals anyway.

Later in his apartment, Roger turned on his computer to three e-mails; one from Kate, one from Becky and one from Sara. So, all three were on to this internet thing. Interesting.

Kate's expressed real concern about Beth. "We're all praying here," she wrote. She went on to say that on Sunday afternoon a number of the members of the congregation had stayed behind for a spontaneous prayer meeting. She concluded her e-mail with "I miss you."

In the first sentence of Sara's e-mail, she wrote that she hoped the "whole abortion thing" would be over soon. The rest of the e-mail concerned Dog Ear's latest musical endeavor.

Becky's e-mail was very short, little more than, "Hi Dad, how are you?"

He answered all of them. Before retiring he rooted around in his small fridge and made a sandwich out of a slice of bread, a piece of rubbery-edged cheese, and a pickle.

For half an hour he lay on the top of the single bed in the small barracks-like bedroom, staring at the ceiling, unable to sleep. He was filled with an overwhelming longing for Kate. On his fingers he calculated what time it would be in Chester. Nine p.m. He wondered what she was doing. Was she sitting at Becky's desk helping her with her homework? Was she sitting in the rocker reading a novel with the television on?

Maybe the girls were out. Maybe Kate was sitting at the kitchen table studying for her real estate license. What was she wearing, her pink terry cloth housecoat? Her old jeans and long sweatshirt? He missed her tremendously.

This was a mistake, he thought, *this coming out here by myself, even if it was only for a few months.* He should have told them that he couldn't come out to St. Matthews until school was over in June. That's what he should have told them.

He reached over, picked up the phone and called her.

"Hello."

"Hi, sweetheart."

"Oh, hi, Roger. How are things? Should I even ask? Are you getting any sleep? I wish I was there."

"I wish you were here, too. I really wish you were."

"Are you any closer to finding that little girl?"

"I don't know. So far, no."

They chatted for a few minutes more, but hearing her voice didn't help. It only increased his longing for her.

Before they hung up, Roger asked, "By the way, what are you doing now?"

"Now? Well, Becky's out. The youth group went out for pizza after church, so Sara and I rented a movie."

"Oh yeah? Which one?"

"You don't want to know. It's a female movie, plenty of Kleenex and romance."

CHAPTER 36

It was shortly after eleven when Matt finally found the chat room he was looking for. They'd changed the name from CFLA1 to CFLA2. Matt laughed. *Brilliant*, he thought, changing from #1 to #2, as if that would fool him! He leaned back, interlaced his hands behind his head and watched the conversation already in progress scroll across the screen:

...had a situation here today.

B. Voice: Explain.

Earth Mother: A Julia Nash from the Pregnancy Care Centre has been wandering up and down Front Street asking too many questions.

Goddaughter: I will move the child immediately. She will find nothing.

Earth Mother: I will have a place waiting your arrival. It is safe here.

Mystic Queen: Why was she asking questions? Surely, she would be on our side.

Earth Mother: We're not certain of that. She never contacted us, as expected.

Mystic Queen: She is secretly on our side or she would have gone to the police.

B. Voice: Perhaps.

West Connect: I have signed on.

Earth Mother: Welcome to this private room, West Connect. We will be moving the plans for the west into full force in a matter of days. But there is the matter of Julia Nash. I say she must be stopped.

Goddaughter: How?

Earth Mother: She has two sons.

Mystic Queen: Perhaps a well-placed call to that ex-husband of hers.

Earth Mother: Good idea!

Goddaughter: You would not be thinking of taking them, too?

Earth Mother: And why not, Goddaughter?

Joan of Ark: Can Goddaughter handle a couple of extra boys?

Goddaughter: I will care for them if I have to.

Earth Mother: We will take them if it furthers our cause.

Goddaughter: Don't ask me to kill Beth. I didn't know there was going to be any killing. I wasn't prepared for that.

Earth Mother: You will.

Goddaughter: She has been telling me about summer camp.

Joan of Ark: I say we take the child away from Goddaughter. She was not a good choice for this part of the operation. She is becoming too attached.

B. Voice: I wish you Canadian contingent would get your acts together. Is anyone out there interested at all in what happened down here?

West Connect: I am. Go on.

B. Voice: The bombing was successful. The equipment has been totally destroyed. My underling has performed well. The video was dropped without consequence.

Mystic Queen: Here, here.

Earth Mother: We need to meet again, maybe tomorrow, but earlier. Eight instead of 11. Things are moving too quickly.

Matt set his printer to print each new screen as it scrolled. By the time Matt climbed into bed and fell asleep, the printouts lay in a scattered pile on his floor.

CHAPTER 37

"Wake up, Beth. We have to go. Hurry now!"

It was late and dark and Beth was curled up, Mrs. Jenkins clutched firmly in her sleeping arms.

"We have to leave now. Oh Beth, please wake up."

"Wha-a?"

"Now, Beth, now!"

Beth sat up slowly and looked around. She asked, "Are we going to see my mom now?"

"Soon, I promise. Soon."

Beth rose reluctantly and with sleepy eyes, she climbed out of bed and grabbed her backpack. Kara was pushing her forward down the darkened hallway.

"We should have a light on," said Beth. "I can't see anything."

"Not now, not tonight. It's too dangerous. They'll see us."

"Are you in trouble, Kara?"

Kara looked down at her sharply. "Be careful on the steps," was all she said. In some ways Kara reminded Beth of Colleen, her camp counselor last summer, who still sometimes wrote to Beth.

The van outside was loaded with boxes, and a computer monitor sat face forward on the back seat.

Kara buckled Beth into the front seat and said, "Beth, I want you to listen to me. We have to go to another place. Right away. And you have to promise to stay with me. If you don't, you won't be safe."

Beth was confused. Nothing that Kara said was making any sense. So stupidly, foolishly she said, "Could we go to the library first?"

"What?!"

"I finished my book and I want to get the next one."

"It's the middle of the night! The library is closed."

"Oh."

Kara's hands gripped the steering wheel, her face grim. Outside, the night air was frosty and dark and Beth shivered. Kara said, "Okay, how about you tell me the name of the book you want and I'll go get it for you tomorrow when the library's open."

"Do you want my library card?"

Kara only frowned.

"Are you scared, Kara?" Beth paused. "Because we could pray if you're scared. Colleen told me that. Do you know Colleen? She's your age I think. I've been praying since I came. But I'm still sorta scared."

Kara's mouth twisted into a grimace and she said, "Yeah, right, pray. I used to pray. That was something I used to do. I prayed all the time. I used to pray for the babies. I used to go to church and pray for the babies. I'd stand outside and pray for the babies. I'd go on the walks and pray for the babies."

"What babies?" asked Beth.

Kara continued, "Everything's going wrong now. I thought I was doing the right thing, but now everything's going wrong...."

Beth looked at her, uncomprehending. Kara continued, "I'm going to take you away to a safe place. In a little while they're going to realize that you and I aren't showing up at the appointed time and place. They're going to start looking. But I know a safe place. You have to trust me, Beth. I'm going to take you back to your family, but I can't right away. Not until it's safe. I don't care about the consequences to me. If I can do this one thing right, then maybe God will forgive me."

"God will forgive you," said Beth, still confused by Kara's long words.

But Kara, with the shiny hair, just frowned.

Beth must have dozed because the next thing she remembered was Kara leaning over her and saying, "Beth, wake up. Come on now." And then Kara carried her in her arms up to an enormous house, bigger even than Uncle Douglas' and Aunt Sheila's. The building was dark and it didn't look as if anyone was home.

"Do you live here?" asked Beth.

"I used to."

From her pocket Kara took a key and unlocked the front door. As they walked through the door, Beth could read the plaque along the top, "St. Matthews Bible School and Seminary. Women's Residence."

Once inside, Kara put Beth down on the floor and put a finger to her lips. They walked down a darkened hallway hand in hand. On either side were numbered doors.

"Is this a hotel?" stage whispered Beth.

"Shh, I'll tell you later."

At the end of the carpeted hall, they went down a flight of stairs. They walked along another carpeted hallway with closed numbered doors on either side. At the far end Kara, using a key from the same key ring, unlocked one of the doors.

Inside were two single beds, one on either side, matching dressers, matching desks and two closets. On the beds were neat piles of folded sheets and a blanket. Beth sat down on one of the beds and Kara quickly made up the other one. When Beth was tucked into the clean smelling sheets, Kara said, "Beth, you'll have to promise that you'll be as quiet as a mouse. This place is safe. No one will look for you here."

"Where are we?"

"This is a school. I used to go here. This used to be my room."

"You get to live at your school?"

"This is a dorm. I went here, that is until I got kicked out."

"You got expelled?"

"Yeah, for being too radical, among other things."

"What's radical?"

"Let's just say my ideas did not sit well with the powers that be. But when I left I forgot to give my keys back. They never asked for them. They must have forgotten or something. I happen to know there are no other students on the floor this term."

"Oh," was all Beth said. It was getting harder and harder to keep her eyes open.

"I have to leave now. Stay put and don't leave this room."

"Where are you going?"

"I have to go now."

Beth's last thoughts were how clean everything smelled compared to the scratchy, smelly blanket of the last place.

CHAPTER 38

It was 11:30 p.m. when Julia suddenly sat up in bed and remembered the address. 703 Front Street! That was it! 703 Front Street. She could see it written across the top of the letterhead. The Christian Freedom Life Army, 703 Front Street. She glanced over at her bedside clock. Emma had asked her, demanded, that Julia call her immediately if she found the address. She looked up Emma's number in the book and dialed it.

"Hello." The person who answered the phone had a crisp authoritative voice. Julia remembered that Emma had said that the police were there.

"May I speak with Emma Knoll, please?"

"Who is this?"

Julia stammered. "This is a friend."

"What's this friend's name?"

"Julia. Just tell her Julia Nash."

A few moments later Emma was on the line. "Hello."

"Hello, this is Julia Nash. I just called to say hi."

"Right," said Emma. She hung up.

Julia looked at the phone before she replaced it in its cradle. Then quickly, quietly she threw on her clothes, pulled on her sneakers, grabbed her keys and left.

By the time Julia pulled into the clinic lot, Emma was already there, leaning against her car.

"So, you've decided to give my daughter back," said Emma, walking toward Julia through the night. There was a darkness about her now, and a rage.

"What?"

"You and that little Christian Freedom Life Army of yours, I know you have her."

"I don't...," Julia stammered.

"And now your conscience is bothering you."

"You have this all wrong. I called you because I remembered the address. I'm not a part of the group that took her. I never would be. I told you that."

"I don't believe you."

"You've got to believe me because it's the truth."

"You gave me this whole song and dance about a lost address and a letter and the feeling you were being watched. When I got home I got to thinking about it and realized what a crock that was. You were just setting me up, making me appear the fool, getting your information by coming to me at the clinic. Never in a million years would you come to the clinic. I know that now. If your story had been true you would have gone straight to the police. Boy, was I stupid. You have Beth and you've had her all along. Now I want her."

Julia was frantic. "No, I don't have her. Honest I don't. You have me all wrong. I would *never* do something like that. Never! I have two sons of my own. All I have is the address. I just woke up and remembered the address. It's 703 Front Street. I'm fairly sure of it. I'm not keeping anything from you. Honest!"

"Oh yes, woke up and remembered the address. How convenient. What a bunch of nonsense. No one wakes up and remembers something."

"I did, honest."

"Fine," said Emma. "Play your little games. But I'm prepared. I brought a gun." Julia saw that Emma was carrying a very small silver hand gun. "Seven-oh-three Front Street? Well, I'm going there. If it's an ambush I've got my gun." She walked back to the car, got in and backed out. Frustrated, Julia got in her own car and followed.

Seven-oh-three Front Street was an ancient brick structure with rows and rows of windows like a chessboard. By the time

Julia had turned off her ignition, Emma was at the front door.

"When do the bad guys pop out and grab me?" she said when Julia approached.

"I've never been here before."

"This is a trap. But I'm prepared. You'll be my hostage."

"It's not a trap. I came alone." Julia was pleading now, frenzied and panicking. "You have to believe me, I don't have anything to do with this. I've never been here before."

Julia followed Emma, pleading, trying to make her understand. Emma walked purposefully to the locked windows. Then she began inching her way sideways through the narrow space between 703 and 705 Front Street, the gun held high above her head. Julia followed. Halfway through she looked up at the dirty brick walls towering high and straight above her and tried not to think about spiders.

The back yard of 703 Front Street was deadly dark. She nearly tripped over piles of debris as she followed Emma to the back door. The wooden door had four small panes of miry glass. It, too, was locked.

Emma smashed out one of the small panes with her gun.

Julia asked, "What are you doing?"

"Getting my daughter."

"But that's breaking and entering," protested Julia.

"Oh, and what's murder and kidnapping and bombing?"

Emma reached through the pane and unlocked the door from the inside.

Julia followed her inside. The room was black and smelled of tires and rancid car oil.

"What *is* this place?" asked Julia.

Emma glared at her. "Well, I've got to admit, you're a good actress."

"I'm not acting. I've really never been here before!"

Emma flicked on a pen-sized flashlight and shone it around.

"You brought a flashlight."

"Brilliant deduction, Watson," said Emma.

Julia muttered, "You don't have to be so sarcastic."

The slender beam revealed a high-ceilinged room, basically empty, except for a few boards and other odd pieces of junk and debris scattered throughout.

"Why'd you bring me here?" demanded Emma.

"This was the address on the letter," said Julia, almost in tears.

Emma was screaming and waving the gun in Julia's face. "I demand that you tell me why you brought me here!"

For the first time Julia felt truly frightened. She said, "Listen, you've got to believe me. I have nothing to do with this. Nothing! How can I make you believe that?"

Julia could see wet tears on Emma's cheeks now. "I just want Beth. I just want Beth."

"I don't think she's here. This is just where their address was. That's all I know. That is the truth. *Please* believe me. I would never hurt a child."

"If what you are saying is true, then I'll examine every square inch of this place. And if any funny stuff happens, I've got my gun."

Examine she did, poking the flashlight beam into musty corners and scaring up brown bugs which scurried away from the light. Emma called for Beth a few times quietly, urgently, but the silence gave no answer. Julia followed her up a metal staircase, casting the beam here and there as she walked.

The upstairs level was much like the lower level, barren and grimy. The light revealed nothing but mounds of boards and junk stacked against the walls. Emma poked and prodded at each one.

Julia was standing at the top of the steps watching her when Emma bent down and said, "Aha!" She rose, holding up two wires. She said, "I knew it! Two phone lines and electric wires. They were here."

"Well, I told you they were here. I told you that much."

"Two phone lines!"

"So, they had two phones."

"Why would they need two phones?"

"Lots of offices have two phones. So what?"

But Emma said, "They were here!"

At the back of the landing was a small room with a door. Emma made her way there and opened it.

Julia followed her in. Emma tried the switch and immediately light flooded the small room.

Emma walked further inside and stood for several seconds, looking around. "She was here," she said calmly. The room contained a single bed with a thin gray mattress and a pillow. Off to the right a doorway led into a small bathroom.

"Here? How do you know?"

"I can sense it. I know it." Now she was walking crazily back and forth, into the bathroom and out again. She ran her fingers on the dingy wall, touching the bed, touching the door. Kneeling on the mattress, she ran her fingers underneath it. She gasped.

"What is it?"

"She was here. Now I have proof. Beth was here. She was!"

From underneath the mattress she withdrew a small paperback book. Julia looked at it. *The Lion, the Witch and the Wardrobe* by C.S. Lewis. "Beth's book?"

Emma nodded. "That was her trick. Putting her books under the mattress. She reads constantly. Every night it's a battle. I come into her room, 'Are you reading?' but by then the book is safely tucked beneath the mattress. This one's her favorite. She's probably expecting Aslan to come rescue her."

"Now we *have* to go to the police," said Julia. "Now there's no question."

Emma did not respond, but she sunk onto the bed, clutching the book and the gun to her chest and rocking like a frightened child, her shoulders heaving. Julia sat down next to her. She wanted to say something, to do something, to reach out to her, to touch her shoulder, but Emma was correct. Julia had no right.

"And the stupid thing is," said Emma, "this isn't a real gun anyway. It's a starter pistol."

Emma's sobs grew more desperate, and Julia handed her a Kleenex from her pocket.

"I'm so sorry, Emma. I'm so sorry this has happened. This is so horrible and unfair." She placed a tentative hand on Emma's shoulder.

Emma did not turn away.

CHAPTER 39

Today was Matt's mother's day off. The last Monday of every month she had off to make up for the first Saturday of each month when she worked. Usually, she devoted these Mondays to house cleaning. It was only 9:30, but she had already finished cleaning her daughter Clarisa's room, carting out two black garbage bags full of old school papers, ice cream and candy wrappers, and outgrown clothing, much of it too ragged even for the thrift shop.

Matt's room was next. She changed his sheets and was gathering up his dirty clothes when she noticed the mess of paper under his computer. "I wish that kid would learn to pick up after himself once in a while," she muttered. As she was stacking them, she became intrigued and began to read. They were all about the bombing of the Boston Clinic, all about the kidnapping of the little girl from this town, and about a person named Julia Nash and Front Street. There was a Front Street in St. Matthews. What was this all about? Carrying the sheaf of computer paper, she went into the master bedroom where she dialed her husband at work.

She could hear him sigh audibly when he recognized her voice. "Alexis, I'm in the middle of an important meeting. Can't this wait until evening?"

"I'm not sure. I don't know. It's about Matt."

"What's that kid done now?"

"When I was cleaning his room, I found some computer

papers, all about the bombing of that clinic in Boston, and about the kidnapping of the little girl."

"So?"

"What do you mean, 'So'?"

"So, what's your point?" He sighed, louder now. "Alexis, that news story is all over the internet. There's probably a web site devoted to the abortion doctor killing by now."

"But Paul, this seems different, somehow, like conversation. Here, I'll read you some of it...."

"Alexis, I don't have time for this. I'm already late for an important meeting."

"You said you were *in* a meeting, Paul. That's what you said when I called, 'I'm *in* a meeting.' Make up your mind, are you in a meeting, or just late for a meeting?"

"I'm *trying* to be in a meeting, Alexis. This whole conversation is completely exasperating. When Matt comes home from school, you ask him about those printouts. Then get him to show you how to find things on the internet."

"Oh Paul, you know I'm hopeless when it comes to computers."

CHAPTER 40

When Roger arrived at the detachment Monday morning, the door to his office was open and through it he could see a dark-haired woman sitting, her hands folded loosely in her lap.

"Who is she?" he asked Kelly.

"Some psychic."

"Some what?"

"Some psychic who says she can help find Beth," replied Kelly.

"Not here," he said quickly. "Not in my detachment."

"Jack authorized it, told her to wait for you."

"Over my dead body. Jack doesn't authorize things around here, I do, and I'm not bringing in any psychic on this case."

Kelly blinked at him. "Police departments use psychics all the time."

"Not this one."

Roger stormed into Jack's office. "I will not have any psychic in this detachment working on a police investigation!"

Jack ran his thick hands through his stubbly gray hair. "And why not? What can it hurt? We haven't been wildly successful on our own."

"I don't believe in any of their so-called powers. We are running short of time and I don't need to waste any of it with a psychic!"

"Calm down. Don't be so touchy. Lots of police departments use psychics."

"Not this one."

How could Roger explain to Jack how he felt without simply sounding ridiculous?—That 90 percent of psychics were quacks looking for a bit of publicity, and more importantly, their methods didn't work. The other 10 percent did not receive their powers from themselves or from God, but from Satan, the Prince of Darkness, himself. *It was fine to believe in God*, he thought. *Everyone did. It wasn't fashionable, however, to believe that Satan, the Devil, really existed.* Roger, however, did. Too much was at stake to even take a chance on bringing that element into this case.

He said, "Jack, you should know the research. Those so-called powers have never been proven."

"Look," said Jack. "The Knolls sent her to us. The media is on our backs. It's got to appear like we're doing everything humanly possible to find that little girl. If word gets out that we turned away a psychic, the general public will crucify us!"

"I don't care. I'm going in there to send her home."

"Fine, but you're cutting your own throat."

"Fine!"

The dark-haired woman sitting in his office regarded him with an amused expression. No doubt she had heard every word. He stood in the doorway.

She looked up at him, "I take it you want me to leave?" Her eyes were large and brown. Her smile was soft, amused.

"No offense—Miss?"

"Risa. Elena Risa. But please call me Elena." She extended her hand. Roger didn't take it. He walked to his desk and sat down behind it.

"No offense, Miss Risa, but I don't make a habit of working with psychics." Something about her seemed vaguely familiar and Roger found himself staring at her, trying to remember.

"So I gathered." She smiled. Hers was a striking face, an articulate face, smooth and swarthy with large brown eyes, thin nose and expressive lips. She smiled coyly when she said, "No offense taken, Sergeant. I am well aware that there are skeptics who view my particular gifts with derision. I assure you that I meant no ill intent. I am also aware that this is a stressful time for all concerned. The life of a precious little child is at stake and tempers flare. But I can help. That's all I want to do, help. And I believe she is alive, but in grave danger."

She leaned forward and the dark silk of her dress fell away from her shoulders revealing smooth skin. She crossed her legs and smoothed her skirt with her long fingers whose ends were flawlessly coated with a dark polish. She told him about other police investigations she had been a part of, of other police officers who had initially been skeptical of her power. "My specialty is child abductions."

As she talked Roger found himself watching that tongue flicking in and out of that mouth, the row of even white teeth, and the soft shoulders. She stopped suddenly and looked at him, "Why are you staring at me, Sergeant?"

"I'm not staring." He pressed his finger tips together hard and looked away, at the wall, at the window, at the ceiling, anywhere but at Elena Risa and her smooth, sensuous skin.

"You are afraid of me, of what I can do." She winked at him. Why did she look so familiar?

He said, "If for one minute I believed that you could help us, I'd be all for it. I just don't believe you can."

"You are afraid of me," she said, and then slowly uncrossed her legs delicately and winked at him. "You are a strange man, Sergeant, full of principle, but full of something else, too. I sense a longing, perhaps. You are afraid, because I know so much about you."

You know nothing about me, he wanted to say. "Miss Risa, I have made my decision. We will not be using your services here in St. Matthews."

He rose and walked to his door, wishing she would leave, yet longing for her to stay so he could look at her forever.

"I will leave then," she said, rising. As she walked past him her skirt brushed his thigh. Again, she winked up at him. "You are a strong man, Sergeant, but a weak man, no?"

When she left, he shut his door, sat there for a few minutes frowning. A strong man and a weak man. She had that much right....

His phone rang. Fine. It would be good to get back to reality, get back to the case, back to the task at hand, get his thoughts away from Elena Risa and onto the missing child.

"Sheppard here," he said businesslike into the receiver.

"Well, hello to you, too!"

Kate!

"Kate, hi, hello."

"You okay? You sound kind of strange."

"I'm fine...just got in."

"Oh, I'm so sorry, that case is really getting you down, isn't it? I won't be more than a minute. I just wanted to catch you. It's real early here, like practically the middle of the night, but I couldn't sleep. I had to call and tell you this. We got an offer on the house!"

"That's great, honey."

"You really sound weird. You sure you're okay?"

"Yeah fine. That's great, tell me about it."

"Last night late, way after we talked, we got a call. I thought it was too late to call you then."

Kate told him about the young couple who was moving to Chester from B.C. They were offering just a little under what she and Roger had agreed on as a selling price. She asked what Roger thought about accepting their offer or counter offering.

"I'll go with your judgment," he told her. "You're more up on real estate things than I am."

"Okay, we'll go with a counter offer."

"Fine," said Roger.

"You don't sound fine."

"It's just that I miss you so much."

"Oh, Roger. It's only for a couple more months."

"Kate, I love you more than you'll ever know."

After hanging up, Roger put his head in his hands. Too much work...worry...and crime. Not enough sleep and definitely not enough Kate.

CHAPTER 41

Sitting across from her at the kitchen table, Constable Jill Mitchell wanted to know where Emma had gone last night.

"Am I the criminal here?" Emma was furious. "Am I under house arrest or something? You can't keep me here. I'm the victim and you're giving me the third degree. Go out and catch the man that has my daughter, make *him* sit here. But no, criminals are free to come and go while we victims are not allowed to carry on our normal lives!"

"You are not under house arrest. This is for your own safety. You could be in danger. We don't know. We don't want to take any chances. All we want to do is to find Beth. But you receive a short cryptic phone call and you're out the door like a shot."

"Did you follow me?"

"I phoned the detachment. They went out looking for you."

"Did they find me?"

"No."

"Yeah, St. Matthews is a huge city. It's really hard to find someone driving around its deserted streets at midnight."

Jill scowled. Emma looked at her high cheek bones, blond hair, and slim, tall build. *She could have been a model. Why did she chose law enforcement*, Emma wondered.

Jill asked, "Has anyone ever told you how sarcastic you are?"

"All the time. I'll quit being sarcastic when you find my daughter."

"Where did you go last night?"

"None of your business."

"It is my business if it concerns Beth."

"I went to meet a man." She enunciated and elongated the last three words.

Jill glared at her.

Emma got up and poured herself another cup of coffee. Her head was pounding, and the edges of her body tingled with fear. She had come so close last night. Beth had been there. She should tell Jill. She didn't know why she wouldn't.

Kathy had called earlier, saying she'd drive over to the clinic, put up a "Closed" sign and be right over. Emma stirred in sugar and cream before she forgot that she had weaned herself from sugar. Jill was still looking at her, concerned and worried. Emma wished Jill would get up and walk out. She needed to be alone.

After she had arrived home last night, Jill met her at the door, along with two other police officers, demanding to know where she'd been. Too exhausted to reply, she had said nothing, just cuddled into the couch, wrapping herself up in Beth's quilt and clutching the book. She could not talk to Jill, not even to Kathy who had arrived 15 minutes later in response to Jill's phone call. Eventually, she fell asleep on the couch with the lights on and people still talking. She had slept shallowly and restlessly while strange images crept in and out of her dreams. At one point she had arrived home from the warehouse to find weeds grown up in her living room, poking their heads through the carpets, around the coffee table, in amongst the chair legs and the television stand; dandelions, Queen Anne's Lace, Lamb's Quarters. She pulled them up and carried them outside to the compost pile. *Things must look nice for Beth's return. Beth was coming. She couldn't come home to weeds in the living room. That would never do.*

But as soon as she was back inside again, new weeds had taken their place; poison ivy, stinging nettles, devil's club. Her hands were raw and red as her weeding became more frantic. The faster she pulled, the more they grew. She awoke, clothed in the sweat of fear.

Earlier, when it was still dark, she had awakened. The house was quiet. She had walked into Beth's room. Empty, of course. What did she expect, that Beth would be there, sleeping soundly, curled up under her quilt, Mrs. Jenkins cuddled to her face? She wandered through Beth's room, touching things, feeling the stuffed bears, flipping through her books, fingering the dolls lined up in a row. At her bulletin board she reached up and ran her forefinger over Beth's cross of colored beads. Last summer she had met Emma at the car, wearing it around her neck, with a "Hi, Mom, come and meet my counselor."

She had been introduced to a smiley college girl name Colleen, who extended her hand and said, "Beth is such a special little girl."

"I know," Emma had said.

She had unpinned the cross from the bulletin board and had held it in her palm. She stared at it a long moment, fingering the beads. Beth's special cross. It was almost as if she could feel a presence then, a lightness, a voice. *I'm taking care of Beth.* She stood up quickly and dropped the cross and looked around. But the house was quiet. *I'm taking care of Beth.*

And then, all was silence again. She picked up the cross from the floor and went out into the living room. With shaking hands she laid it beside the thick white candle that still burned for her daughter.

This morning she thought of these things as she sat silently in the kitchen, watching Jill read the morning news. She remembered the voice, *I'm taking care of Beth*, and felt strangely calmed.

CHAPTER 42

It was an unusual morning, that Monday when Julia sat behind the desk at the Pregnancy Care Centre. The rain had let up, but it was still overcast, with lines of misty gray seeming to drip from the sky in strings.

Earlier, Julia had seen both her boys off to school with their lunch boxes, and had said good-bye to her mother, who said that despite all of the pressing things she had planned to do this week at home, she'd stay with Julia and the boys. She could do that much, after all, until the whole thing "blew over." Julia had said it wasn't necessary, but her mother waved her hand in front of her face and said it was the least she could do.

Julia had come home the previous night at about 1 a.m. to a dark and silent house. She had tiptoed through the kitchen and into her room. If her mother *had* heard her, Julia was fairly sure she would have said something about it at breakfast. But she hadn't. "I was out smashing windows in an old warehouse at midnight with the manager of the Shanahan Clinic." No, she shook her head, her mother wouldn't have believed her anyway.

The house was quiet in the morning when she woke, showered, and made coffee. She usually did this, rose early, got ready, and then with her coffee she'd sit down with her Bible and her journal and write out her meditations and prayers. But this morning, her thoughts had been tumbled down and scattered. She read the passage in Luke about Jesus blessing the children. She thought of Beth. She thought of her own boys. How could Jesus allow this to happen? An innocent child, Beth, taken by a brutal gang of terrorists? Why were there so many innocent victims on this fallen planet; kidnappings, bombings, accidents, abortions?

Please keep Beth safe, she prayed. *Lord, keep her safe.*

She was still praying that same prayer as she sat behind the reception desk at the Pregnancy Care Centre, where she had once more looked in vain for the missing letter. Why didn't I call the police when this first happened? And why can't I pick up the phone and call the police now? What am I so afraid of?

Her thoughts were interrupted by a very quiet and reticent Shelly, who entered her door, a newspaper in hand. She laid Monday morning's *Canada Today* down in front of Julia. "You were right. Maybe there is a list."

It was a front page story, well not the interview with Julia, but the murder and kidnapping, of course. Hers was a prominent side bar. "Anti-abortionist Surprised She is on List." Julia scanned it, hardly able to breathe.

Julia Nash, coordinator of the St. Matthews Pregnancy Care Centre expressed surprise Saturday that she is one of a number on a list of anti-abortionist terrorist groups.... RCMP will neither confirm nor deny the existence of such a list.

"Oh Shelly, this is horrible!"

"I don't really think it's that bad."

"Not that bad? How could you possibly say it's not that bad?"

Shelly leaned over the desk and placed both hands on the article. "Any thinking person will just see how ridiculous this is. No thinking person could ever possibly believe you are a terrorist."

"Most people who read papers aren't thinking people, Shelly."

"Still, you gotta look on the bright side."

"What bright side? There *is* no bright side," protested Julia.

"Sure there is. This will mobilize pro-life groups to really come out and make a stand against this kind of violence. We'll be *forced* to make a stand, that to be pro-life means just that, that killing in any form is wrong, including murdering abortion doctors. You can't fight death with death. That's what we'll tell them, that we pro-lifers don't protest evil by more evil. Two wrongs don't make a right. You just sit down right now and write a rebuttal to the editor explaining *your* side of the story."

"They'll just change it all around. They always do."

"Well, if you don't write anything, I will."

After Shelly left, Julia picked up the phone. It was definitely time to call the police. Definitely time. But she didn't do it. She replaced the phone in its cradle and was startled when it rang immediately.

"Hello, Julia."

"Mason." She tried to keep her voice even.

"Did you happen to read today's *Canada Today*, Julia?"

"I happened to read it, yes."

"I'm concerned."

"Everyone's concerned, Mason."

"I think it might be best for all concerned if the boys come out and stay with Judith and me for a while. We would love to have them. Judith loves them."

"I'm sure she does. But, my mother is staying with me now, and they have school and activities. There is nothing to be concerned about."

"That's not what I heard."

"Mason, that reporter was just manufacturing things."

"I'm not talking about the article."

"What, then?"

"Let's just say that someone called me in connection with this whole thing, warning me that my sons could be kidnapped next."

Julia willed her body to remain calm, "What?"

"You heard me, that Josh and Jeff, that my sons, might come to harm unless you quit your snooping around."

"What!"

"What have you gotten yourself into Julia?"

"Who called you saying that?"

"I have no idea, they had blocked their number and my call display didn't pick it up. I immediately called the police, however, as would any good law-abiding citizen who has information about unlawful activities."

Julia sat down in her chair and could not speak.

Mason was continuing. "As I said before, Judith and I would love to have the boys, and I should let you know that I've put a call into my lawyer about caring for them until this threat to them is past."

When Mason finished with his threats and had hung up, Julia put her head in her hands and wept.

CHAPTER 43

In the case room, Roger sat with his second cup of coffee, leafing through the files and reports that were scattered on the top of the long wooden table. He was writing notes in his small notebook and trying to get his mind away from Elena Risa and Kate calling and houses selling.

There was an air of frantic in the place, uniformed and plainclothes officers frowning and scurrying here and there, everyone aware that the clock was steadily ticking toward Tuesday 1 p.m. They had not heard from the CFLA since the bombing last night in Boston.

Shortly after Kate had phoned, Steve had come in with a blue van update. They had eliminated all but about a dozen, which they were personally following up on. Roger picked up the long fan-fold computer list of vans. Those which had been eliminated were struck through with red. He scanned through the list of individuals not checked yet:

Bill Meals, o/c: fisherman, Saint John, New Brunswick

Kara Scoretti, o/c: student, Loggieville, New Brunswick

Ronald Pederman, o/c: Dept. of Highways, Fredericton, NB

The list continued. Nothing familiar, none of those names matching any of the names in Des' famous address book, none matching any of the names in Shanahan's personal files.

Another officer had reported that Mason Nash, ex-husband of Julia Nash, employed at the Pregnancy Care Centre in St. Matthews, had received an anonymous call that his wife may "know something" about the murder.

"Sounds like it could be a vengeful ex-husband trying to make trouble for his former wife kind of thing, but we're checking it out anyway."

Francine had come in to say that that morning she'd talked with a store in Moncton who, in the last six months, had rented out three costumes; an Easter Bunny, Snow White, and one used in the musical Cats, to a woman named Joan Aarkman who gave a Woodstock address. She had paid cash for the rental. The manager of Copyright Costumes described Joan Aarkman as medium height, mid-thirties, shoulder length brown hair, no glasses, and no distinguishing marks that she could remember. And surprise, surprise, the costumes had never been returned.

"That lady, the manager of the store, asked if we could get her costumes back if we catch up to Joan Aarkman," said Francine. "She was mad, I'll tell you."

Police in Woodstock had gone to the address given by Ms. Aarkman to discover that no such address existed.

"Didn't she have to give the costume place some sort of deposit?" Roger asked her.

"Yeah, normally they require a credit card imprint, but Joan Aarkman seemed so pleasant, had this big story about leaving her wallet at home and needing the costumes for her high school play, and asked if it would be all right this one time. I think that's why the lady's so mad. She got taken big time. Do you have any idea what those costumes are worth?"

"None," said Roger.

Francine grunted, "Plenty, I can tell you. Let me tell you the rest of the story. We did a computer check on Joan Aarkman. Turns out there really *is* a Joan Aarkman, current address Florenceville, holds a current N.B. driver's license. No blue van, however. Turns out she hasn't been at her place of residence for a couple of months, that's according to neighbors. They also say she keeps to herself a lot."

"Anything else?"

"Yeah, neighbors reported seeing a blue van there in front a few times."

"We're getting somewhere," said Roger.

"So we got a search warrant and, as we speak, her place is being systematically searched. We're also doing a computer search of her relatives, family, places she could have gone. We'll find her."

We'll find her, thought Roger, but in time?

About 45 minutes later, at 12:20 p.m., a call came in from Boston. They had a suspect in custody in Boston. They got lucky. An employee from O'Keefe's Funeral Home just happened to be gardening in the back. He was there when the building was bombed. He was the one who dialed 911. He said he was just coming out of the back door and spotted this woman walking up and placing a video on the steps of the bombed out building. He was able to get the license plate number. A woman, Beverly Winter, was picked up shortly after that and was now in custody at the police station in downtown Boston. They asked if Roger wanted to come down and have a chat with her.

"We can't get a straight word out of her," said the Boston detective. "She keeps spouting off these religious sayings. We heard you are an expert in religion. Thought you might be able to help."

"Well, I don't know if I'm an expert in religion," said Roger, "but I'll be on the next plane out of Fredericton."

CHAPTER 44

It wasn't all at once, a sudden astonishing thing that caught her by surprise. No, Mason's leaving Julia was more subtle than that. When he told her, when he finally came right out and told her, she wasn't surprised. They were standing together in the front yard examining the new crocus buds when he said, "I'm leaving you, Julia."

She didn't look up when he said those words, but watched as he kept jabbing and jabbing at the dirt around the purple blossom with a long stick. She was not surprised when he told her. It would explain nights working late, business trips that she could not verify by calling his office, little things. Lots of little things, like, he never touched her anymore. He never reached for her in the dark. At night he would roll away from her. Sometimes she would face him in the darkness of their room, face his back and run her hands over him, an inch above his skin, but not touching. Never touching. If her hand slipped, if it fell onto the flesh of his back, he would flinch. She wondered what he dreamed.

Words refused to form in her brain. All she could do was to stare at the crocus. When she finally said something it was ludicrous and out of place. "You're hurting the flower."

"Did you hear me, Julia? I found someone else." He was looking at her now, but her eyes refused to meet his. She stared at the flower, bent out of shape and bruised by his jabbing. Why was he doing that to the flower?

Her whole being became filled with silence and a strange urge to get this over with as quickly as possible, to help him through this, to make it easy for him, not to question him too deeply.

Later she would wonder about that urge, questioning where it had come from. Later she would replay those moments. Over and over in her mind she would rehearse what she should have said, cutting remarks such as, *You found someone else? You mean you went looking?* or *What about till death do us part? What about the vows we made before God and our families? What about that? What about all that?*

That's what she should have said. She should have stood in front of him and demanded that he answer her. She should have grabbed the stick from him, stood there and made him answer her.

She thought about all of this as she sat with her head in her hands on the desk. Gloria had helped her deal with all the rage, all the unsaid things, the anger that would not go away.

Thou wilt keep him in perfect peace whose mind is stayed on Thee.

She had grabbed a handful of fear from the olden days when every subtle nuance of Mason, every look, sent her scurrying, running, wondering what was wrong with her that she could not keep "her man?" What kind of a wife was she? *God, I'm sorry. If You give me another chance I'll be a better wife to Mason. I'm sorry, I'm sorry. Please give me another chance.*

It was Gloria who had gotten her to finally stop praying that prayer, to stop writing that in her journal. She closed her eyes. *Perfect love casts out fear.* Gloria had told her that God loved her with a perfect love, and nurturing herself in God's unconditional love would cast out the fear in her life, the fear of Mason.

She picked up the phone and called Shelly. It was a start.

CHAPTER 45

Alexis sat at the dining room table, the computer printouts spread in front of her. She was reading them through carefully again. Maybe Paul was right. Maybe she was over-reacting. After all, what did she really know about the internet anyway? A big fat zero. She stacked up the papers again, noticing for the first time the date and time written across the top of them. She grabbed the stack of newspapers from the kitchen counter. If the dates across the top of the computer printouts were right, then those computer printouts had been written *before* the events had happened! *The time for the bombing of the B. Clinic has been moved up. It will now be destroyed tomorrow at 6 P.M. instead of Monday....* With a kind of horror she dropped the paper. What on earth had Matt gotten himself involved in now?

She dialed the school number and asked for him to be paged, calling it a family emergency.

"Mom, what's the emergency?" asked Matt, breathless when he answered.

"Matthew King, what on God's green earth are you involved in? You tell me! Now!"

"What are you talking about?"

"Do you want me to turn you in to the police?! Who are you, their computer specialist?"

His voice sounded panicky. "What?"

"Bombing, shooting, kidnapping!!"

"Mom, what are you talking about?"

"Your father said this wasn't important, that I should wait until you get home, but I read the printouts. I'm not stupid...."

"Mom...."

"Don't 'Mom' me! You want me to go to the police right now and tell them what my own son, my own flesh and blood, has gotten himself involved in, or will you? I told your father it was a mistake to get you a computer, but no, no one listens to me around here. I knew it was a mistake and now you've gone and gotten yourself involved in something criminal!"

"I didn't do anything!"

Matt's mother lined up the computer printouts in order, fairly sure now of the dates.

"Matthew, don't play dumb with me. I'm talking about this stack of computer printouts I found next to your computer. Bombing, killing, kidnapping, Earth mother. This is serious stuff, Matthew. You shouldn't have involved yourself with people like that."

"But that's just people playing a game."

Alexis sat down and put the palm of her hand on her forehead. People playing a game? Her voice was sad, tired when she said, "What kind of a game is this, Matthew?"

"You know, like Doom, Dungeons and Dragons on the internet. Only in this one they use the names of real cities and stuff. Can I go now? The bell's going to ring."

"No, Matthew, you may not go. You have to tell me more about this game."

"I don't know much about it. I just found it one night. Really, Mom, I don't know why you're so ballistic!"

Maybe it was a game, maybe the dates along the top of the printouts were incorrect.

"How accurate are the dates of these printouts?"

"What dates?"

"The dates along the top of the pages."

"Yeah, they're right. I found this group on Friday night. Mom, I gotta go now...."

Friday night. The day Shanahan was shot!

"And these people write letters to each other on the internet?"

"More like chat, Mom."

"In my day we called written communications letters."

"It's live chat, everyone's on at the same time."

"How did you get hooked up with this group?"

"My friend and I invented a way to log into private rooms."

Alexis touched her forehead again. "Matthew, explain these terms to me. I don't know what you're talking about."

"Mom, I gotta go. I'm already late."

"You and your father. Everything's more important than my questions. Look, if you get in trouble with your teacher, you tell him to call me."

"It's a she."

"Okay, get *her* to call me. Now tell me, what's this chatting line you're talking about?"

"It's live chat. It means that you have a bunch of people...."

"Friends? People who know each other?"

"Well, they would have to know the location of the room."

"What room? You mean the room where the main computer's located?"

"What main computer?"

"I don't know. Go on," she said tiredly.

"Okay, it's called a room, but it's really not a real room. They're just called rooms because people meet in them...."

"But they're not really there, they're just writing letters to each other?"

"Sort of, but you'd have to know the location of the room, like where to find it on the internet."

"Like what buttons to press?"

"Sort of, but all these people are on live, talking to each other back and forth, writing stuff."

"Okay," Matt's mother was talking faster now. "How did you find these people playing that game on the computer?"

"WhizKid and I wrote this program where you can find the passwords of private rooms, even rooms not on a regular chat network."

"Who's WhizKid?"

"A friend."

"From school?"

"No, from the internet."

Alexis sighed. "Was it hard to find these people 'chatting'?"

"It was a breeze."

"But, I mean, for the normal person hooked up to the internet. Would it be easy say, for your dad?"

"He wouldn't have a clue."

"Could the police get on?"

"Don't think so, not without the program WhizKid and I wrote."

"Thanks Matt, you've been a help."

After she hung up, Alexis King bundled all of the printouts and placed them in a file folder to take to the RCMP.

CHAPTER 46

When Shelly pulled into the Centre parking lot, Julia hurriedly put a sign on the door, "Back at 1:00" and hopped into the passenger seat.

"Shelly, thank you so much for coming. Thank you."

"Julia, you're shaking. What's wrong?"

"It's Mason. Can you drive to the school?"

"What about Mason?"

"I'll tell you on the way. I called you because I needed to talk to someone, someone who could bring me back to sanity. But first, the school."

Shelly put the car in reverse and backed out. "Why the school?"

"I have to make sure the boys are okay."

Shelly looked at her quizzically and then turned out onto the main road.

As they made the short drive between the Centre and the elementary school, Julia, in breathless spurts, told her story. She began with the letter, with the feeling that she was being watched, about knocking on doors on Front Street late at night.

"Wait a minute." Shelly put her hand up. "You went up to every house on Front Street in the dark?"

"Yes."

Shelly shook her head and went back to her driving. "You're nuts. Do you know how dangerous that is? Front Street of all places!"

"Thank you for that vote of confidence."

"Why didn't you come to me? I would have helped you."

"I felt like I had to do this on my own. I can't explain it."

Shelly shrugged. "Go on, sorry for interrupting."

Julia told her friend then about visiting the Shanahan Clinic, about meeting Emma Knoll, about the midnight foray of the two of them....

"You mean to tell me you were actually *inside* the Shanahan Clinic?"

"I was actually inside."

"Oh, Julia...."

"What are you 'oh Julia-ing' me about?"

"The Shanahan Clinic." She put a hand to her chest. "You were actually *inside*. My goodness, I drive by that place, I sense evil, I really do."

"I wasn't thinking about that when I was in there."

"Maybe you should have. That's the enemy camp. You shouldn't have gone in there without a lot of prayer."

"Shelly...."

"I'm just saying what's true, Julia."

"For Pete's sake, Shelly, Emma Knoll is a normal, regular human being who's intensely confused and hurting beyond belief. I tried to be a friend."

But Shelly was shaking her head. "We, as Christians, should not associate with evil."

Julia was impatient to go on, to finish her story, to get to the part about Mason's threat, the part where she was now, but Shelly could not stop muttering about evil and the Shanahan Clinic.

Finally Julia blurted out, interrupting Shelly's rantings, "Shelly, Mason called. He's going to take the boys. You want to talk about evil, he's evil!"

Shelly looked at her. "Julia, I'm sorry. Here I'm going on about the clinic. What did he say?"

"Just that his lawyer is going to be in touch with me."

"But you have custody...."

"Someone called him. I don't know who. Someone told him I was snooping around and if I didn't stop snooping around they would take the boys like they took Beth."

"Those pro-abortion people called him. Shanahan's people. To get even."

Julia put both hands on her head. They were at the elementary school now and Shelly was pulling into an empty "Visitor's Parking" spot.

Julia said, "I gotta go. I'll be right back."

"Julia, you have to be careful. Satan is slicker and smoother than you realize."

"Well, tell me, why would Emma call Mason and tell him I've been snooping around when she was snooping around herself?"

"I don't know. But I'd be careful. That's what I'd be."

She opened the passenger door.

"Wait, I'm coming with you."

The normal, noisy chatter of children had been replaced today by a somberness that was almost tangible. The halls were quieted and Julia wasn't at all sure what she should do. Tell their teachers that they were in danger? Take them home? Tell her teachers to keep an eye on them? Go talk to the principal?

"Shelly, what should I do?" she whispered.

"We'll go and see their teachers. Where are their rooms?"

"Down the end on the right is Josh's. Jeff's is around the other wing."

"Fine, we'll go to Josh's first."

Josh's classroom door stood open and inside the students were bent quietly over their desks. The teacher, a young woman in a long denim skirt topped with a white cotton sweater, was writing on the board. Shelly knocked quietly.

She walked toward them.

"Hello, Mrs. Nash. Did you need to see Joshua?" She looked worried and tired.

"I just want to know, is there someone watching the kids on the playground and during lunch?"

"We've been keeping them in today. Principal's orders. Because of Beth."

Shelly spoke. "How are the children reacting to what has happened to Beth?"

The young teacher frowned. "Not well. Her own class is really struggling. Beth was always so...so cheerful, such a bright light. The District office is sending us counselors. It's really tough because no one knows for sure what has happened to her."

Shelly said, "Can we see Joshua for a few minutes?"

"Certainly."

"Hi, Mom. Hi, Aunt Shelly," said Josh as he met them in the hall.

Julia bent down and held his little face in her hands. "Josh," she said, "I have to go back to work, but Grandma is going to pick you up right when school gets out, right at 2:30. Do you hear? Don't walk home. You look for Grandma in the parking lot. Okay? You know you're never supposed to get into a car with a stranger, right? This is especially important today. Don't get into the car with anyone but me or your grandma. Not anyone else!"

She did the same in Jeff's class, telling him over and over that under no circumstances was he to get in a car with anyone else, not under any circumstances. He nodded soberly.

Julia left then, and on the way to the police detachment, she turned to Shelly. "I made a mistake. I should have taken them out. I should have taken them to the Centre with me. I know I should have taken them with me."

CHAPTER 47

"Do you believe in angels?" Emma was sitting in a rocking chair, Beth's book in her lap, and Beth's blanket around her shoulders, rocking slowly and looking at the beaded cross. The candle, although shorter, still burned.

Jill looked up from the paper she was reading. "Angels?"

"Well, spiritual visitors, that inner dimension, I don't know, epiphanies?"

Jill looked at her. "I don't know. Maybe."

"I know what you're thinking, 'This lady has finally gone around the bend.'"

"No, I wasn't thinking that."

"I've never gone much to church. Churches are full of hypocrites."

"If you want to know the truth, the whole world is full of hypocrites." Jill went back to her paper.

"Maybe you notice them more in church, where you think they're not going to be. But then, since I don't go to church I really can't say for sure. But I think we all have a spiritual dimension, don't you?"

"Why're you asking me?"

"There's no one else to talk to."

Jill folded the paper, laid it on her lap and looked at her.

Emma was saying, "I was in Beth's room in the middle of the night and I had this spiritual experience."

Jill blinked at her.

"I know what you're thinking, that I dreamed the whole thing. But I was awake." She looked at Jill then. A beautiful woman, she was. She had encountered two beautiful women in the last two days. Elena and Jill. Elena was a small, fine-boned, exotic beauty. Jill was more a California-girl blonde beauty. She asked, "How did you get to be a cop?"

"I applied. I was accepted, went to school in Regina...."

Emma shook her head. "Not how, but why did you want to be a cop?"

"My dad was a cop." She didn't smile.

"That is how you pick an occupation? If I did what my father did I'd be an alcoholic wife beater."

Jill said nothing, just looked away.

The phone rang.

Jill jumped for it, but Emma had already picked it up, giving Jill a look that said, *This is my house and I'll answer my own phone, thank you very much.*

"Mom?" A tiny, scared voice.

"Beth!" Emma rose from the chair, dropping the blanket and book onto the floor. "Oh, my goodness, Jill, it's Beth! Beth where are you, are you okay?"

"I'm okay."

"Where are you?"

"I'm at Kara's school."

"Who's Kara?"

"The lady who's taking care of me while you're sick."

"But I'm not...."

Jill had gone into action. Over the cellular she kept clipped to her belt she had dialed the detachment and they had dialed the phone company, who was already tracing the call.

"You sure you're okay?"

"Some people took me, they said you were sick."

"Beth, Beth, don't hang up." She was following frantic hand signals from Jill, who said to keep her on the line.

"Were you sick, Mom?"

"I'm fine, Beth. I've been so worried about you."

As they talked, Jill nodded and mouthed the words, "We gottem."

There was a click.

"Beth? Beth! Are you still there, Beth? Do you hear me? Oh, don't hang up."

Jill took the phone and said. "It's okay. We have her. We have the exact location where she is being held. We're already on our way over there."

"Where is she?"

"St. Matthews Bible School and Seminary."

Emma made fists of her hands. "I knew it. I knew those people were involved. I knew it."

CHAPTER 48

Even though Kara had told her not to, Beth had ventured out into the hallway. It was like Kara had said, no one was around. She tried some of the other doors. All locked. At the end of the hall she saw a large room, like a living room, with a couple of old couches and chairs. There was a fridge in there and an ironing board and a TV. A TV! She turned it on, settled into the couch and watched. Sesame Street. Mr. Dressup. She was too old for these programs, but there was nothing else on. Bored again. She walked to the fridge. Empty.

It was then that she spied the telephone on the counter. She could call her mom! She pressed the numbers, but nothing happened. She tried again. Nothing. And then she saw the little notice on the wall above the phone. "Don't forget to dial 9 first."

She pressed nine. Nothing happened. Just a dial tone again. She tried her number one more time and got through!

Her mom! Her mom was okay. And then....

"Beth!" Kara had disconnected them and was dragging the little girl, along with her backpack and doll, down another hallway, a low hallway with cement walls and the sounds of dripping.

"What's the matter?" asked Beth timidly. "I wanted to call my mom."

"I told you not to. I told you not to leave the room. Beth, I don't want to scare you, but your life is in danger. They'll kill you if they see you." There were tears in Kara's eyes. "I know they will. You have to stay with me. I don't want to hurt you,

Beth, but you can't go home yet, not just yet. Not until I take care of things. It won't take me long, but I have to do it right."

"Where are we?" The corridor was getting smaller, and even Beth had to crouch down. Kara, who was small, moved along swiftly, like she'd walked this hallway before.

"A secret passage."

"Secret passage?" Beth's mind was filled with wardrobes that opened into magic lands and snow queens and mighty lions.

"Well, a root cellar anyway. I don't think anyone in the school knows about this place. In these old houses, there's tons of secret hallways. I needed a place to hide out and collect the stuff for the group."

"What group?"

"The group I belonged to. The group I'm keeping you safe from."

"Oh," was all Beth said.

They walked down a hallway that became narrow and dirtier. Beth had to crouch down more. Finally they reached a small cement room with a dirt floor. On one side dirty wooden shelves reached the low ceiling. Piled against the side were a few boxes which contained papers and books. It felt very cold in there and Beth shivered.

"Here, Beth, I brought a blanket. It'll only be for a while. And I have to lock you in. I'm sorry, but I'll be back. I have to do a couple things. I have to talk to someone. You'll be safe here."

CHAPTER 49

While Roger was in the air on his way to Boston, the St. Matthews Seminary and Bible School was being completely surrounded by squad cars, and SWAT teams with high powered rifles. Into this pandemonium, Alexis King determinedly walked into the police detachment and dropped off the internet printouts. Eventually they found their way to the case room, and half an hour later they were buried underneath a stack of Shanahan's files.

Into all of this, as well, came Julia and Shelly.

"Is there someone available to talk with us? We may have information regarding the kidnapping of Beth Knoll."

Kelly took their names and addresses and told them to wait for a minute. They waited more than a minute, sitting on the bench provided and looking at the glass display of old badges, guns and red uniforms. This detachment building was brand new. Julia wondered where a brand new building would get such a display.

"What's going on here?" said Shelly to an officer who introduced himself as Corporal Jack Boyce.

"We may have a break in the case." He led them through the door, past a bank of computers, down a short hall and into his office. When they were seated he folded his hands and looked at them. "So, you may have information that can help us?"

"I don't know, it may be nothing," said Julia.

"It's something," said Shelly.

"But he said they already have a break in the case."

Boyce spoke. "How about if I'm the judge of that?" He looked down at his notebook and said, "Julia Nash. Pregnancy Care Centre, right?"

Julia nodded.

"Your husband called the Ontario Police about your sons being in some kind of danger?"

"Ex-husband."

"Okay, ex-husband."

"Yes, he was threatening me. He will use anything against me, but that's not why I'm here. I found out some things and didn't come to you sooner. And for that I'm truly sorry, especially, when I could have put a child's life in danger."

Jack Boyce was still looking at her name in his notebook. "You the same Julia Nash in today's *Canada Today* story?"

"That's me," she said, but her voice sounded far away, even to herself.

He looked at her. "Talk to me then. I'm listening."

Julia swallowed and looked at Shelly. The air felt hot in the room. She looked at his face, a large face, gray and whiskery, limpid blue eyes, half smile cocked on his mouth, jaws hanging slack, big hands folded on the desk. The room was closing in on her.

"Are you all right, Mrs. Nash?"

"Yes," but her voice caught at the edges in a whisper. "Maybe you don't need me anymore. You said you had a break in the case...."

"Why don't I just listen to what you have to say?"

She could tell that he was getting impatient. He leaned forward and she could smell coffee on his breath. He looked tired. Maybe they were all tired. Maybe everyone in the world was tired. Shelly grabbed hold of her arm and looked concerned.

"Okay." She breathed deeply and began. She started at the very beginning, about being called about the list, and then becoming afraid. And then about finding the letter and going back to find it was gone.

"I would have come sooner. I should have come sooner. I

don't know why I didn't. I was just so scared...."

"Mrs. Nash, go on...."

"Okay, all right." She fished for a Kleenex in her purse and continued. She told him about someone having been in the clinic, about feeling afraid. She told him about meeting Emma. His face sparked interest when she told him about the midnight warehouse excursion and about finding the book.

"Why didn't you come to us then?"

Julia began to cry. "Stupidity. Fear. I don't know. A lot of things. I'm usually a really good citizen. I don't even speed."

He sighed. "Well, you're here now. I guess that's important." He went back to his notes. "We're pretty sure we found Beth now, and we're fairly sure she's okay, but it would have saved everyone a lot of grief if you'd come right away."

Julia swallowed and nodded, feeling like an errant high school student in the principal's office. "Am I in any kind of trouble or anything?"

He rose and looked at her. "I'll be back shortly. If we need you, we know where to find you."

CHAPTER 50

It was a clear day when Roger touched down in Boston. All he had with him was a small navy blue duffel bag that he carried. As a result he didn't have to wait for the baggage carousel, which made him one of the first people through customs. Out in the terminal it wasn't difficult to spot Boston Police detective Max Whitehead as he scanned the crowd. A big man, he stood head and shoulders above everyone else. He was a well-muscled mustached man about Roger's age. He reminded Roger of how Boston's fictional detective Spenser might look.

"Sergeant Sheppard?" The large man extended his hand.
"Max Whitehead?"
"Was the last time I checked." He chuckled.
The two walked through the terminal to Max's waiting car, double parked and blocking in two very unhappy cab drivers who were honking and glaring and shouting obscenities.

It was rush hour when the two drove towards downtown Boston. It was slow going, but Max didn't seem to notice as he wheedled in and out of traffic, changing lanes, pulling up, then pulling back. Roger wondered if he'd ever driven cab.

Max said, "I used to drive taxi. That's where I learned all these bad habits."

Then he turned to Roger, "Let me tell you about the suspect we have in custody. We got a positive ID. Someone from the funeral home spotted her dropping the video on the front steps of the place. By this time the place'd been gutted. The fellow looked at her and even got the license of the car."

"What kind of car?"

"Little Chevy thing. That important?"

"We're looking for a blue van." Roger told him about the blue van at the *Courier* office.

"Sorry, no blue van."

"Do you know if she planted the original bomb?"

"That we couldn't say for sure. Our witness didn't see that, only the video thing. So, we're going with what we have."

Roger nodded. "Tell me about her."

"Yeah, well, okay. Her name's Beverly Winter, unemployed nurse. No previous record, not so much as a parking ticket. Single, age 27, though she looks half that. Parents live in Kansas. Someplace near Wichita. She's got a brother in the army. Out west somewhere. No family close by."

"Nurse," said Roger thinking. "She ever work in an abortion clinic?"

"We're trying to find that out. You're thinking what I'm thinking. Maybe she took those pictures, staged them a bit for effect. That we don't know. We're still digging into her life."

"What's she saying?"

"That's the thing. Nothing. Nothing that makes any sense anyway. Talks about a 'voice' telling her to do things. The lady's wacko."

They were driving through cement streets with cement buildings, people lounging against the outside of them, leaning into them like immovable sculptures of cement.

"Nothing?"

"Yeah, not like, 'I won't talk to the cops without my lawyer present,' but nothing, as in gibberish, platitudes and religious sayings. That's why we called you, you being an expert in those matters and all."

Roger grinned and shook his head. "I'm no expert."

"Your reputation precedes you, the way you broke that crooked evangelist murder a few months back."

"The Sterling Jonas case, but I had a lot of help."

Max turned to him as he passed a large delivery truck on the right. "You used to be a priest or something?"

"Not me. Not hardly. My religious knowledge you could put on the head of a pin. Now my wife, she's the religious expert. She's got a degree in theology."

"She a minister then?"

"No, she's going for her real estate license."

"No kidding! What's she gonna do, sell churches?" He laughed at his own joke.

Roger grinned. "Might not be a bad idea. I'll tell her the next time I talk to her."

It felt good to talk about Kate, about her accomplishments that he was so proud of. He had been to Bible School for one year, that's where he and Kate met. She was just finishing up her four year degree and he was trying to find himself after a few unhappy years working in his father's hardware store. After a year in Bible school he applied to the Royal Canadian Mounted Police, was accepted, and had loved the work ever since. He wasn't cut out to manage a hardware store, nor was he cut out to sit around discussing theological concepts. He was a doer. This job fit him perfectly.

They were nearing the downtown precinct and Max was giving a running tour of Boston, to which Roger was only half listening. "You'll be staying at the Park Plaza Hotel, which is really only walking distance to the precinct. And from there you can walk up to Copley Square and tour churches. You being interested in theology and all. You want to see the suspect or you want to check into your room first?"

"I'll see the suspect."

"We'll head there now."

The precinct house was an old cement structure with wide steps, stained from years of being stepped on and spit on. Sitting on the steps was a couple of guys with dreadnoughts woven into their black hair. They wore colorful caps and sat in silence. Roger wondered if they were waiting for a friend inside.

As soon as he entered he was met by a woman officer who

turned to him immediately. "Are you Sergeant Sheppard from Canada?"

Roger nodded.

"There's an urgent message that you call a...," she looked down at her note pad, "...a Corporal Jack Boyce immediately."

Max led him to his office phone.

Jack told him that Beth Knoll had phoned her mother, the call was interrupted, but not before they found that it positively came from the St. Matthews Seminary and Bible School. RCMP had been there for an hour, but they hadn't located the girl or her captors. They were still searching every room, every square inch.

"Their president, a Dr. Milliard Conan I think his name is, is some upset, I can tell you that much. He denies any knowledge of anything."

When Roger hung up he frowned and looked at Max grimly. St. Matthews Seminary and Bible School had always been thought of very highly in the community. It's reputation was spotless. He hated to think that someone there was actually involved with this whole mess. And he hated to think what a field day the press would have with this one.

Max raised his eyebrows. "Bad news?"

"They may have found that little kidnapped girl."

"Well, that's good news, isn't it?"

"At a seminary."

"Yeah?"

He shrugged again. "Yeah, I guess you're right. It is good news. I just never thought those people could be involved."

"Yeah, well, one thing I've learned in this business, you can never tell about people."

"I guess not."

When he saw her, Beverly Winter was handcuffed and sitting stiffly, knees together in a small interrogation room which was bleaker and grimier than any he had worked in. There was a faint smell of something unpleasant about it, too, but he couldn't positively define it.

What immediately struck him about Beverly Winter was her

size. She was tiny, not more than four feet and maybe 80 pounds soaking wet. Her feet barely touched the floor and her thin wrists looked like they could easily slip through the metal handcuffs. Was this little thing responsible for the bombing? Her eyes were closed and she moved not a muscle when Roger approached. He wondered if she was asleep.

Max spoke first. "Okay Bev, we brought someone in to talk to you. Someone who knows religion."

Max placed the tape recorder on the table and pressed RECORD. "Just to let you know, we're recording this conversation."

"Miss Winter," said Roger softly.

No response.

"Miss Winter, what can you tell me about the bombing?"

No response.

"You were seen placing a video at the clinic. What can you tell me about that?"

Still no answer. Maybe she really was asleep.

"What can you tell me about St. Matthews Seminary?"

Her head moved ever so slightly, but her eyes did not open.

"Miss Winter, have you ever worked in an abortion clinic?"

It was like talking to a wall.

Roger spoke quietly, gently. "If you open your eyes you'll notice that I'm not wearing a uniform. I'm not even carrying a gun. I'm from Canada. And I know a little about believing in a cause, believing in something so deeply. I guess, if you'd ask me personally, I'd say I have to agree with you about abortion. I think it's wrong, too. Really, I do. Hundreds of unborn babies are killed every day. The law should be changed...."

She opened her eyes. They were deep blue, piercing. "You're wrong. It's thousands. Millions," she said. Her voice was high pitched, like a child's.

"Thousands, millions, what?"

"Thousands and millions of unborn humans being murdered and we do nothing. We have to do something."

Roger leaned to her, moved his chair closer to her. Her eyes shifting, she regarded him warily. She reminded him of a cat; tiny, wiry. He could imagine her crawling in and out of small places.

He said, "Murdering the murderers is not the answer. Others will just rise up and take their place. A year from now that clinic in St. Matthews will be up and running. A year from now the clinic here in Boston will be rebuilt. The law has to be changed from the inside out. That's the only way. Murder's not the way to stop murder. But I think you know that. I think you've gotten yourself involved in something way over your head."

Her eyes regarded him, so blue they were, like ice.

She said, "Thou shalt break them with a rod of iron; thou shalt dash them to pieces like a potter's vessel."

"Why did you say that?"

"A rod of iron will destroy the murderers."

"What do you mean?"

"Shanahan is destroyed. Hundreds like him will be. He is the first."

"You're going to get rid of all the doctors and nurses who perform abortions? That's a tall order."

"They will be dashed to pieces. God's law will prevail."

"What do you know about St. Matthews?"

"Saint Matthew was the tax collector, a collector of souls."

"St. Matthews is a town in New Brunswick. Dr. Douglas Shanahan lived there. His family still does. He has children and grandchildren who will never see their father and grandfather again. He has a wife who will never see him again."

"The unborn are now safe from his horrors." Her voice was becoming frailer and Roger had to strain to hear.

"It's Earth Mother," she was whispering. "And the voice. The voice which says I must take vengeance out on the death of the children. She has scattered and destroyed the wicked places, bringing them down, laying them waste, damming up the evil places. It is she who I must listen to."

"Miss Winter," Roger was persistent. "Who placed the bomb at the clinic?"

"She has scattered and destroyed, Earth Mother and the Queen, the mysterious one." Her voice sounded tired, like she was running out of steam.

Roger glanced at Max who was leaning against the wall behind her. He was circling his forefinger beside his ear in a "she's crazy" gesture.

"Who is the Earth Mother?" Roger asked.

She had closed her eyes, and now her head was bowed on her chest. "The mother of us all. She has seen her babies ripped apart. She has risen up to kill the killers. The voice has told me."

"Do you know Beth Knoll?" he asked.

"Child of evil. But she has gone. The daughter has taken her away from Earth Mother and they don't know where she resides." Her voice was so faint he could barely hear her.

"What is the voice telling you to do now?"

She looked up, surprised. Roger continued, "Did the voice tell you to bomb the clinic?"

She shook her head. "No, just to lay claim to it."

"Who is Earth Mother?"

"The mother of us all."

"Is Earth Mother a real person?"

"Earth Mother will dash them to pieces. She will cast down the evil from the high places...."

"You mentioned a queen. Is she the queen?"

Beverly gazed into Roger's eyes. They were almost translucent in their blueness. "The queen of the universe," she said.

"What is the voice telling you?"

"I am merely the underling, the maidservant of the voice. I do what the voice tells me."

"What is the voice telling you to do now?" Roger glanced up at Max, who was lounging against the wall behind her and shaking his head.

Beverly bowed her head. "I can speak no longer. The voice is quiet to me now. In this place it cannot commune with me."

She closed her eyes.

She had finished speaking. Her chin was resting on her chest, breathing deeply as if asleep. Roger and Max stayed with her another half hour, prodding and probing and repeating their questions, but she said nothing more.

CHAPTER 51

The building at 703 Front Street was owned by Bay Enterprises in Saint John, New Brunswick. They had leased it to the Christian Freedom Life Army four years ago when they wanted the space for an office. A year and a half ago the Freedom Life Army had pulled out. The building was now abandoned and had recently been declared condemned by the town of St. Matthews.

Corporal Jack Boyce was telling all of this to Julia and Emma who sat in the back of his patrol car as they drove out to the site. Constable Francine Myers was in the passenger seat.

Emma sat quietly looking out the window. Julia wished she had had a chance to talk to Emma alone, before the police found her waiting outside of the seminary. She would have told her how she felt the police should know what they found.

"My daughter's at that theological school and you are taking me away from her."

Jack turned slightly in his seat. "We are checking every room in the building. It may take some time."

"What am I doing here if you find her? I should be there."

"If they find Beth, they will contact me immediately and we'll turn around. We'll be there before they bring her out."

"If she is there, why are we going to the old building?"

"Clues," said Jack. "We also have a murder to solve."

Emma sat back, looking a little more relieved. Julia glanced over at her, but Emma seemed to be lost in her own thoughts.

Jack parked the patrol car in front of the condemned building.

"This the place?"

Julia said, "Yes."

The inside of the building looked different by day, less ominous, less full of dark angles and goblin shapes. By day it was just an ordinary, dirty, condemned building.

Inside, the two officers were full of questions. "What did you see? Where did you go? Is anything different or out of place now?" Julia took the lead in answering the questions.

Upstairs the police officers paid considerable attention to the room where the book was found. They filled plastic evidence bags with floor dust, the electrical wires, and even the gunk inside the sink.

"We're going to come back and fingerprint the entire place," said the corporal. He turned to Emma. "Do you have the book? We told you to bring the book."

"I don't have the book."

"Why not? Where is it?"

"It's mine. I need it."

"Don't worry. We'll get it back to you," said Francine.

Emma looked from one face to the other, horrified. "I know, but I need it. Don't you understand, I need it now."

Julia watched the exchange. She watched Emma become more and more frustrated. She watched her slender fingers interlace behind her back, then fall stiffly at her side. She watched her eyes dart from one to another, swallowing nervously.

Julia said to the police officers, "What will the book tell you? Nothing. It was hidden underneath the mattress. Beth's captors didn't touch it at all. If they did, they would have taken it. They would never have left it to be discovered. Why don't you let her just keep the book."

Jack shrugged and looked at Francine. "Fine. How about you just bring the book by for a few minutes and we'll have a look."

Emma nodded.

CHAPTER 52

The gardener who had positively identified Beverly Winter was a tall, thin man in his mid-70s. His yellow-white hair was sparse and fine and stuck to his smooth pink scalp like a skull cap. He was wearing beige walking shorts, knee high black socks and a long-sleeved white shirt. He was standing in the lobby and smiled at Max and Roger as they walked toward him.

"Gentlemen," he said.

Max nodded. "Mr. Stanley Smallwood, this is Sergeant Roger Sheppard from the Mounties in Canada."

Roger extended his hand. Stanley Smallwood's hand was soft and cool. His face was round and pink with limpid eyes. The beige shorts looked incongruous, as if Mr. Smallwood hadn't fully dressed that morning.

"This is our star witness," said Max.

"It's nice to meet you," said Roger.

"My pleasure."

Roger was curious. "I know you've been asked these questions a million times by now, but would you humor me and answer a few more?"

"No problem. Glad to be of help. My wife and I visited your wonderful country once a long time ago. Beautiful place. Always happy to help a Canadian."

Roger smiled. He said, "You were across the street from the clinic and yet you were able to positively identify Beverly Winter and her car?"

"Oh, yes. My eyes are the one thing that is perfect.

Everything else is gone, but not my eyes. I don't even wear glasses."

"Do you work at the funeral home?"

"I'm what you call a freelance gardener. I was returning to the fronds and Miss Winter pulled up in her car. I thought she may have something to do with the authorities. They had been there. For some reason there were no police officers there then...."

Roger looked at Max who shrugged.

"So I watched. She walked up to the steps and laid the video down. Then she left. I rose from my position and noted her license number."

After Stanley left, Roger and Max listened again to the recording in Max's office. Was there meaning in those disjointed sentences? In his notebook Roger wrote down Earth Mother, Rod of Iron, underling of the voice. But he could sense no design in her words. At the bottom of the page he doodled a large question mark.

He called the detachment in St. Matthews and was surprised to discover that Julia Nash of the Pregnancy Care Centre plus Emma Knoll had taken a midnight "tour" of a warehouse that may have housed Beth.

"The two of them? Together?" said Roger into the receiver.

CHAPTER 53

When the police officer dropped Julia off at the Centre, the phone was ringing. It was Shelly.

"Tell me what happened," said her friend.

"We just went out to the warehouse and looked around. That's about all."

Julia wanted to be alone. She was tired of her friend's constant talk about evil presences and "strongholds of the enemy." When Julia told Shelly about Emma's book, about sticking up for her, Shelly said, "Oh, don't let Emma get to you. She appears nice, doesn't she? But the enemy is not stupid. She will appear nice, friendly even, but that's one of Satan's tricks. Julia, I'm going to be praying for you that you will be given discernment in this."

"Thank you. I can always use prayer."

When she hung up Julia wondered if she had been taken in by the enemy. *But I'm just trying to be a friend.* She thought of Jesus here on earth, He readily associated with sinners and tax collectors. He walked right up to people with evil spirits. He didn't shun them, keeping his distance like the rest of the established church did. He treated people like people, not like "strongholds of the enemy." *Give me discernment*, she prayed, *but most of all help me to see people the way You do.*

She turned on the radio and listened for any word of Beth. The news stated that the police were still at the seminary. St. Matthews Bible School and Seminary was an old, established, well thought of institution. She couldn't believe that they had anything to do with this.

She took out her Bible from the shelf and began reading through Matthew. She would start at the beginning of the New Testament and not stop until she finished. She didn't know how many minutes had passed, with her bent over the Word of God, but when she looked up she saw Emma Knoll through the glass in the top of the door. Julia rose and walked toward her.

"Hello," she said, opening the door wide.

Emma had been crying. Her eyes were red-rimmed. She said, "They haven't found Beth."

"I thought she was at the seminary. What happened?"

"They couldn't find her." Emma was clutching Beth's book close to her chest.

"I'm so sorry."

"They're still looking."

"Would you like to come in. I could make some tea."

Emma stepped into the room and then stood there looking around, almost in wonder. Julia saw her look long into Tanya's painting on the wall, at the little tole painted and needlework designs which covered the walls. She also saw Emma gaze at the small stained glass cross which hung from a window. It had been a gift from one of the mothers they had helped. Emma said nothing and it occurred to Julia that Emma would feel as strange and as out of place in this building as she did in the Shanahan Clinic.

Emma spoke, "I wanted to thank you about the book."

"That's okay. I don't know why the cops feel they have to take every little thing...."

"You know," said Emma, "I was thinking. You and I are basically in the same business."

Julia raised her eyebrows.

"We both want to give women their lives back. We both want to make things right for pregnant women. I was thinking about that earlier."

Julia nodded, not knowing what to say.

"I was thinking about something else, too. You seem to me

to be a spiritual person. I had a spiritual visitation the other night. From outside of this place."

Julia looked at her. She could almost hear Shelly's voice, *Be wary, Julia, be wary.*

Emma continued, "I was in Beth's room and I heard a voice. I don't think I was dreaming. I don't think so. And I remembered that your place has a cross on the front. I remember that from walking past once. I wonder if maybe you could say a prayer for Beth."

Julia whispered, "I'd be happy to. Would you like me to pray right now?"

"Now or later, it doesn't matter."

Right where they stood, Julia bowed her head and prayed to the God she knew, asking that Beth be kept safe, asking that they find her quickly, and asking that God protect and help Emma. By the time she was finished both of them were weeping. Julia touched Emma's arm.

Emma said, "I have to go. It is strange for me to be here."

"The stronghold of the enemy," Julia whispered.

"What?"

"Nothing."

CHAPTER 54

Since there seemed to be no reason to stay in Boston overnight, Roger canceled his hotel room and booked himself on the next flight north. Beverly Winter was scheduled for a psychiatric evaluation later that Monday afternoon. Roger would be leaving before then. It was easier, Roger thought, to have a suspect that lied, than one who spoke gibberish or one who remained quiet. You could trap liars in their lies.

On the way to the airport, Max drove Roger to the crime scene. The clinic was little more than a partially standing pile of rubble now. Max nodded good morning to the uniformed officers who stood guard and lifted the crime scene tape. The two of them ducked under. The place had attracted a number of "rubber-neckers," as the police called them, spectators who stood there, looking. Always there was a group which found its way to a crime scene. In one of his more cynical moments, Roger suggested that police departments could make a lot of money if they set up food stands at crime scenes and sell coffee, hot dogs and ice cream.

Today's group didn't have that awful pall that surrounded crime scenes where a death had occurred. A building had been bombed, but no one was killed, no one was hurt. Just a building. Have a hot dog.

Max and Roger crunched through the blackened bits of ash as they made their way toward the building. At the front of the sooty building a clump of yellow daffodils was blooming in defiance.

Max introduced Roger to the fire inspector who was on his knees methodically sifting through the rubble. He was a tall and rather thin man, about Roger's age, with a wide, unsmiling face. He extended his hand. "Howard Thomas," he said, still not smiling.

"Roger Sheppard, Royal Canadian Mounted Police."

"The place where this all started, I presume."

"I suppose, but it's not a wonderful thing to take credit for."

"Plastic explosive," he said, bending down again. "Whoever set this puppy off knew exactly what he was doing."

"This whole operation has that smell about it," said Roger. "But they're going to slip up. A lot of what they're doing is for show."

Max said, "Yeah, leaving the video on the front steps was a nice touch. Too bad they didn't make sure the coast was clear."

"We think some of them are holing up at a local seminary in St. Matthews. I'm headed back there now."

"A seminary? Who would have thought."

"Yeah."

On the way to the airport, Roger listened as Max tried to make sense of the bombing. "Tell me," he said, turning to Roger. "Do you think any of what Beverly Winter said made sense? Like, do you think she was talking in riddles, like maybe she was so spooked by her superiors that she was trying to give us veiled hints?"

Roger nodded. "Maybe, but I wouldn't count on it."

"But you'll listen to the tapes again and let me know if you get a brainstorm?"

"Yes."

There was a short silence and then Max spoke again. "You're pretty new to the east aren't you?"

"Brand new. Only been in New Brunswick a few months."

"And all this happened."

"All this happened."

The rest of the way to the airport, the two remained silent. Roger thought back to his rather unceremonious introduction to the Maritimes and to New Brunswick in particular. It had been a long flight from Calgary, an all day procedure with a two hour layover in Toronto and another four hours in Montreal. Plus, they were making planes smaller these days, he was sure. He always asked for an aisle seat, where he could stretch his legs into the aisle if need be, but sitting in the chair, seat belt dutifully on, his knees came up right to the seat in front of him. Yes, they were making planes smaller. Flight lunch used to mean a hot meal, now lunch was half a cold ham bunwich, a rectangle of cellophane wrapped cheese, a white square bowl of fruit and coffee in a communion cup. On the final leg from Montreal to Fredericton, he had to walk what seemed like miles down the corridor to a forsaken little waiting room at the farthest end of the terminal.

"This is where you get the plane to Fredericton?" He asked this of a bald headed man who was engrossed in a *Sports Illustrated*. There were no attendants in sight.

The man looked up. "That's right."

"The end of the line, huh?" asked Roger, sitting down.

"The end of the world, more like it." He went back to his reading. Roger had finished his book, the latest John Grisham paperback, so he leaned his head against the wall.

He must have napped, because when he opened his eyes a blue suited flight attendant was taking tickets. He glanced out the terminal window. No super jet awaited them, complete with the indoor carpeted walkway onto the plane. Their plane was outside on the tarmac. And it was raining. Of course it was raining. It had to be raining. Whenever you have to walk outside to a plane it's raining.

There were only about twenty on the flight. The balding man, a young couple who held hands, a woman wearing a long rain coat and carrying a briefcase, a couple of young men in military fatigues, and a few families with children of various ages.

He was being met at the airport by RCMP Division 2 Staff Sergeant Mal Jarvis who was going to "show Roger the ropes" in Fredericton before driving him down to St. Matthews the following day.

Roger settled himself and read through the in-flight magazine for the fifth time that day. But as they made their way through the sky, Roger moved over to the window seat and gazed down onto the unfamiliar landscape.

After coffee and peanuts, Roger could feel the plane descending. Now that he was closer to his new home, he was anxious to start; new location, new challenges. But he could have sworn the plane was going back up again. He looked around to the other faces. People were looking around. "That's Grand Lake," said the balding man, pointing. "What are we doing over Grand Lake?"

Right on cue, Roger heard the crackling of the pilot's mike, "Good morning, ladies and gentlemen. We're on our way to Moncton. The runway in Fredericton isn't capable of receiving us at this point."

"Wha...? What's going on?" That came from a young man in jeans and a faded purple sweatshirt who was sitting opposite Roger. His face was creased with sleep.

As the plane rumbled forward, Roger busied himself reading the a magazine article about what to pack for a Caribbean cruise. Twenty minutes later the pilot's voice again came over the loudspeaker saying that they were on their way to Halifax. He said something about no maintenance people in Moncton. Something about the flaps. When the plane landed thirty minutes later, Roger knew why. They careened down the runway and kept careening. Head back against the cushion, he glanced out the window to see the world go by and by and by. "We're going to crash into buildings!" said the young man across the aisle.

"We'll be fine," said Roger.

"How do you know? Are you a pilot?"

"No, I'm a police officer."

"Oh."

When the plane stopped, they were told that they were being put onto another flight to Fredericton in one hour and that their boarding passes qualified them for a $9 lunch.

As a group, they walked toward the cafeteria. Thrust together by common disaster, they shared flight horror stories.

At the counter Roger ordered soup, a sandwich and a large Coke.

"Yours is $9.05," said the short, squat woman behind the cash register.

Roger handed her his boarding pass and began to walk away. She called after him, "That will be five cents, sir!"

"You want five cents?"

"Yes sir, the voucher was for nine dollars. Yours was nine dollars and five cents."

Roger reached into his pocket. No change. He knew without looking that all he had on him were two twenties. His last stop had been the bank machine in the Montreal airport. He pulled out his wallet.

"This is all I've got." He handed one to her.

She took the twenty without comment, rang it into the cash register and gave him $19.95 in change, carefully counting it out in his hand.

Roger smiled, nodded good day and took a seat next to the two in military fatigues. But before he left he heard the guy behind him, the balding man, say, "What did that guy have?"

"Soup, sandwich and a large Coke."

"I'll have the same, but all I've got is a fifty. Hope you don't mind."

Roger was still thinking about that when half an hour later he was seated in the waiting room in the Boston airport. Funny, how disaster pulls strangers into commonality. He had been surprised when Jack told him earlier that Julia Nash, one of St. Matthews strongest pro-life proponents, had been out with Emma at the warehouse.

Today, the flight from Boston to Fredericton was totally uneventful. Roger sat with his head against the back of the seat and slept.

CHAPTER 55

After she left Julia's, Emma continued her walk. The afternoon was gray and grizzled and mist covered her hair like lacework. She ignored the sloppy sidewalks and the sound of her wet Keds squishing on the pavement. She wondered about the rain and angel visitations. Was there something in common about the two? It had been lovely, extraordinarily bright and warm until Douglas had been killed and Beth had disappeared. Then the rain had come, mourning rain. She wondered if the sun would ever come out again in her life.

Emma's head was down as she walked, numbed with the wet, deadened by the chill. The sidewalk was dirty and she had to walk between slugs and worms who were inching their grimy way across the pavement, leaving glistening trails behind them.

They had not found Beth, even though they had torn the seminary upside down in their search. They told her that perhaps the kidnappers were using very sophisticated equipment that made it *seem* as if the call came from the Bible school, when in actual fact it had come from some other place. They even talked to her about the possibility that Beth hadn't called at all, that perhaps her voice had been recorded and then the sentence fragments had been digitally pieced together to make it appear that she was saying something over the phone. A constable named Steve Malone told her this.

"So we're back to square one?" This was said by Glen. He stood with his arm around Emma in the rain outside of the seminary. Kathy and Sophie were also there, and Sophie was still ranting about women and girls as victims of the fundamentalist right. She pointed to the school when she said this.

Constable Malone said, "Not entirely. Our sergeant is down in Boston talking to a suspect. We're hoping to get a lot of information from that interview."

Glen nodded.

That the sergeant was down in Boston getting a lot of information didn't really change things. Beth was still missing. Beth was not here. Beth was out there alone somewhere. But alive. She had to be alive! *I'm taking care of Beth.* Funny, she was telling fewer and fewer people about her visitation. When she mentioned it she noticed that people's eyes glazed over and then they would head her to couches, sit her down, cover her with blankets and say, "Rest, dear, you need rest." So, she had stopped talking about it. The last one she spoke to about it was Julia (of all people, Julia Nash!), but she felt a strange calm knowing that Julia had said a prayer for Beth.

Emma had always believed that human beings had a spiritual dimension. She believed in the eternality of life, of souls. That gave her some comfort in her job at the clinic, that maybe if they did have it wrong, that maybe life *did* begin at conception and not at birth, then an aborted baby's soul would simply enter another human being. This wasn't a belief she held to with any religious zeal. It was just a feeling. She had never gone to church much. Beth sometimes went with her friend Melissa. At first Emma had some reservations about allowing her to do so, but when Beth came home not spouting off any weird beliefs, she continued to let her go.

Emma kicked a stone in her path. She had always been a feminist and a strong proponent of the rights of women. And this was just one more right. Wasn't it?

CHAPTER 56

It was turning into a strange day, but Julia felt calm for the first time since this whole ordeal began. She had been to the police. She had told them the story. And then Emma had come in *asking* Julia to pray for her. Even Mason's accusations held no threat for her this afternoon. She was humming, singing actually, when the woman walked in.

She looked to be in her early thirties with dark blonde hair cut in a Dutch-boy style. Her skin was pale, limpid and she did not look well.

Julia approached her. "Hello, can I help you with something?"

The woman just stood there, staring at Julia behind thick glasses, eyes unfocussed. Julia waited.

The woman edged back to the door. "I shouldn't have come here," she said.

"Are you okay?" Julia moved toward her.

"No, I'm not okay." There was a muddled silence. The woman was whimpering. Julia led her to a chair. She sat down and brought her chubby short fingered hands to her mouth. Her eyes darted from one thing to another in the Centre.

"I'm not pregnant," she said.

Julia said, "Would you like to talk about it?"

"I don't know." Her voice faltered and she spoke each syllable slowly as if she were just learning how to talk. "I've never talked about it to anyone."

"I understand. If you want to talk, I'm right here. And if

you just want to sit for a while, that's okay, too."

"I had an abortion."

Julia waited.

"It was a long time ago. Almost four years ago."

"And that's why you're here?"

"Yes, I was told I'd get over the feeling, like I'd murdered my child, like I'd committed murder. They told me I'd get over feeling that way, but it's only gotten worse." She clenched her fists and put them on either side of her head. "I get headaches. I dream about my child sometimes. I think about her. I know it was a her. I was married...I *am* married. I have two other children. So, it's not like I was an unmarried mother on welfare and all. We had planned for only two children, and then I got pregnant again. At that time my husband said it would be best if we didn't go through with the pregnancy, that we get rid of it. Get rid of it, as if 'it' is some mass of tissue or something. It was a baby. A baby! And I killed it...her."

"You didn't know. They told you wrong, they always do."

"And here's the kicker. I had just started a new career, a new job, and of course, the baby would get in the way of things. That was our thinking. That was my husband's thinking. And so, I got an abortion, so I could get on with my career. And then you know what? I got laid off." The woman had risen now and was pacing in the empty front room. "Nothing ever turns out right for me." She turned to Julia. "I came here because I saw the ad in the paper about the post-abortion support group."

Julia nodded. "We'd be happy to have you come. The facilitator is a woman, a pastor's wife here who had an abortion. She's wonderful to talk to."

"So there are others who feel like me?"

"Lots. It's one thing they don't tell you over there."

"Over there, yeah, over *there*." She spat out the last word. "Do you know who I am?"

Julia shook her head.

"My name is Lois Claymore. Dr. Douglas Shanahan was my father."

Julia opened her mouth and stared at her.

"You're shocked, I can tell. But it's true."

"I believe you."

"My father told me that what I was feeling had to do with other problems in my life, and had nothing to do with my abortion. Even my mother told me that, too. And I haven't been able to work. Not since then." She was sniffing now, and had grabbed a Kleenex from the box on the desk. "And this is a stress to my husband because we're barely making it financially. Sometimes I hate the unfairness. My parents won't help us at all and my dad's gotten rich off the pain of other women. That's what it's all about. He's gotten rid of thousands of babies, he's murdered them and gotten rich off it. And we just get poorer and poorer and I can't work. My husband thinks I'm crazy. So do my parents."

Julia looked at her sadly. She had no reason not to believe that this wasn't Shanahan's daughter. "You're not crazy. There is a large group of women who have had abortions, who know what it's like. You would be welcome to come to the group. And no one need know who you are if you prefer it that way." Julia handed her a brochure and a card telling her about the support group.

"Yes, I prefer it that way. But I have to go. Rod is waiting. He doesn't know I'm here. I told him I was at the china store across the street. I'll have to come up with some excuse about coming here on a Monday night. I'll have to make up something."

"Maybe that's part of the problem, lies. Why don't you just tell him the truth?"

She shrugged. "You know, deep down somewhere in his mind I think he's going through a lot with this, too. We never talk about it. That's one thing we never talk about."

"There's a name on that card, the facilitator of the group. Gloria Tilden. You can call her at any time."

Lois nodded and left. Julia watched as she ran through the rain down the street.

At 2:46 the phone rang.

Her mother.

"Julia, did you say the boys would be out of school at 2:30?"

Something tightened in Julia's stomach. "Yes. I told them to meet you there right at 2:30."

"They're not here yet. There seem to be no children here anymore. I'm in the principal's office. No one has seen them. We were just wondering if they called you. Perhaps they walked home after all."

Julia sat down. *Oh, God, no*, she prayed.

"Get the principal to call the police. I'm on my way."

CHAPTER 57

By suppertime, Roger was back at the detachment. It had been a long day and it was going to get longer. While he was in the skies somewhere over New England, Josh and Jeff Nash failed to show up at 2:30. Their grandmother had frantically called the department. Four officers were assigned to the case and were still out there talking to neighbors and talking to a very distraught mother and grandmother.

Jack filled him in. "Their grandmother was there to pick them up at 2:30 and neither one of them met her. We don't know what to make of it. We've called that husband in Toronto, the one who got the anonymous phone call. We're trying to follow it up from that end."

Roger was stunned. Why had her children been taken? He was standing in the case room going over the reports, reading the interview transcripts again. He even listened to his interview with Beverly Winter. But nothing was making any sense. Today was Monday, only four days since this whole ordeal had begun, but he felt like it had already been years. His mind went back to a week ago, just a week ago, when the biggest thing on their minds was trying to figure out whether St. Matthews should hold a regimental charity ball this year. That was a world away.

Roger slowly, methodically began working his way through the piles of Shanahan's folders, notes, computer printouts of terrorist organizations and blue vans, the latest on Joan Aarkman, which was that she was no where, even though a North American wide search was on for her and her car. He added his own notes and tapes from Boston to the mix.

"Where are these people holing up?" he muttered out loud.

"Good question." Jack had entered the room carrying a sheet of paper. "We got something on one of the blue van people. It could be nothing, but it could be a link."

Roger looked up.

"One of the blue van people, a Kara Scoretti, used to be a student at the seminary."

"Really."

"Yeah, it's not much of a link. Motor Vehicles gave her address as being in New Brunswick, yet the seminary lists her as from New York. We called down to her New York apartment, to the phone number the Bible school gave us, and someone who is subletting her apartment said that as far as they knew she was a student at the seminary."

"Interesting."

"Thought I'd tell you that before I contact the seminary. They'll love to hear from us again."

Roger smiled. "That not go so well?"

"What do you think? Two dozen armed officers go storming into the place, into a *Bible* school. No, it did not sit well. Even though now she doesn't appear to be there. Maybe we should have done it differently. Maybe we should have called first, warned them we were coming or something."

"You did the right thing."

Jack nodded. Roger was idly leafing through the computer printouts from Matthew King's computer while he talked to Jack.

"Let me know what the school says about Kara Scoretti."

He left. Roger sat down and continued to leaf through the printouts. What were these? All about bombings, with strange names, Earth Mother, Goddaughter. *Earth Mother*! Beverly Winter talked of an Earth Mother. At the time Roger thought it was a veiled reference to "mother earth." He picked up the sheets. What were these? He read them through carefully.

The phone rang three times at the King household before a tiny female voice answered. Roger asked for her mother or father.

"MOM!" The sound pierced Roger's eardrums and he moved the receiver away.

A few minutes later Alexis King answered in a tired voice. "Hello."

"Hello, Mrs. King. I was just going over these computer printouts that you brought in. Can you explain to me what these are all about?"

"I'm not sure. My son says they're people playing a game. He got onto their chatting line by accident and found they were playing a game called Doom or something."

Roger held the receiver away from his ear. What she was saying made no sense at all. He really wished Steve were here, Steve, the computer expert. But Steve was still following up at the elementary school.

Roger said, "Do you think you could explain that to me in layman's terms. I have to admit to not being an expert in these matters, and our officer who is an expert is out on another important matter."

"I'll try, but it may be the blind leading the blind." Then she told Roger about finding them in her son's bedroom and what her husband and son had told her, about games and private rooms and things.

"I guess what got me thinking that these printouts may be important is the dates across the top. They seem to be *before* the actual events occurred," she said.

Roger scratched his head. "Is your son there?"

"He gets home from school in about half an hour. He's at the high school if you need him."

"What about your husband?"

"He won't be home until 6 or 6:30, but I'll give you his work number. I'd be *happy* if you were to phone him at work. Yes, I'm sure he would be *delighted* to hear from you."

He jotted down Paul King's number. He worked at Fundy Bay Computer Systems. But when Roger called his extension, he got voice mail. He left his name and number and asked him to please call as soon as possible on an urgent matter.

Jack was waiting in the doorway when Roger hung up. He said, "Get this, Kara Scoretti was a student at St. Matthews seminary for one semester. She was asked to leave in January for, get this, 'dangerously radical leanings.'"

Roger looked up. "What does that mean?"

"She participated in a number of pro-life rescuing operations that turned ugly."

Roger stood. "No kidding!"

"We're narrowing them down, Rog, one by one we're narrowing them down. We got Joan Aarkman. We got that lady down in Boston. Now, we got Kara Scoretti."

"May I remind you we haven't *got* any of these people. Do we know where Joan Aarkman is? No. Is the lady down in Boston saying anything worth listening to? No. And have we got Kara Scoretti? I would bet no."

"We got the New York Police department checking her out. But so far all we know is she left New York last summer for school here and has never shown up since. The sub-letters of her apartment deposit their rent into her account in New York, which she accesses from here with her bank card."

"Can we trace her through her bank card?"

"This is the information age, Sergeant. You can hide forever behind voice mail and talk mail and bank cards and e-mail."

Roger looked down at the printouts. "So I'm learning. Virtual hiding places. Maybe all these people have amorphized into computer robots and live inside their machines. Maybe that's why we can't find any of them."

"Well, we got a North America wide search out for Kara Scoretti. We'll find her. We'll find that Joan character, too."

But in time? wondered Roger.

CHAPTER 58

Roger called Steve to come back to the detachment.

"I've got a computer problem here, like you to have a look at it," said Roger when Steve returned.

"Computer problem? You wanted me to come in because of a computer problem?"

"A situation. You know anything about chatting lines?"

"Chatting lines? You mean chat lines? IRC?"

"You know anything about that stuff?"

"A little." Steve eyed him curiously.

"Good. Your 'little' is better than my 'none at all.'"

Roger handed him the printouts, telling him Alexis' story. "What do you make of these?"

For ten minutes Steve studied them, his brow furrowed.

"Do you think these are important?" asked Roger. "I don't know much about this stuff."

"I'll say these are important. It looks like it could be conversation between the terrorists. People on chat lines normally give themselves a handle. We've got Earth Mother here and Joan of Ark." He looked up.

"Joan Aarkman," said Roger.

"It looks like someone has either accidentally, or on purpose, found their secret meeting place."

"You're kidding!" said Roger.

"Not kidding at all. Remember that brochure we got a couple months ago? About that conference down in Bangor on computer crime?"

"Yeah, I was going to send you. Does this fall under that category?"

"We've known for years that various terrorist groups throughout the world are meeting over the internet using private codes. As soon as Interpol or the FBI finds them, they move on to another place. You mean this 14 year-old *kid* got into their room?"

"Apparently."

"We should hire that kid."

Roger opened the phone book. "I'm going to call that computer company, not Paul King's voice mail, but their main number. When I get Paul on the line I want you to talk to him."

"I'm sorry," said the receptionist to Roger. "Mr. King is currently in a meeting. Would you like to leave a message on his voice mail?"

"This is the St. Matthews RCMP and we need to speak to him immediately about an urgent matter."

Roger handed the phone to Steve.

"Mr. King," said Steve when Paul came on the line. "We have in our possession some computer printouts that allegedly came from your son's home computer. These were dropped off by your wife. Do you have any knowledge of them?"

A pause, Steve smiled at Roger.

"It seems your son may have accidentally, or on purpose, logged into the private chat room of the terrorist organization, the Christian Freedom Life Army."

From where he stood, Roger could hear the loud "What!" emanating through the receiver.

"Yes, it appears that, way. No, Mr. King your son appears to be in no danger that we know of. But we would like to talk to him and to you. Can you meet us at your house in say, 10 minutes...? Yes, we'll need you there. No, there will be no other way.... Yes, we're fairly sure about this. Yes, I'm sorry about your meeting. Fine, that would be fine, sir. We'll see you there."

When Steve hung up he smiled at Roger. "The guy's in a

major snit. Probably I'm taking him out of a meeting with Bill Gates or something."

Ten minutes later Steve and Roger were in Matt King's bedroom, watching while Matt turned on the computer and modem and logged around the internet. Matt King seemed small for his age. He had a child's cherubic face and wore a backwards Blue Jays' baseball cap and plain white t-shirt.

Behind him stood Mrs. King, hands folded in front of her, a triumphant look on her face. Next to her stood a glowering Paul King. Roger could only guess at what was going on between them.

Roger was standing behind the computer and gazing onto the monitor screen. Steve pulled up a chair to the computer and was chatting with Matt in computerese. Roger could make little sense of their conversation.

Matt seemed pleased to be able to show off his computer expertise. He was flicking a bunch of keys. Various configurations appeared across the screen. Finally he said, "They're not on now."

"What does that mean?" asked Roger.

"I think they're coming on at eight. I was on last night with them and they said they were meeting at 8. So we have to wait until 8."

Steve looked at his watch. "Okay, I want you to keep trying that room at half hour intervals until eight. We'll be back here at 8."

He turned to Matt's parents. "I'd like you to stay with your son. If they log on any earlier, call us immediately. Do you hear?" He gave Matt one of his business cards. "We'll be back around 7:45. Okay?"

"Okay," said Matt, taking the business card. He seemed to glow in the recognition.

Before they left, Roger turned to Matt and casually asked him, "Could you log onto say, a private person's e-mail? Say, my own personal e-mail to someone?"

"Are you logging onto a chat room, the web or are you using

mail box software?"

He looked helplessly at Steve.

"He's using e-mail software," said Steve.

Matt said, "Then no, I can't. Not yet."

CHAPTER 59

It was on the six o'clock evening news, that her sons were missing. Missing since 2:30 that afternoon when their grandmother was supposed to pick them up. The police weren't saying much, but it was known that the boy's father, who lives in Toronto, had received an anonymous call stating that they were in danger. Julia and her mother sat side by side on the couch and watched. Julia could not stop her shivering, and her mother placed her own cardigan across her daughter's shoulders and sat there. Sitting across from her were a few friends and people from her church. Shelly was there, along with Tanya, Gloria and her pastor husband. Even neighbors had dropped by to say how sorry they were and to please let them know if there was anything they could do.

Her mother turned to her. "Does Mason know?"

Julia shook her head.

"He'll see the news, Julia. Would you like me to phone him?"

"I should," said Julia, rising. Even though the room was warm, Julia shivered. She couldn't get her mind away from the fact that her boys were missing. Both of them. Just like that. And that no one had seen them. Not one person.

She said to no one in particular, "Beth Knoll called Emma. So we know that Beth is okay. If the same person took Josh and Jeff then maybe they're okay, too."

She picked up the kitchen phone and dialed Mason in

Toronto. Judith answered with a soft "Hello."

"I need to speak to Mason."

"What it is, Julia?" he said when he came on the phone.

"Mason, something terrible has happened. The police are out looking. A whole lot of people are."

"What has happened, Julia?"

"The boys are missing."

"Missing! My goodness, Julia, and when did this happen?" His voice was full of accusation, which only added to Julia's pain. Her shivering increased. Her mother placed her arm around her shoulder. It felt odd for her mother to act this way, not making tea for everyone and waving her arms. For some reason her mother was being still and just holding her. Her mind was too numb to think much about it, but she felt comforted.

"Mason, I took all the precautions. I contacted the police. I went to the school to make sure the teachers would watch them. I did everything right. They were to get in the car with my mother and my mother only...."

"You had your mother, that superficial, antique hunting lady? You trusted my boys with her...?"

"Mason...." Julia was near tears. "I was at work."

"And your work is more important than my sons?"

Why were the old patterns emerging? Why was she feeling like she needed to defend herself and her every action. *I did my best. I tried my hardest.* She was conscious of Gloria watching her from the living room.

"Julia, I'm taking the next flight to Fredericton."

"Do you want someone to meet you at the airport?"

She could hear him sigh. "Not your relatives, they'd probably get the times wrong. I'll take a cab."

"You can't take a cab all the way here from Fredericton."

"Oh, for crying out loud, I'll rent a car."

After Mason hung up, Julia burst into tears, crying for several minutes while her mother hugged her for a long time. In the living room Gloria and her husband led the group in prayer. Julia asked them to also pray for Beth. That they did, plus they prayed for the Shanahan family, and for the terrorists themselves. They also prayed that the police would quickly put an end to this.

At 7:14 the door bell rang. Julia raced for it. It was Emma, who stood there alone, her hair curling and wet around her cheeks.

"I heard about your sons," she said. "I just wanted you to know how sorry I am."

"Thank you." Seeing Emma brought on a rush of fresh tears. "Would you like to come in?"

Emma glanced past Julia into the room of strangers. "No, I wouldn't be welcomed there. I would feel strange. I just wanted to come over and say how sorry I am."

Emma hugged her then, and in the fading light, the two women held to each other, tears mingling on each other's shoulders.

CHAPTER 60

At 7:30 that night Roger and Steve showed up at the King household and were assured by Matt that the group wasn't on yet, although he had faithfully checked every half hour.

"They're pretty punctual," Matt said with his newfound importance. "If they say they're going to be on at a certain time, they usually are."

It was a long half hour, sitting there in Matt's bedroom while his mother and father stood behind them. His father was taking more of a keen interest now, talking to the officers as if he were the one that had cracked the code of the Christian Freedom Life Army. "Yeah," he said at one point during the half hour, "I'm pretty proud of my son here. A regular computer genius, he is."

Matt had looked up at Steve once and said, "Am I going to be on television?"

At five minutes before eight o'clock the computer issued a series of beeps.

"What was that?" asked Roger. "Does that mean they're on?"

Matt said, "No, I set an alarm, to remind me to log on." This he did, pressing several keys. Then he sat back, crossed his arms and waited.

"What are we waiting for?" asked Roger.

"We can't log into an empty room. With my program I have to wait for conversation to already be in progress before I can get in."

"Oh."

"So, I have to keep trying."

"Oh."

"Sort of like redial."

"Oh."

When he pressed the keys a few minutes later, the monitor screen brightened and lines of conversation scrolled across it.

"They're on," said Matt, making a fist and pounding the air.

Steve said, "Set the printer to print every word."

"Already done," said Matt.

Earth Mother: We have had some complications to our operation which may require some revising on our part.

Mystic Queen: I'll say, having the maidservant get caught! What foolishness. They will laugh us to scorn. They will sneer at us in derision.

Earth Mother: She won't say anything.

Joan of Ark: How do you know?

Earth Mother: Because B. Voice has trained her well. She knows when to speak and when not to speak. She won't speak.

Mystic Queen: Where is B. Voice now? She should be here.

Earth Mother: She is on her way.

Joan of Ark: They've been asking about the costumes.

Earth Mother: They are well hidden, are they not? And you are no longer there. I don't see a problem.

West Connect: What happened to the girl?

Joan of Ark: Another foul up. She's gone. Earth Mother thought she had chosen well, chosen someone who could care for the child and carry out our wishes. It turns out our little Goddaughter has turned on us.

Earth Mother: We will find her. The police are looking at the seminary. That is Goddaughter's old haunt. If she is there we will find her. We have ways that the police can only dream about. The atheist police force believes that we are the ones who still have the girl. Let them think that. They don't know we've lost her. We can keep threatening. We also now have the boys. WE have the boys.

West Connect: And they are safely away from police eye?

Earth Mother: Yes.

Joan of Ark: Where are they?

Earth Mother: Out here. They are safe until the time comes for more displays of our strength. We are almost ready for the ultimate display. When we are all assembled. When B. Voice arrives here and West Connect.

Mystic Queen: What do we do if we find Goddaughter and the child?

Earth Mother: Kill them on sight. It is the only way.

Roger watched the lines of communication in amazement. He was actually witnessing the inner secret meeting of a terrorist group, although from the sounds of the conversation, they were small and scattered and had experienced major setbacks. He was astonished to learn that they no longer had Beth. Leafing through the old printouts they had brought with them, it appeared that Goddaughter, her keeper (Kara Scoretti?), had taken off with her.

He said, "Can we trace these calls?"

Matt looked up. "What calls?" he asked.

"The calls into the computer, the modem calls, these calls."

Matt looked at him blankly.

Roger persisted, "Is there no way to know where the conversation is originating from?"

Steve spoke, "Afraid not."

Roger shook his head. "Well, there should be," he said.

More conversation scrolled across the screen. He picked up and read the printouts as they came from Matt's computer. He was puzzled. Earth Mother? B. Voice? The daughter? Beverly Winter had talked about Earth Mother. She had talked about listening to a voice, about being the maidservant of the voice. At the time Roger thought she was just speaking gibberish. Could she have been telling him something? Could B. Voice be the voice she was talking about? And who is Earth Mother? He read the transcripts carefully, slowly.

He stopped suddenly on one word. He raced to the King's hall phone.

"Jack," he said when he reached the detachment. "Get me that Elena person."

"Who?"

"That psychic person."

"I thought you didn't want to use her."

"Where'd she come from anyway?"

"She came at the request of the Knoll family."

"We must have her name and number on file. Get it, and get back to me as soon as you find it. I'm on my way to the detachment just as soon as we're finished here."

He went back to the bedroom where the computer was still spewing out pages of conversation across the screen, all printed by Matt's printer. Roger scanned the pages, looking for anything else.

At 8:20, when the Freedom Life Army signed off and the chat room emptied, Roger stacked the pages. He and Steve headed back to the detachment. While they were still in the patrol car, Jack called.

"I couldn't find a number for her here. I checked with Kelly. Looks like we never got it. I called the Knolls. Found out they didn't call her, she called them. She left her card. Kathy, Emma's friend, is going to phone back with her number."

"She mentioned Houston, that she'd worked with police in Houston. I assume that's Houston, as in Texas. Call them, maybe they have her phone number. I'm getting a bad feeling about this, Jack. Steve and I are heading over to Emma's now. Call me if you find anything."

When Jack hung up Steve turned to him. "What's this all about?"

"I don't know. A hunch. A word. Could be nothing. But I think it's significant that the Knolls didn't call Emma, she called them."

"Yeah, so?"

"I don't know. As I said, it could be nothing."

CHAPTER 61

Emma was there, along with Glen, Sophie and Kathy. The four of them were sitting around the kitchen table when Roger and Steve entered. Kathy eyed him warily. She said, "You didn't want to use her before, and now you want to find Elena immediately? Now it's suddenly so important?"

"That's right," said Roger, feeling no need to explain himself.

"No," she said shaking her head.

"No, what?"

"No, I don't have her card. She gave it to me. I put it down on the coffee table next to the candle and now it's not there."

"Let's have a look," said Roger. The coffee table, a pale rough pine, was empty, except for a stubby white candle and a cross made of beads on a leather thong which lay beside it. He knelt and ran his hands underneath the table. Nothing. Kathy and Emma had followed him in. "Are you sure you left it here?" he asked them.

"Positive," said Kathy. "I put it down right next to the candle. I remember doing that."

"Someone moved it," said Roger.

"Or it blew off in a breeze," said Glen.

Sophie spoke now. "What breeze?"

Glen shrugged. "I don't know. When the door opens. Anything."

Roger asked them each in turn whether they had seen the card. Sophie said she saw Kathy put it down on the table, she was sure she did. Glen said he had never seen it at all, had never even met this Elena person. And Emma said she had never really noticed the card, just that Kathy took it. She didn't remember it being on the table at all. "I sit here a lot. I look at the candle," she said, indicating the couch. "I would have noticed it, I think."

"Then someone moved it," he said.

For the next quarter hour all of them ran their hands underneath couch cushions, on the floor, along the wall baseboards, in the magazine rack, in the box of videos beside the TV, underneath the stereo, along the window sills. Their search, conducted in silence, moved to the kitchen and then into the bedrooms. All the while that nagging feeling in the pit of Roger's stomach grew. "Elena Risa," he muttered, "where are you?"

The phone rang. It was Jack and what he said was something Roger had already guessed.

"We called Houston. Sheriff's department, State Patrol, even the FBI. They never heard of her. They never had a case where a boy was abducted by his father and found later in the Arizona desert. She said she was from Maine. We're running a check on her there."

Roger frowned. *So close*, he thought. *So close*. Why had no one thought of checking on this Risa character? They had just accepted her story without question. Even him. Her smooth manner, her persuasiveness, her seemingly genuine concern. Who was she? He thought of her face again and shut his eyes. Why was her face so familiar? Had he seen her before? Where?

"Kathy," he said, turning to her. The tall woman's hands were folded into fists in front of her face. There were dark circles under her eyes and her long hair looked uncombed. He wasn't the only one not getting enough sleep, he thought. Roger said, "Did you look at the card before you put it down? Do you remember anything on it? Anything at all?"

She moved her fists away from her face, but kept them clenched at her side. "I did. I glanced at it. I remember seeing her name, Elena Risa, and then something like 'lost children, lost loves, lost lives,' something like that, then an address in Maine."

"Where in Maine?"

"That I couldn't tell you. It wasn't a familiar place. I would have remembered it if it was Bangor or Playa Brisa or something, but it was a town I didn't recognize. Why is finding her so important? Do you think she can help us now?"

"Sit down," he said. "I should fill you in. You, too, Steve," he said, turning to the young bewildered constable. "Sometimes I get a hunch, call it intuition, call it whatever, but when she came to see me she used a word, not a common word. She used the word 'derision,' that I held her gifts or something 'in derision.' He looked at Steve now. "That same word, 'derision,' was used by one of the participants in the internet discussion, Mystic Queen."

Glen raised his hand. "Whoa, hold on a minute. What are you talking about? What internet discussion?"

"You're right. I need to fill all of you in on this. Sometimes I like to wait, see if my hunches pan out, but I should fill you in...."

He told them then about finding the chat room, the discussion, and about Jack's call. He even showed them copies of the printouts.

"And now we have two more missing children, Jeff and Josh Nash." He shook his head remembering Earth Mother's words, *Kill them on sight.*

He pointed to the most recent sheet. "Here someone named Mystic Queen uses the same word. Derision. Mystic. Mystical, Psychic. I think Elena Risa is the Mystic Queen."

Kathy, looking tired and faint already, suddenly collapsed into the nearest chair. She said quietly, hands in front of her face, "I didn't know. She seemed so genuine. I thought she was really trying to help. I thought...I thought she was someone who could help us. She seemed so...sympathetic. I can't believe I was so fooled."

"She fooled us all," said Roger sadly.

CHAPTER 62

Beth was sitting beside Kara in a van and Kara was driving fast along a narrow road which wound beside the waterfront. Beth looked over at Kara, at her eyes darting from side to side, her trembling lower lip, at the way she would grab handfuls of her dark hair with stiff fingers and fling it back behind her.

"Are you afraid, Kara?"

"Beth, *please*! You must stop talking. This is the most dangerous part."

"Dangerous part of what?"

"Of our journey. I'm taking you to safety, to a nice place, nicer than the root cellar where you were. I couldn't leave you there alone."

Earlier that evening, Kara had come into the root cellar with a sandwich for Beth. When she had pushed open the heavy wooden door, Beth had been crying. It was cold and black and spidery and she just couldn't help herself. Even praying didn't seem to be working. She missed her mother and her friends and didn't know why those people had taken her. That was the way Kara had found her, all scrunched up and cold against a dirty wall. "I want to go home. I want my mom. I have to go to the bathroom, Kara."

Kara had run to her then. "I can't leave you here. I can't." She had wrapped Beth up in a gray woolen blanket and placed Mrs. Jenkins and Beth's blue jacket in the Pocahontas backpack. Then she had picked her up and carried her down the grimy dirt floor hallway, the backpack dragging behind her.

When Kara stumbled, Beth had said, "I can walk."

They had walked a long ways down another hall, and had come out at a doorway. They climbed into the van, which was parked behind a stone fence and hidden in underbrush.

"I never knew you had a van like this," said Beth.

"It's mine. It's mine all right, but my friends have been using it."

Now Kara was shaking her head from side to side. "I'm sorry I got involved with all of this. There's no sense to it. You're an innocent child and there's no sense to it." Kara wiped her eyes with the back of her hand. Beth noticed there were no other cars on the road.

"Why are you crying?"

"Keep your head down, Beth. Please stay put."

Beth obeyed and leaned her head against the back of the seat. Eventually, Kara turned right and drove slowly down a steep gravel driveway. At the bottom they were met by a tall man in a plaid shirt.

"You got to get her to back off!" Kara was practically screaming to the man, even before they got out of the van. "I never thought there would be killing. There wasn't supposed to be any killing. No one told me that he was going to die! I didn't know that was part of the plan!"

The man took a step toward them. "What did you think the armory was for, then?"

Kara said, "I don't know. I didn't think." Kara was biting her lower lip now to keep it from trembling. Then she covered her head with her splayed fingers and yelled, "I'm stupid, stupid, stupid! Can't you get her to stop?"

"I can't get her to quit doing nothing she don't wanna quit doing."

"I know, but we can't let them go on."

"So, what do you want me to do?"

"Take care of Beth. I know I can trust you. Make sure she gets some clean clothes. Get her some of mine. I've got some in my room. They should fit her okay. And there's an extra

toothbrush there and some shampoo. I'm going. I'll be back. I
don't know how much the police know, if anything. I don't
know how long before they find this place. Please don't let
anyone know she's here. No one!"

Kara got in the van and drove away quickly then, the back
tires spitting up gravel as she drove toward the road. In the
darkness Beth could smell the sea, as the strange looking man
with the plaid shirt and gray beard took her hand and led her
inside.

CHAPTER 63

Walt, of Walt's GraphArts, and his wife Marion, a thin brown-haired waif of a woman, lived in a square box house by the wharf. His multi-media studio was in a separate building that looked like it had more square footage than his house.

"He's expecting you," said Marion, who met them in the driveway. "I'll walk you there." Her voice wore a slight Maine accent. When Marion opened the door, Walt looked up.

"Ahh," he said smiling. "Here already." Walt was sitting cross-legged on his computer chair and hunched into the monitor. He was a roly-poly man in his mid-thirties and was clad in khaki shorts and a plain white t-shirt. He reminded Roger of the Pillsbury doughboy. The single room housed a number of computers and computer looking equipment. Everything was that beige-gray plastic that all computers are made of, no matter what brand or stripe.

"And you think you can come up with a computer generated likeness of a person?" said Steve, bringing Roger back to the present.

"Yeah, I think so. I'm working on that now." A pair of half glasses were perched crookedly on the end of his fleshy pug nose.

Steve and Roger pulled up chairs and sat on either side of Walt. Roger watched as an egg-shaped empty head appeared on the screen. Walt said grunting, "I've never done this before, so let's give it a try."

Roger had worked with sketch artists before, but never an

artist who drew his pictures using a computer tablet. As he remembered details about the face of Elena Risa, Walt filled them in on the computer head. Steve contributed as well, because he had also seen Elena, although briefly. Eventually, between the three of them, the face of Elena Risa began to take shape on the screen.

Walt printed the finished product on his color printer and handed it to them, along with a disk. "You can download it and send it across to the FBI or whoever you are hooked up to."

"Fine," said Steve, taking the disk. Roger took the picture and stared down at it. It was a surprisingly good representation of her face. He shook his head. *Amazing what computers can do nowadays*, he thought.

Back at the detachment, Steve went to work, downloading the contents of the disk to Interpol in Ottawa while Roger faxed them the printed copy. He added the question, "Where is this woman?"

This completed, Roger allowed himself five minutes at his desk, eyes closed, head back. He could not give into the fatigue that was seeping through him like a bad case of the flu.

He opened his eyes to see Kelly placing a ham sandwich and coffee on his desk. "I thought you could use some nourishment," she said.

He smiled up at her. "Thanks. How did you know I was hungry?"

"I could tell," she said, smiling. Her long strawberry-blonde hair was piled up on top of her head in a blue ribbon. She looked so very young, not much older than his eldest daughter, Sara.

"I just want you to know," he said, grinning, "I'm not the kind of boss that demands that his women employees get him coffee."

"I know. I can tell. I'm just doing this out of kindness. You can make coffee for me sometime."

"I will, for sure. But why are you here so late?"

"I've got nothing to do at home and there's so much going on. With all these extra officers here, I figured everyone could use my help. But I'll be leaving soon."

"Good, go home and get some sleep. We need you in top shape tomorrow." He began reviewing while he ate.

Later, his sandwich long since eaten, his coffee long since gone, he was still bending over the reports and the printouts. He was reading through them methodically, carefully, line by line, like he'd done a hundred times already. What was he missing? Mal Jarvis from Fredericton had called him at one point and together they reviewed the case. Mal had done a few more checks on Kara Scoretti, and Roger wrote down this new information in his notebook. But there was still nothing on Joan Aarkman and Elena Risa.

Finally, Steve came in smiling.

"We got her," he said.

"Elena Risa?"

"I don't mean we physically have her or anything, I mean we know who she is. And her name is not Elena Risa. It's Irene Needham. She's an actress from Toronto."

"An actress!"

"Yeah, she's with ACTRA. That's how they found her."

"ACTRA?"

"That's the actor's group in Canada, sort of like the SAG in the U.S."

"What's SAG?"

"Screen Actors Guild."

"How come you know so much?"

"I watch a lot of TV."

"I never heard of Irene Needham."

"She hasn't exactly made it big. A few bit parts in Canadian TV shows, some commercials, local stuff. That's about it."

"You ever see her in anything?"

"Yeah, I think so," said Steve. "Maybe that's why she looked familiar to me."

Roger nodded. "Looks like her biggest acting role was playing a psychic right here in St. Matthews."

"Looks that way."

Steve went on to tell him that a search was being conducted of her Toronto apartment. Like the others, she wasn't there and hadn't been for a month.

When Steve left, Roger took a new sheet of paper and began scribbling:

Goddaughter: AKA Kara Scoretti, owner of a blue van, registered under her name in Loggieville, NB. One time resident of New York City, former student at St. Matthews Seminary, expelled because of radical leanings, that is, advocating violence in the matter of abortion. Comes from a wealthy family, parents live in New York. According to Mal, her parents have been questioned, but don't believe their daughter could have had anything to do with the CFLA. They don't know where she is. They thought she was still at the seminary. Family owns various properties and summer homes in NB, some they rent out. These properties are systematically being checked now.

Earth Mother: Identity still unknown, seems to be the ringleader of the group. Who is she?

B. Voice: Identity unknown. On her way to the "hideout" at Earth Mother's. Put extra manpower at customs.

Beverly Winter: Maidservant of the Voice, in custody in Boston, talking nonsense, fear she is psychologically unbalanced. Listen to tape again.

Joan of Ark: AKA Joan Aarkman, whereabouts unknown. Former teacher. Rented the costumes, never returned them, address in Florenceville, NB.

West Connect: Identity unknown, possibly out west??

Mystic Queen: AKA Elena Risa, AKA Irene Needham, an actress, whereabouts unknown. From Toronto, hasn't been there in a month.

He also looked at the recent reports from Des Thillens' address book. Renee Blanchard of Vancouver, B.C. had been questioned and released, along with Martin Cranmore, and a few others from Des' list. Roger was beginning to think that this was a whole new crop of abortion protesters, and that they were wasting their time looking up the old ones....

Wait a minute.... He looked down at the computer printout in his hand, the conversation that the group had had that evening and suddenly he knew where they were....

CHAPTER 64

It was now late at night and Julia couldn't stop shaking. She hadn't eaten a thing since lunch, even though people kept pressing food on her. "You've got to eat. You need you're strength," they kept saying. *What for*? she wanted to ask.

Gloria was there, along with her husband. Shelly had been there, but was gone now, home to put her kids to bed. She said, "I'll be back." Julia looked at her. Was there a hint of "I told you so," in Shelly's eyes? *You tempt evil, you play with evil and it will destroy you.* Was that what Shelly really wanted to say to her?

Gloria had stayed with her, holding her hand and not reciting any of the Christian platitudes that Julia feared hearing, things like this being "God's will," or that "Good would come of this." No, Julia knew that Gloria herself had been through too much to worry about saying the "right" things. To Gloria, God was a Strong Rock, a Tower, and could not be defined or confined by our feeble sayings. He had been there for her, and she knew Him.

It was her mother who surprised Julia the most, however. Her giddy, shallow, tea-making mother never left her side. It wasn't her mother who was pressing food on her. It was other people, people from her church who came in and out with their casseroles saying, "If there's anything I can do...."

Instead, her mother was taking charge, sending people away, inviting them in, shielding Julia, listening to her talk and praying with Gloria and her husband.

Julia was standing at the window now, knowing that at any minute Mason was going to come traipsing through the door, accusing her, belittling her. Mason, who went to church every Sunday, and who still, as far as she knew, taught Sunday school (partly because no one else would teach that particular class of boys). Mason, who left *her* and not the other way around, and had *refused* to try marriage counseling, even though she had begged him to. Mason, who was so concerned with appearances, would at any time, come waltzing into her little house and take over. He would order the police around, order her mother out and use his sharp tongue to knife into her again and again. That's why her hands shook as she stood by the front window and gazed into the night.

The phone must have rung. Julia didn't hear it. But now she could hear her mother saying quietly, "No, I don't think she is able to speak to you right now, Mason."

Mason! Julia stood still. So he was here already! He had gotten here fast.

"No, I don't think it would be wise for you to talk to her right now."

Julia took the phone from her mother. She'd have to face him sooner or later.

"Mason?" she said into the receiver.

"Julia, I'm glad that mother of yours has consented to let me speak to you. Listen, it's not convenient for me to fly to St. Matthews right now. I was going to get right on the next plane. Those boys mean everything to me, to both myself and Judith. But then, I got a call from the company. They're flying me out to Washington later. It's something that can't be put off. So, it looks like I'm not going to be able to come down."

"Fine, Mason." A part of her was immensely relieved and a part of her was angry that his work still came ahead of his family. Nothing had changed.

He continued, "I want to let you know something. I've talked with my lawyer about matters of custody and he agrees with me that the boys would be safer here. I'm also in the process of hiring a private investigator to check into their disappearance."

"The police are working on that, Mason."

"The police are typically overworked and don't have the time to check every little detail. I've called a reputable firm in Fredericton. They're already on their way there."

"I don't think they'll find anything the police haven't. But go ahead. It's your money."

"Now Julia, that attitude will get you nowhere."

When she put the receiver down, wet tears threatened at the corners of her eyes. Gloria looked up at her quizzically. "Are you okay?" she asked.

"He hasn't changed much, Gloria. He's not coming. Work is interfering."

And then she cried, long sobs, while Gloria and her mother sat beside her, one on each side.

CHAPTER 65

Roger was used to playing his hunches. Sometimes they panned out. Sometimes they didn't. But as he left the detachment in a patrol car with Steve beside him, and Eric and Jack following in another car, two things troubled him. First of all, was he taking them all out on a wild goose chase when they should be back at the detachment working head to head on the case? Secondly, should he have called out absolutely everybody, all the detachments, the SWAT team and the military? Turning onto the gravel road he caught a glimpse of the back seat with the three teddy bears he had grabbed from their stock of stuffed toys and dolls donated by a local charity. He sincerely hoped they would get some use this evening. On the highway north, toward the Connor Settlement Road, he shared with Steve why it was he thought the hideout might be out there.

Steve turned to him and said, "I'm learning a lot about you. You're a smart cop."

But Roger's eyes were on the road. "Smart enough, I hope, to get there before it's too late."

Roger relied on his memory as he drove down the rutted gravel dirt road that led out to their destination, the cabin of Des Thillens and Betsy Schellenberg. About a half mile from the cabin, they doused all lights and depended on the stars and the moon light to guide them.

The two patrol cars parked about 50 yards from the cabin and the four of them kept their flashlights off as they walked silently toward the building. Through the uncurtained front windows the inside of the cabin appeared deserted. Perhaps Des and Betsy had already retired for the night. They walked around to the back. But no, the back windows revealed two undisturbed beds.

"Do we go in?" asked Steve.

Roger nodded and tried the front door. Like the last time, the door was unlocked. Inside, Roger shone the flashlight around the front room, and then into the back rooms. The wood stove was cold to the touch, a metal pot of tea at the back of the stove was stone cold. They did a hasty search, rifling through papers on the table, letters, magazines and anything that would give them a clue. Nothing did. In the entire cabin there was no reference to the Christian Freedom Life Army.

"But you think the two of them are really involved?" asked Eric.

Roger frowned. He could be wrong. But....

Jack grumbled, "I can't believe they don't even have electricity."

Electricity! Roger looked at Eric. The last time they were here, Eric had asked about electrical wires. Roger went out and stood on the front porch.

"We follow the wires," he said to the others.

"What about the sheds?" asked Jack.

"Nothing in them but shed stuff. No, we follow the wires."

The four of them walked quietly, steadily, following the path of the overhead wires. They walked downstream, the wires criss-crossing the stream, first on one side and then on the other. Perhaps fifteen minutes later they came to a foot bridge which looked like it had been newly constructed. They crossed it. On the other side it opened onto a clearing. As they trudged through the low grasses, heads down, Roger nearly strangled himself on a long piece of wire which was strung between two trees. Pinned to the wire were large square pieces of cardboard. Frowning, Roger pulled one off. Targets!

"Well, it can be argued," said Eric to him, "that lots of people shoot targets for fun. It may not prove anything."

"Bulls eyes, all of them," said Roger, gathering the targets as he followed the wire.

A few minutes later Jack called. He had wandered north of the shooting range and was shining his light onto the ground. At first it looked like a row of 2'x 6's laid side by side on the ground. A closer look revealed that this was some kind of doorway, a covering, maybe for an underground vault of some kind.

Using a thick pole for leverage, Jack hefted up the banded boards. Underneath was a square opening leading into a fairly shallow underground vault. He shone his light into it. No children. But what they did see were several wooden boxes piled on top of each other. Roger let himself down into the earthwork cave and pried opened the topmost box, lifting the cover off. Arms. Grenades, rifles, and boxes and boxes of ammunition!

Jack peered in and whistled. "There are enough weapons here to arm a small country!"

After examining all of the boxes, and exclaiming over each one, they closed up the cave and replaced the lid. They would come back for this stuff. They had not come to the end of the overhead wires. They still had not found the children.

They followed the stream, up and down and through gullies. A bit of wind had come up, an added chill on this damp evening. Roger shuddered. Soon they found themselves on a well-worn path. Roger stopped.

"I smell wood smoke," he said.

"I don't smell anything," said Jack.

"Faintly," Roger said. "Ever so faintly."

Following the overhead wires, the smell of wood smoke increased with each step. Wood smoke meant a chimney and a chimney meant a house. They were getting closer.

Finally, Eric stopped and pointed. In the distance, down in a gully and surrounded by dense brush and scraggly trees, was a small square cabin. Its lights were on.

"Come to papa," said Jack as they climbed down.

The cabin was larger than they first thought and reminded Roger of gingerbread cottages in the forests and of witches capturing children. They crept closer.

The cottage was fronted by a wooden porch. Slowly, almost not daring to breathe, he and Steve moved silently, imperceptibly near the front porch, while Jack and Eric went around to the back. In front of Roger was a figure sitting on the porch steps, elbows on her knees. Creeping on his belly, he edged so close he could see the red tip of her cigarette and hear her clear her throat. She was a large woman with a thick body and gray hair cropped short and unevenly. He didn't recognize her. Was this Joan Aarkman or had they stumbled onto some stranger's cabin in the woods?

They waited, the two of them, Roger and Steve, crouched in the underbrush. The only sound was the rustling of the wind and the bubbling of the creek. Roger felt his left leg cramp. He grimaced and attempted to stretch it out, thankful for the camouflaging sound of the wind. A few minutes later the door banged open and a woman came out, hands on her hips. Elena Risa! or rather Irene Needham, frowned down at the woman on the porch. She didn't look at all like the Elena Risa who had come to visit him, with her layers of silk, her long mismatched earrings and her coy smile. This Irene wore a pair of loose jeans and a sweatshirt. Her dark hair was tied back in a rubber band, no earrings, no silk scarves. She truly was an actress. A rage so intense filled him then. She had deceived him, had played him like a violin, plucking each string with her smile, her words.

The woman on the porch did not look up when Irene approached.

"Come in, Joan," said Irene.

So it was Joan!

"Why?" said Joan, still without looking at her.

"Betsy wants to talk to us. Des has run off."

"Des is always running off. If he's not running off by foot, he's running off at the mouth."

Elena, or rather Irene, gazed out toward the night, facing Roger suddenly, as if she could see exactly where he was lying. "I hear something," she said.

Roger held his breath.

"The wind's come up. That's all."

"I wish you'd come in. Brenda will be here soon. And the others."

"I'm tired of Betsy always calling the shots."

"The whole thing was Betsy's idea from the beginning."

"The revered Earth Mother," said Joan, raising her hands in mock worship.

"This was a foolproof plan," argued Irene. "How did we know Goddaughter would take off?"

"The plan is falling down around our feet," said Joan.

Good, thought Roger.

Irene was pacing now, walking back and forth across the porch. "Betsy thinks it's significant that Des has left. He and Kara were always friendly. They could be together now."

"And your point is?"

"You know he always opposed this. Betsy's afraid he'll go to the police."

Roger was finding this conversation most interesting.

"I think we can still recoup." Irene's voice was plaintive, urging. Joan sighed, rose, brushed off her jeans and the two women walked inside.

Within minutes Roger radioed the RCMP in St. Matthews. Through the uncurtained front windows, Roger could see Irene strutting and gesturing wildly with her hands. Joan had plopped herself into an overstuffed couch. Next to the couch he saw a desk with a computer. *Command Headquarters*, he thought.

Roger heard the squawk of his walkie talkie and adjusted the volume. Eric was speaking quietly, "I can see through the bedroom window back here. There are two kids sleeping on a cot. Betsy is sitting next to them. She has a rifle across her lap. She is talking, I presume to the two in the living room. I can't make out what she's saying."

The walkie talkie crackled again. It was Jack this time. "It looks like there are just the three women in there, and the two children."

Eric was talking, "I've got an idea. Call it foolishness. Call it stupid, but here's my plan...."

CHAPTER 66

The phone rang. Julia picked it up. Mason again. She frowned.

He was saying, "I've contacted that police force of yours and everybody seems to be out. No one can tell me anything. I asked specifically to speak to the sergeant in command and the fools there told me he was out. First the phone rang and rang and then when I did get someone they told me the sergeant was out."

"They're doing everything they can."

"They're doing nothing. My sons are missing and the sergeant apparently has gone home to bed. And those fools in the office won't give me his home number."

Julia sighed. "Why did you really call, Mason?"

"I'm leaving shortly for Washington. I'm taking an overnight flight rather than waiting until tomorrow. I just wanted an update on my sons before I leave."

"You want to know if the police have told me something that they haven't told you? Well, the answer is no. I don't know anything more than you do."

"I don't trust them, Julia."

"And that's why you hired a private detective?"

"Actually, no. When the firm quoted me their price, I argued that it was exorbitant."

"But arguing didn't make them change their minds, I take it?"

"Julia, there's no need to be sarcastic, especially now when our sons are missing."

Julia was tired of talking. It was nearly midnight. Shelly had come back and was now making coffee in the kitchen. Throughout the evening Tanya, a few people from the Centre, neighbors, and people from her church had stopped by. Julia felt buoyed up by their presence. But, if anything were to happen to her boys.... She put a shaky hand to her head.

"Mason." Her voice was tired. "I'm going to hang up in case the police are trying to call."

"Promise me this, Julia. Promise me that you'll call just as soon as, the minute, you hear anything."

"Okay then, just give me your number in Washington."

"It will be difficult to reach me there."

"Your hotel there? Don't you want me to call you there?"

He coughed. "I'll not be staying at a hotel."

"Then just give me the number where you'll be."

"I can't."

"Why not?"

"It's rather, um, it's rather, uh complicated."

He coughed again.

When Julia hung up she suddenly felt very, very sorry for Judith. But she felt something else, too. She was beginning to see just how empty his threats were, how very weak he was. She really was the strong one. With that knowledge, however, came another understanding, too. That Mason was not to be pitied, but prayed for. No one, no matter what they've done, is too far away from God's love and care. She should pray for Mason. And for Judith.

"What are you so deep in thought about?" asked her mother.

"Mason," was her reply. "I feel so sorry for him, for him and Judith. She's going to be hurt so deeply."

Her mother said nothing, just looked at her.

"I don't know what happened to him," said Julia, who now included Shelly and Gloria. "He wasn't always like this. When the boys were babies, he was gentle and good."

"But moody," interjected her mother. "Don't forget moody."

"Everybody gets moody," said Gloria. "That doesn't give someone permission to go and have an affair. It's not your fault, Julia."

"I know that, Gloria, I know that now. Thank you for everything you've done for me."

Their midnight kitchen table conversation was interrupted by a knocking at the door.

"Who could that be at this hour?" said her mother. But Julia had raced for the door. Josh? Jeff? She opened it wide to the figure of Lois Claymore standing there alone, her arms hugging her body.

"I saw your lights were still on," she said in a small voice. "I took a chance you'd still be up."

"Lois."

"I just wanted you to know how sorry I feel, and if there's anything I can do," she said. "Boy, the wind's picked up, hasn't it?"

"Come in."

"I don't mean to intrude." But she entered tentatively and stood against the wall.

"This is my friend, Lois," she said to the group at the table.

"I should leave."

"Nonsense," said Julia's mother. "There's coffee."

"Yes, please have a cup. We're just up...waiting," said Gloria.

"Well, one cup, I guess. I was just up at my mother's. She's having trouble sleeping, but my other sister's there and my aunt. I usually end up feeling like I'm getting in the way over there. I thought I'd leave and come for a drive."

"Does your mother live in town?" asked Gloria.

Lois' face reddened, and she looked over at Julia.

She said, "Around here. Up the road."

No one pressed her.

CHAPTER 67

Some rescues were easy. Some rescues were difficult and required the very accurate timing and precision of a well-tuned and well-honed piece of working machinery. Some required the knowledge and skill of a trained hostage negotiator. He'd give a four out of ten to this particular one. Inside were three women, one of them armed, and outside were four police officers, all of them armed. Inside, the three knew nothing about the four outside. Should be a piece of cake. Except for the fact that they had two hostages.

They *could* wait for the hostage negotiator and backup, play it safe, do it by the book. They could. But Eric's plan made sense. It *could* work. They *could* pull it off. "As long as it didn't put the little boys in danger," Roger had said.

"I don't see how it can," Eric replied.

Jack spoke next. "I don't know. It sounds a little John Waynish to me."

"A little what-ish?" asked Steve.

"The Duke. Never mind, you're too young."

"Let's give it a try," said Roger, settling the matter. Eric grinned.

The wind was stronger now. The three officers stood quietly behind the stand of trees, watching, waiting, while Eric walked down to the stream. A few minutes later he was back, carrying his dripping wet jacket.

"That's too wet," said Roger.

"I'll wring it out. I was planning to."

The three watched, saying nothing, as Eric wrung out his jacket, tied it securely to his belt and walked determinedly to the large maple tree which leaned against the cabin. Inside, Roger could see Irene and Joan. Joan was sprawled on a couch watching TV, and Irene was still walking back and forth talking. They could not see Betsy.

A little to the right, he could see Eric making his way slowly up the tree, a black shadow against the trunk. Roger held his breath. Inch by inch he rose, until he was able to step onto the roof of the house. Roger hoped it would hold. It did. He watched Eric take the jacket and carefully place it over the chimney, completely cutting off the flow of smoke. He turned, gave them the thumbs up sign and shinnied down the tree.

"Now, we wait," he said when he returned to them. The four of them took their positions near the front door.

It didn't take long. Within minutes, Irene was at the fireplace, poking it with the poker, fiddling with the flue. She said something to Joan and Joan nodded.

Irene opened the front door. When she came down the steps and turned to look at the chimney, Roger and Steve grabbed her from behind, cupped a hand around her mouth, and quickly cuffed her hands behind her back. A look of surprise crossed her face, but Roger and Steve were too strong for her. Steve took her around to the side of the house.

When Irene didn't return, Joan walked to the door, calling for her. She descended the steps, still calling for Irene. They grabbed her from behind, cuffed her and led her squirming around the side to join Irene.

"Two down, one to go," whispered Eric.

Roger watched through the window as Betsy walked to the front room. The irritated look on her face was evident, even from where Roger stood on the porch.

"How convenient," whispered Steve. "She put her rifle down."

"Let's go in then," suggested Eric.

"Let's wait...she's still too near the boys," said Roger.

For several minutes they watched as Betsy, hands on hips, frowned at the fireplace. Then she picked up the rifle again and carried it toward the front door walking slowly, looking around her. Did she suspect something? Roger and Steve were instantly alert. She tentatively opened the front door, carrying her rifle, nervously calling for Irene and Joan. If the two were making any noise around the side of the house, it could not be heard.

"Thank you, God, for the wind," breathed Roger.

Two steps down the porch and Steve and Roger grabbed her from behind. They didn't need to cover her mouth, but moments later, Roger wished they had for the sake of the sleeping boys. Her mouth screamed obscenities and she spit square into Roger's face.

Entering the house Roger wiped his face with his sleeve, doused the fire, and grabbed the sleeping boys. He carried them out, one in each arm.

By the time the party of four had reached the first cabin with their new companions, there were three more patrol cars, lights out and waiting. The boys were placed in the back seat of Roger's car and swathed in blankets, each clutching a new teddy bear.

On the way home Roger said to Steve, "We keep this quiet, out of the news for the time being. Then when the others arrive, that Brenda and the one from the west, we pick them off here, one by one...."

"Like I said, you're a smart cop."

Roger frowned. "Not smart enough. There were three missing children tonight. We only have two of them."

CHAPTER 68

"I have no idea what's going on," said Kara when she returned to the old rambling house by the water. "I know you don't know too much about their plans, but I was just headed out there. I was going to confront them and I saw a bunch of police cars on their way to your place. So I turned around and came back here. No one saw me."

Beth opened her eyes and looked over at them. She had been afraid and cold up in the big dark bedroom, and had persuaded the man, who said his name was Des, to let her sleep on the couch downstairs. She woke up when Kara returned, opened her eyes, then closed them again, pretending to be asleep.

"Why would the police go there?" said Des softly.

He was a strange man, thought Beth, kind of quiet, but he seemed nice enough.

"Isn't that where they all are?"

Des shook his head and put his hands up. "I don't know much. I always kept out of it. Betsy was the strange one. I kept out of her way mostly."

"I can't imagine you didn't suspect anything."

"I didn't."

"Well, I didn't know that Shanahan was going to get shot. I didn't know that."

"Betsy practiced her shooting every day, every single day. Sometimes three and four hours at a time."

"So, she shot him."

"Maybe. Maybe not."

"She did."

"Maybe."

Beth opened her eyes. Were they talking about Uncle Douglas? She hugged the blanket around her. It felt so cold. Everything felt so cold. Why couldn't she just go home?

"She *did*, Des."

Des spoke slowly. "You're right. Betsy done it. I found out that much."

"Then why didn't you *tell* anyone? Why didn't you even tell me?"

He stroked his thick beard. "I told Betsy I wanted to stay out of it. My time doing all that is past."

"Des, I didn't know that Shanahan was going to be killed. I didn't even know he *had* been killed until that night. I had Beth in the warehouse and no radio."

"She was trying you out. She told me."

Kara rose now and walked around the kitchen. Her movements were jerky, just like in the van.

"I'm going to take her in."

"Who in?"

"Beth. I'm going to take her home tonight. Right now. Are you coming with me?"

"Right now? But it's the middle of the night."

"I'm sure her mother will be delighted to see her no matter what time of day I take her home."

"Then what, you think you can escape the police?"

"I'm not going to even try. As soon as I take her home, I'm going to turn myself in. Go right down to the detachment. I'll have to go to jail. Maybe I'm even some sort of an accessory to murder, I don't know."

"And you want me to go with you?"

"Only if you want to."

"I'll come."

Kara walked into the living room and gently shook Beth's shoulders. She sat up.

"Beth, the nightmare is over. I'm taking you to see your

mother. We're going right now. I'm just going to drop you on your porch and then I'm going to leave."

On the way into town Beth, fully awake now after a few hours of sleep, plied Kara with questions.

"Where are you going after you drop me off?"

"To the police."

"But why don't you come in first? You can meet my mom."

"I don't think I'd be too welcomed at your place."

"Will I see you again?"

"I don't know."

"Well, can we be pen pals then?"

Kara turned and took a long look at the little girl who was sitting beside her. "Maybe."

EPILOGUE

Roger: Well, how do you like this chat line?

Kate: I'm absolutely amazed that you are on the computer and chatting with me over a chat line. You even got the word right!

Roger: Steve set it up. Says it's foolproof, which in my case means dummy-proof.

Kate: All except for teenagers like the one who crashed the terrorist organization.

Roger: Who, Matt King? We hired him.

Kate: You hired him?

Roger: Well, not exactly, but if we ever have another case involving computers, we're going to use him. He and Steve have turned into great buddies.

Kate: Steve's the computer nerd?

Roger: I wouldn't call him a nerd, the guy's 6' 2".

Kate: Okay, he's not a nerd. Do you know they're calling your constable Eric Jamison a maverick?

Roger: We took a chance. It worked. He's now putting in for a new RCMP jacket, cited smoke damage on his form.

Kate: That's cute. And the way you ambushed all those other arriving Christian Freedom people, one by one. They're saying that you brought wild west policing techniques to the staid and proper Maritimes.

Roger: It was Eric who came up with the idea. I just okayed it. Oh, and "Christian"? That's one thing those people are definitely NOT.

Kate: They used the word "Christian."

Roger: Anybody can use the word "Christian" in their titles. It doesn't mean a thing. When we arrested her, Betsy, the ringleader of the group, let out a string of four-letter words that would make a sailor blush. No, I would not call her a Christian.

Kate: Are things back to normal up there?

Roger: Almost. Josh and Jeff are back with their mother. Beth is back with her mother. Kara, the girl who brought her in that night, dropped her off at three clock in the morning. Then she came over to the detachment and turned herself in.

Kate: I know. I read about that part. But you weren't there then?

Roger: No, I was out at the cabin. So was practically everyone else. Kelly was there, however.

Kate: Your receptionist? That late?

Roger: She stayed all night. I sent her home a couple of times, but she stayed there, wanting to help. She's a good kid.

Kate: I'm so glad the children weren't harmed.

Roger: Yes. Weird thing, though. When I took the boys to Julia's house, Shanahan's daughter was there.

Kate: Shanahan's daughter?

Roger: Yeah, strangest combination of people. And here's another one. The other day I saw Emma Knoll and Julia Nash having lunch together down at the waterfront diner.

Kate: Emma and Julia. Really??

Roger: Yeah. And last Sunday I saw her daughter at church.

Kate: Whose daughter?

Roger: Emma's. I didn't see Emma, but I saw Beth come in with another girl, some friend I presume. I'm still so new there, can't remember names of the church people.

Kate: We'll get to know them. What's happening at the Shanahan Clinic?

Roger: It re-opened the other day. Emma's not there anymore.

Kate: Why not?

Roger: From what I understand she's quit that job. Said she doesn't want to put her family in that kind of danger anymore. That clinic has one of the highest tech security systems in town, and they hired some fancy security company in Toronto to come help them make it even more secure.

Kate: How sad. A sad commentary on people who call themselves Christians and feel they have to resort to so much violence that the clinic has to be built like an armed fortress. So far removed from what Christ said and lived.

Roger: Agreed.

Kate: Just wondering, how did you KNOW they were out at that cabin in the first place? That part was never in the news.

Roger: One word, well actually, two words. "Out here." When we were at Betsy and Des' place she used the words "out here" in reference to their place. She used the same words on the computer printout.

Kate: And you went with that?

Roger: Yeah, it was a long shot, but it panned out. Hey, this chat line is fun. We could talk all night this way.

Kate: I'll be out there in less than two months, dear.

Roger: Can't wait....

Other books available
in the RCMP series by Linda Hall:

AUGUST GAMBLE

NOVEMBER VEIL